# FOREWORD

Charismatic is the final book in the Arcane Mage series (yes, that means no more cliffhangers, you can rest easy!). This is a paranormal reverse harem series where the heroine doesn't have to choose between her men. It contains explicit sex, cursing, crazy grandmothers with awesome (if questionable) taste in clothes, and a lot of magic.

No mailbox opossums were hurt in the makings of this book.

The author cannot be held responsible for any spontaneous combustions, cursing, crying, or sleepless nights.

# CHARISMATIC

### BOOK 6 OF THE ARCANE MAGE SERIES

T.S. SNOW

Charismatic by T. S. Snow

Copyright © 2022 by T. S. Snow. All rights reserved.

No portion of this book may be reproduced in any form or by any electronic or mechanical means, including information storage and retrieval systems, without written permission from the author, except for the use of brief quotations in a book review.

This book is a work of fiction. Names, characters, businesses, places, events, locales, and incidents are either the products of the author's imagination or used in a fictitious manner. They are not to be construed as real. Any resemblance to actual persons, living or dead, or actual events is purely coincidental. The author acknowledges the trademark owners of various products, brands, and/or stores referenced in this work of fiction which have been used without permission. The publication/use of these trademarks is not authorized, associated with, or sponsored by the trademark owners.

Cover Design: CJ Romano @CoversbyCJRomano

*To my mom,*
*Who not only ignored every single foreword, but also recommended my books to all her friends.*
*I love you, you rebel.*
*Thank you for believing in me.*
*But please stop telling your friends to read my books.*

# 1
## CHARISMA

*Charisma, it's time to end this foolishness. Tomorrow, we'll announce your status as the Silverstorm heir. You'll be expected to return to your duties effective immediately and find a suitable male to start producing a new heir. We know your magic is weak, but we have someone in mind whose Elemental magic should be strong enough to ensure the Silverstorm line is carried through, and your child will be the new heir the minute they're old enough to begin their duties.*

My father's words, or rather, his ultimatum, ran through my head like some terribly catchy song that would live rent-free in my mind forever.

And the fact both he and my mother were standing there, staring at me like this decision was a done deal and that I was supposed to just smile and say "yes sir" like a well-trained doll only aggravated the situation.

I didn't know which part was worse or more delusional. If it was the fact they thought I'd just submit like a good girl and slink back into the family after all the shit I'd gone through, acting like the last five years had never happened. Hell, they acted like the last *ten* years—since they'd brought

Cara to our house to groom her as my replacement once all their attempts to force my magic to get stronger failed—had suddenly ceased to exist. Or if it was the fact they wanted me to be some broodmare whose only role would be to keep the seat warm until I gave them little powerful grandbabies, and then I could be cast aside again. As if I'd *ever* give up any child I might have one day to them so they could put my kid through this hell. My son or daughter would *not* be some sacrificial lamb, bred for the purpose of being raised to the throne or some shit. Despite their plan, there was no guarantee my child would have strong magic. As I'd already proved, no matter how powerful the couple, the kid could still be magically weak. There was no way I'd ever turn them into a magical guinea pigs, hiring all kinds of psychopaths to torture them, claiming the "unorthodox" methods would strengthen their magic. Nor would I allow my parents to do that to their grandchild.

No fucking way.

Any kid of mine would have better than this. No matter what magic they had, or how powerful they were—or *weren't*—they'd be loved for who they were. Come hell or high water, no matter what I had to go through to ensure it, they'd be cared for and protected until I drew my last breath.

This, I vowed.

All that, and I wasn't even bothering to consider the fact they'd found a "suitable candidate" to be my husband. Probably a male version of Cara. Some power-hungry, twisted Elemental who cared about nothing and no one except their own sense of self-worth.

I couldn't believe they expected me to give up the life I'd built for myself, and my growing relationships with men I loved, so I could go back to … to being *miserable*.

Actually, no. That wasn't true.

I could totally believe it. Because it was just like my parents to think only their needs were important and only their wishes mattered. It was *exactly* like them to expect I'd jump at the snap of their fingers while asking how high. After all, they were the *Silverstorms*. They were used to getting their way. And for most of my life, I'd done just as they'd told me to because I wanted their approval. Desperately so. But it never mattered what I did or how quickly I could overcome the obstacles in my way. I'd already failed at a fundamental level for lacking magic power, even if there was nothing I could do to change that fact. It was who I was.

It had taken me years to come to terms with it and accept the fact I wasn't lacking, I was just different, and that was okay too.

Even though it had taken me an awfully long time, I was finally finding my backbone. I was not going to roll over and let them walk all over me. I'd already stood up to them once, back when they'd wanted me to make Cara her MET–and thank fuck for that, considering how my twisted cousin had ended up trying to kill me–I could do it again. I'd be *damned* if I'd force a child to go through what I did.

I felt my magic stirring inside me as if in approval, a low hum that warmed me all the way to my soul and kept the biting cold from my mother's magic at bay. I was no longer freezing. In fact, I felt all warm and fuzzy inside.

Closing my hands into fists, I stared my father in the eye. He hadn't changed, not even a little bit. Sure, his blond hair may have more white in it than before, and there were bags under his silver eyes while wrinkles marred his once-smooth face. But, underneath it all, he was still very much the same.

Unfortunately for them, I was not. I'd grown, changed,

and fully intended to continue doing so. I was no longer a teenager desperate for approval, for affection.

I was no longer a Silverstorm.

I straightened my posture and said the one word I'd wanted to say since I was a teenager.

"No." I didn't leave room for argument. I didn't sound unsure. I didn't raise my voice. I didn't even drop my gaze to avoid the prolonged eye contact.

"Of course," my mother said, ignoring me, or just incapable of hearing anything that wasn't the sound of her own voice. "You'll have to break things off with your ... friends. We can't have any rumors that you've dated someone from another family. We'll also need to make the announcement soon. I'll call the Brants and set something up. We could have a nice wedding organized soon, or maybe we could announce you two eloped, and get this over with. It'd make for a nice story. People would find it romantic, I think. I'll also have to call—"

"No," I repeated, this time a little louder, cutting her off before she could continue with her delusional planning.

My mother's selective hearing skills were out of this world, however. She just kept pacing and rambling about all the shit that had to be done so I could be married by the end of the week. It felt like now that she had something to do, she'd go all out, giving her imaginary task her all, the same way she'd always done.

Except, this time, she was wasting her time. I had no intention of going through with this bullshit.

While my mother kept rambling and ignoring me, my father had most definitely heard me. And, if the look on his face was any indication, my "defiance" had not pleased him.

*So rude of me to want to make my own choices regarding my*

*fucking life and my future. Clearly, I'm just going through a rebellious teenager phase ... in my twenties.*

I swore I could see that train of thought, or something very similar, going through his mind.

How had I ever thought coming here today was a good idea? Why had I thought this would go any differently than any of my previous interactions with them? How could I be so damn naive as to think, against all odds, that they'd suddenly had a change of heart and attitude after twenty-three years?

I couldn't even be mad at them. I mean, they were acting exactly like expected, really. I'd been a fool once again for thinking something would've changed just because they'd been slightly nicer on the phone than they'd been in years.

This was on me. Fool me once and all that crap. I should've known better.

Still, the little part inside me that had dared to hope was hurting. Goddess, how it hurt. I thought I'd built up my defenses against them, but I'd been wrong. Despite everything, after all this time, the little girl inside had still held out hope that we'd finally be acknowledged for who we were, finally have their approval. It didn't matter how much I'd tried to pretend that part of me was dead, I'd only been lying to myself, and that, too, hurt.

I wanted to rub the spot on my chest where it felt like I was being stabbed, but I refused to give them the satisfaction.

Not that they would care, anyway. But I had *some* pride.

"It's not a request, Charisma," my father said almost harshly. It was, maybe, the most emotion I'd heard from him in ten years. Usually, Mother was the one who did most of the speaking, and my father just tagged along to look down his nose at me and be judgemental. "We're merely informing you what's going to happen. I expect you to be all packed by tomorrow. Tell me your new address, and I'll send a driver to pick you and your things up. We'll hold a press conference in a week. It should be enough time to finalize any plans and ensure you and your future husband are up-to-date."

My mouth hung open, and a weird, strangled sound came out.

This was ridiculous.

Why on earth was I sitting here, listening to this bullshit? Why was I just letting them ignore me and plan my life?

I didn't *owe* them anything. I ... I actually had no reason to be here listening to this at all. I could just ... walk out, walk away.

They couldn't *force* me to do anything I didn't want to.

It didn't matter what my father was saying or that my mother was already picking up her phone and scrolling through whatever to-do list app she used while she went on and on about flowers and dresses.

Much like Dobby, I had no master. I could do whatever the fuck I wanted.

Clinging to that thought, I stood up.

That one action managed to do what none of my denials did. Both my parents stared at me, and the silence was enough that I'd have been able to hear a pin drop.

My mother's perfectly shaped eyebrows were pulled together in a frown, while my father's silver eyes were swirling with a vortex of emotion I was not going to bother trying to read into.

Because I didn't have to.

"I've said this before, and I'll say it again for the last time: No. I'm not going to end my relationship with anyone, and I will not return to being a Silverstorm. *You* cast *me* out and forced me to find a way to keep living." Seriously, it was like they'd forgotten all about it. As if teenage me had decided to just run away from home and leave *them*. "At eighteen, I had to find a house, a job, and figure out a way to keep paying tuition for the Academy, and you never bothered to even ask me if I was okay or needed something. I'm no longer Charisma Silverstorm; I'm Charisma Carter and have been since I was eighteen." Even though my heart was shattered, somehow, I managed to keep my voice steady and calm rather than emotional. And if I curled my hands and dug my nails into my palms, well, they couldn't see it, so it was fine.

I was done here. Whatever hope my heart had clung to that after all these years, my parents would miraculously see reason and finally behave like caring parents had just been snuffed out completely. Once and for all.

I didn't need them; I had a family I'd found and built for myself. One that was still growing and that loved me for me and supported me. One that respected me as a person and didn't treat me as merely a tool.

And the sooner I got out of here, the sooner I could get back to them. Cuddles and ice cream. That was all I needed.

I held my father's gaze before moving on to my mother's, wanting to make sure my words would be heard and understood. The final nail in the coffin had to hit home, or else I'd just be stuck in this toxic vortex until I died. "I'm Charisma Carter, self-made Magical Engineer, and I'll never be a Silverstorm again. I don't *owe* you or the Silverstorm name anything, because in order for me to have any family obligations, we'd have had to be an actual *family* first."

I took a deep breath and pushed my shoulders back, correcting my posture.

"Sorry, but you'll just have to find another heir to fix

your reputation. I'm sure there's a cousin somewhere whose life you can upend. And who knows? Maybe this time, you'll do a better job of it than you did for either me or Cara." My mother flinched at that, but it didn't give me any satisfaction at all. In fact, I was kind of numb. Unable to feel anything.

Maybe *that* was why I sounded so level-headed.

"One thing is for sure, though; I'll not be going through with this charade, and before you get any ideas, let me make one thing very, *very* clear. If I ever have a child, they'll never be put through this. Even if they have Elemental magic, even if it's stupidly strong, they will never be a Silverstorm, and they'll never live this life. They'll be a Carter, always and forever. Good luck finding the next heir, though, or trying to fend off all the challenges. We're done here."

And then I walked out, ignoring their calls and accusations, ignoring the fact the doorknob was completely frozen over as I pulled the door open and the cold steam coming from my mouth.

I didn't look back. I didn't dare.

Instead, I wrapped my magic tighter around me, making sure its warmth would protect me, and I kept walking.

Once I was far, far from here, I'd call Blaze and ask him to pick me up.

Hell, I'd walk home if I had to, but I was *done*.

## 2

## THEO

Annie. Wouldn't. Stop. Talking.

Ever since I'd woken up in the hospital, she'd been ranting at me about how irresponsible and stupid I'd been and a bunch of other shit. The only time she'd made herself scarce was when the matriarch had paid me a visit. Then, my sister suddenly remembered she had some very important ghost business and poofed out before our grandmother entered the room.

More than once during my grandmother's visit, I wished I could've just poofed out of the room, too, but unfortunately, I'd been stuck here.

"I know you're listening, you know. I can see your eye twitching from here." I saw her crossing her arms in front of her and stomping her foot in irritation, and I knew I was in trouble.

Even though I'd had time to get used to the fact my sister had died and was now a ghost, I still struggled to wrap my head around it. It felt like being glad she'd chosen to stick around after passing was a betrayal to her, somehow. A selfish impulse that had forced my sister to be stuck here when she could've crossed over. Every time I looked at her ghostly form, I was hit with so many mixed feelings all at once.

Just another one of my sins, I supposed—another smudge on my soul.

Sighing, I ran a hand over my face, pressing my thumb and pointer finger against my eyes before finally turning to face her.

"I don't know what you want me to say, Annie." I sounded tired, probably because I *was* tired. The past few weeks had been hell, and my little hospital stay wasn't exactly helping me rest. Not when Healers were coming and going, as well as a shit ton of ghosts.

I hated hospitals. It was like they sucked the energy right out of you.

Still, it had been worth it. I hadn't planned on being captured by the resistance—and I doubted Logan had, either—and I felt like crap for being the reason Char had been kidnapped. However, because we were there with her, at the resistance's mercy, I'd been able to intercept an attack meant for Char. I'd managed to protect her, even if just a little. There was no way I'd ever regret that.

Annie dropped her arms to her sides, and I gave a weary laugh at the shirt she'd chosen to wear. "This is *boo*-shit!" it said, with a little cartoon ghost that looked a lot like the poop emoji.

She'd always shared Charisma's fashion sense. That was for damn sure.

Annie walked, well, floated closer until she was hovering over the bed as if sitting beside me. "Why are you constantly self-sabotaging, Theo?" This time, there was no judgment in the question, none of the usual bite that tended to follow.

I knew what she was talking about. The same thing she

always did. Annie wanted to know why I acted all over the place whenever Char was near me and like a fucking creep when she was away. So far, I'd always evaded the actual reason. However, this time, I felt I had no choice but to be honest.

I closed my eyes, knowing I couldn't bear the look on her face when I answered.

"I don't know. It's not ... It's not on purpose. Sometimes, when I'm near her, and she gets that look in her eyes, I just ... " I trail off, shaking my head.

Goddess, I'm ridiculous. "I don't know what comes over me, and I'm always left with a bitter taste in my mouth. I love her, Annie. Always have, always will. And because I love her, I can't hand her over to Grandmother on a silver platter."

I'd never forgive myself if something happened to Char because I'd been selfish enough to want her in my life. This hadn't changed in the past five years, even if everything else had.

Besides, now she'd found her other soulmates. They made her happy. She didn't need me and the burdens I carried.

I didn't care if I had to keep playing the bad guy in order to push her towards them, so long as they made her happy.

Even if just thinking it made my mouth taste like ashes. So, I was a little bitter about the situation; I could live with that.

"You're such an idiot."

I opened my eyes at the mocking tone to find Annie rolling hers.

"I never claimed to be smart, Annie," I pointed out, making her scoff.

At times like this, she seemed so full of life, so much like her usual self, it physically hurt.

Then, she surprised me by placing her hand on my arm.

It felt weird, bizarre. My powers meant I could feel the weight of her hand on me, and there was a tingly sensation, but there was no heat coming from her and no actual contact.

The pain in my heart intensified, as it often did these days.

I'd give anything to be able to bring Annie back, even if it meant changing places with her, but I knew it was an impossible dream. Even Char's Necromancer couldn't make that happen, and even if he could have, I didn't want my little sister to be someone else's puppet. Not now, not ever.

"Why are you so sure Grandma would do something like that to Char? Did she say something?"

Should I tell her? Admit to Annie that Aunt Kate hadn't been the only person Grandmother had placed a soul-binding on. That when I was little, I'd seen her place one on our parents, too? I'd been too young to understand back then. In fact, I'd been so young that I'd all but forgotten about it until recently.

My darkest, dirtiest secret.

I'd seen the matriarch bind my mother and father so they'd never attempt to overthrow her.

No. I couldn't tell her.

No good would ever come out of Annie knowing how twisted our grandmother could be. Not when there was nothing she could do to change it.

Honestly, part of me even questioned if what I'd seen was true. It had happened years ago, and the only reason I thought my grandmother had bound their souls was that she'd uttered the command while magic circles had surrounded my parents. Once the magic had vanished, they'd looked meeker, somehow. Changed.

All I could do now was hope to grow strong enough to one day challenge my grandmother, or wait until she stepped down. The last thing I wanted was for word to get out to our matriarch and for her to bind *my* soul.

That would be a disaster in so many ways.

And though the matriarch had threatened to do just that if I didn't stay away from Char, she hadn't gone through with it.

After all, I'd given her no reason to.

"Theo?" Annie's gentle coaxing almost managed to undo my resolve, but I held firm.

Shaking my head, I gave a bitter laugh. "I don't know, Annie. Call it a gut feeling or sheer paranoia, but I refuse to risk it."

"Urgh. You're so damn stubborn! So, rather than being happy, you decided to meddle so she could have other men?"

Surprised, I turned to stare at her, but she raised an eyebrow in a "bitch, please" way. "I used to be able to see auras too, you know."

Right. Not like I could've ever forgotten. Annie and I had been considered the trump cards for the Soulbinders. The golden heirs. The first children to be born with the gift of reading auras after generations without it being seen among Soul Mages.

A power that only manifested once every few generations, and somehow both Annie and I had been born with it.

And yet, neither of us had ever been allowed to talk about it with others. Instead, we were instructed from a young age to keep this marvelous gift a secret.

I opened my mouth to say something, but Annie suddenly jumped from the bed. "Someone's coming!" she whispered before vanishing.

Frowning, I picked up my phone to check the time.

Three in the afternoon. The Healers weren't supposed to check up on me for another hour.

Who could it be?

I didn't have to wait long.

In a flurry of activity, the door to my hospital room was opened, and an old lady barged in as if she owned the place, looking determined. She was almost beside me on the bed when two other people entered my room, rushing after her.

Forcing myself to act nonchalant and not show just how fucking alarmed I truly was, especially when I recognized Andres Illudere as one of the men in my room, I put my phone down.

"Can I help you?" I asked, trying my best to be polite, even as I called upon my magic.

Big mistake.

My blood froze when I noticed the sheer number of ghosts suddenly appearing in my room as if attracted by an unseen force. However, rather than flocking around me, they did their best to stay close to the old lady.

When nobody responded, I opened my mouth, intending to demand answers, but the old lady had finally reached me and put her hand on my arm.

I tensed, eyes flickering from her to the strange male, then to Andres, the only one I recognized.

Andres had the *nerve* to give me a little wave, and I lost it.

"Illudere, what the fuck is this?" I asked, trying to break the woman's hold on my arm when she stopped humming, but she had a death grip on me.

I didn't give a shit how old she was. If she didn't release

me in the next five seconds, I would use my magic to force her to let go of me.

I was so focused on calling up my magic I didn't realize the humming had stopped until the woman holding me spoke.

"What a mess," she said, giving me a pitying look.

What. The. Fuck?

"She's bound you to seek your soulmate, but also to keep away from Charisma? Just how fucking stupid *is* your grandmother?"

If I'd been tense before, now I was completely frozen in place. I wasn't even breathing.

Had she ... surely she couldn't have ...

No. She couldn't be right. Not only was there no way my grandmother would've placed a soul bind on me without me remembering it, but there were no other living Soul Mages who could see auras.

I was the last one standing.

But, even as I thought all that, a little voice inside of me protested.

"What the hell are you talking about?" I directed my power to my eyes, switching so I could read her aura, but found she had none.

"Who are you?" I asked, turning to check on Illudere and the other male.

Andres's aura was the only one I could see, which meant I hadn't lost my abilities, but somehow, they'd managed to block it.

What was going on here?

"Manners, boy," the old lady admonished as if I were five or some shit. "I could've been your grandmother too. Show some respect."

*I beg the fucking pardon?*

My grandmother? There was no way.

*This lady is batshit crazy.*

My eyes flew to Andres, a million questions on the tip of my tongue, but the woman's grip on my arm squeezed even harder, her fingers digging into my skin.

"You've been soul-bound. Ironic, isn't it, considering your name? Now hold still. I'm going to fix the mess Esme made, and then you're going to help me teach your grandmother she cannot simply fuck with people the way she has been. She's not a damn puppeteer."

Any blood I still had left my body, and I felt lightheaded from shock.

No, shock was too tame a word to explain what I felt over the bombshell that had just been dropped on my lap.

My first instinct was to jump up and deny, call her crazy and her accusations baseless, but ... were they really?

There was a loud, shrill noise in my ears that seemed to reverberate inside my head. Around the room, the ghosts grew restless, their forms flickering in and out of my sight. A splitting headache formed as if my brain was trying to crack my skull open. Without my permission, my magic resurfaced, forming a thin layer under my skin as if ready to act on my behalf. Fuck. I was losing control.

But maybe ... I tried to find the woman's aura, tried to get a reading out of her, but found nothing.

Illudere's aura was still the only one I could see. Its gentle, playful, slightly chaotic strings a weird comfort in the room when it felt like the very ground was being swept out from under my feet.

Pain on my arm brought me back to the present, helping me focus on something other than my internal turmoil. "Calm down, boy, you're scaring the ghosts." I didn't give a shit about the damn ghosts, and whether or not they were scared right now, I had bigger things on my plate.

But the woman just kept talking, not expecting an answer to her words. "We mean you no harm, so you can stop trying to read me. It won't work, no matter how much you try."

My mind was already spinning so damn fast, trying to comprehend everything, that the fact she could tell I had the power to read auras and that I was trying to read hers didn't even register.

"Now, here's what's going to happen. Andres is going to lock the door and drop the illusion he placed on us, and you and I are going to have a chat. Once we're done, you can choose whether you'll want to let me unravel the binding or not."

Then she shrugged as if it was no big deal either way.

As if she hadn't just ripped the fabric of my reality to shreds and then stepped on the pieces until they were nothing more than dust.

This whole time ... had I been nothing more than another one of the matriarch's pawns?

And just who was this woman who knew so much about us?

# 3

## BLAZE

I hadn't gone to the meeting.

Something in my gut had warned me that leaving Char was a terrible, terrible mistake, so rather than go to my parents' house to face whatever new scheme my brother had come up with or hear the bullshit on how I should find a suitable woman to marry and breed heirs with, I'd stopped just around the corner from the Silverstorms and waited.

The waiting paid off when, not long after, I saw Charisma storming out of the house like a woman on a mission.

The wind blew her pink hair around her face, but she didn't seem to notice the strands whipping her skin. Her shoulders were stiff, tense, and her hands curled into fists at her side as she power-walked out of the Silverstorm gates.

Every time I looked at her, I fell in love all over again. To think there had ever been a time where Char hadn't been mine.

I was so glad I'd gotten my head out of my ass and decided to give this whole poly relationship thing a chance —or whatever the proper name was; Blair called it a harem.

It was much better to have her, hold her, love her even if I had to share her, rather than not have her at all.

Turning on the car's engine, I waited for Char to see me and head over so we could drive home, but instead, she turned in the opposite direction and just kept walking.

Had she not seen me?

I put the car in gear, rolled the windows down, and drove until I was beside her.

"Char," I called out, but she didn't react to it.

So I tried again. And again. On my fourth attempt, it worked.

She turned her head in my direction, and there was a moment before her brain came back to the here-and-now, and she noticed it was me. I could tell because her eyes widened after a few seconds, and she tripped on thin air, catching herself before she fell—thank fuck.

"Blaze?" she asked, pushing the hair from her face and staring at me.

I stopped the car because she'd finally stopped moving, and then I leaned over to open the door for her.

"Get in, Little Spitfire. I can drive you faster than you can walk."

She did, but after she put on the seat belt and closed the door, she just kept staring at me with her hypnotic silver eyes, her eyebrows furrowed in adorable confusion.

"Weren't you meeting your family? Did it already end?"

I shrugged. "I didn't go. I wanted to be near in case you needed me, you know? I figured facing your parents would be hard for you, no matter how much you said it was fine." I gave her my best sheepish grin. "Worst case scenario, I was going to be outside like a creep until you called me to pick you up." But considering she'd stormed out of the gates and walked with no clear goal in mind, I was more glad than ever that I'd bowed out of my family meeting.

"So, where do you want to go, and do you want to talk about it?" I offered.

Char pressed her lips to mine, smiling. "Thank you. Let's just go home. I'll fill you in on the way."

"Home" was actually Char's other boyfriend, Bastille's house. After Char's apartment had blown up and she'd *finally* stopped being targeted by the resistance, Char had sort of moved in with Bast. So, when Andres began dating her too, and then I joined her growing harem, Bast's house became the place we all hung out.

Even though both Andres and I had our own places—which were significantly bigger than Bast's—we wanted to be where our Char was.

Some day, assuming our relationship with her continued to grow more serious, I hoped we'd reach a point where we'd all officially live together. In order for that to happen, though, we'd all have to sit down and address the lack of space in Bast's apartment, and a permanent solution to our living situation. The fact both Andres and I were heirs and would be sharing a roof with a Necromancer—the head of the Tumbas, no less—complicated things, too.

But I was getting ahead of myself.

If and when it became an issue, I knew we'd all work together to find a solution. We had to, if we wanted to continue to make Char happy.

"I can't believe your parents had the nerve to tell you to break up with us." I was *seething*. More than once, while Char had recounted the events, I'd had to stop myself from turning the car around so I could storm the Silverstorms' mansion and give them a piece of my mind. "And they wanted you to date *Brant*? Did they mean Agent *Lucien* Brant? He's way too old!" He wasn't, not really. Brant was thirty, or in his early thirties, so probably just a little older than Blair, or my brother Dean.

"You know him?" she asked, and I almost snorted.

"You don't? Char, he's worked for AMIA longer than either of us. He's part of a special ops team—him and Callum Goldcross—and they specialize in tough missions. They're kind of legends around AMIA. I'm surprised you don't know them."

Char frowned, tilting her head to the side, deep in thought. Then her eyes cleared. "Oh. Big, burly dude with super long locks whose partner is a Legolas wannabe? That's Brant? Oh wow. I've worked with them a couple of times; he has crazy strong Elemental magic."

It was my turn to frown. I didn't like the awe in her voice, nor how she'd mentioned how burly he was.

I didn't even fully register what I was doing until I had Char pinned against the door of the car, our faces inches apart. I ignored the awkward positioning, and the handbrake digging into my leg. My whole focus was on Char, and the way her lids fluttered down. She licked her lips, as if anticipating my kiss, but I didn't give in to the temptation. Not yet, anyway.

"Char?" I purred dangerously. My jealousy was slightly appeased by her breathy "hmm?"

She raised her hands to my shoulders, clinging to me in preparation for what was to come. Her hooded gaze met mine, and there was so much longing in them, so much want.

"Did you have Legolas fantasies as a teen, or were you more of a big, burly hunk type of girl?"

I hated myself for asking, but the green-eyed monster inside me *demanded* to know. Just because I was learning to share her didn't mean I wasn't still possessive of her. I wanted Char to myself, and I was learning to be okay with her relationship with Bast and Andres—though I didn't know why I was okay with her being with them and wasn't going to dwell too deeply on it. The thought of her with someone like Brant, however, made me sick.

"I was more of an Aragorn kind of girl," Char admitted, and then she blinked, adorably confused. "Wait, what? Why are we talking about Lord of the Rings instead of making out?"

She put pressure on my shoulders to get me to close the distance between us, but I wasn't done with her yet.

"Aragorn, huh?"

Char narrowed her eyes at me. "Blaze, are you ... jealous? Of fifteen-year-old me and her crush on fictional men?" When I didn't say anything, she pushed me back. "No, wait. That's not what this is about, is it? That wasn't what we were talking about, not really. It was Brant and Goldcross. Are you ... did you feel jealous of them? Oh, Blaze." Her expression softened, and she cupped my cheek, but I averted my gaze, suddenly embarrassed.

I would've sat back in the driver's seat, but Char kept her other hand on my shoulder, holding me in place.

"Blaze, honey, look at me."

I did as she asked. Char was staring at me with so much emotion and love that it stole my breath away.

"You have nothing to worry about, Blaze. I know our relationship is unconventional and complicated. I know I'm asking for a lot from you and the others. And I know it might be hard to believe when I've already asked the impossible of you, and you're already sharing me with Bast and Andres. But Blaze? I love you. Big time. If you believe nothing else, please believe this: I love you, you dummy. I'm not going to break up with you or the others so I can marry Brant or anyone else, for that matter. We're not at risk. And as for Brant, even before I'd met you or started dating you, I was still not attracted to him. There's nothing to be jealous about. I'm yours."

Then she kissed me, pouring all her love into it, and soon enough, I could think of nothing else.

"I love you too, Char," I said, brushing my lips against hers once more. "Let's go inside. I need to make love to you."

Char smiled against my lips. "I thought you'd never ask."

# 4

## ANDRES

There was a lot I didn't understand about what was going on, especially the whole soul-binding thing.

No, that wasn't true, I'd heard horror stories and rumors about the Soulbinder's ability to control others against their wishes, but I'd always assumed that was all they were. Rumors.

Besides, it wasn't like Theo was acting any different now than he always did. I mean, sure, he was a complete asshole to my girl. When he wasn't being a jerk to her, he acted like a kid whose ultimate Christmas toy was way out of budget, so all he could do was stare longingly at it from afar, never allowed to touch or play with it.

A shitty analogy for the borderline stalkerish behavior, but one that fit him, nonetheless. Especially when he acted like a five-year-old who thought she'd give him the time of day if he pulled her pigtails.

I'd probably never understand what Char saw in him, but if being with him, or at least making peace, was what she wanted, then I'd do everything I could to make it happen. Even if I thought Char was too good for the likes of him.

He had, after all, ghosted my girl and treated her like shit, not even bothering to explain why he was being an ass. Granted, all that had happened years ago, right before we'd all enrolled at the Academy. Back then, I'd just assumed he'd ghosted her because her family had shunned her.

I was ashamed to admit I hadn't done much better. Back then, I barely knew Charisma, and while I thought she was cute, I was too full of myself.

It wasn't until I truly got to know her over the last year that I learned what a fool I'd been. I could've been with Char all these years. Although, she would've probably dick-punched me if I'd tried to pursue her then. I was kind of a cocky bastard and a player.

So, rather than voice my concerns or call Theo all the names he deserved to be called, I followed Gran's orders, locking the door to ensure our privacy. After all, if Gran was right that Theo was Char's soulmate, and if Char forgave him, then I might have to forgive the dumbass.

Once I locked the door, I turned and stared at Theo so I could see his face as I dropped the illusion on both Gran and Bast while making sure their auras remained hidden.

If he tried to attack them in any way or so much as lifted one hostile finger in their direction, I'd end him and get us out of here.

Theo's gaze narrowed as he looked from Bast to Gran, back to me, then to Bast again.

"What are *you* doing here? What do you want?"

How the fuck did Theo know Bast? My hand moved of its own accord towards my MET, and I braced myself.

If I remembered correctly, the one time Bast had

appeared in public near Char had been when we'd rescued our girl, but Theo had been unconscious, slung over Logan's shoulder like a sack of potatoes.

Bast tilted his head to the side regarding Theo.

"We never properly met, but I'm Bastille. Don't worry; I have no business with you. I'm just here as her ride," he tilted his chin in Gran's direction, causing her to roll her eyes at him.

More like Bast was here to make sure she stayed out of trouble, but there was no need for Theo to know that.

"You're Char's Necromancer boyfriend," Theo said, his expression impassive.

Well, fuck.

Trying to break the tension and divert attention despite my blood running cold, I threw an arm over Bast's shoulder, forcing a dazzling smile. "You mean *one* of Char's *boyfriends*. Bast here is my brother-husband. My boyfriend-in-law."

If Bast noticed how sweaty my palms were or how strained my voice sounded, he pretended not to.

I kept rambling about peas in a pod and any other random bullshit I could think of, desperately trying to think of a way to bribe Theo's silence.

He shouldn't know about Bast being a Necromancer.

*No one* should know. It was one thing for Blaze, who was madly in love with Char, to be in on the secret. He'd never do anything to hurt her, even if it went against all we were taught growing up.

But Theo?

Theodore Soulbinder had nothing left to lose when it came down to Charisma Carter. He'd made sure of it.

"Andres, enough!" Gran's command was so uncharacteristic that I stopped mid-sentence.

It was only then I realized I was the only one freaking out in the room, both Gran and Bast were oddly relaxed, and Theodore had made no move to attack or run away screaming about the evil Necros.

"You have nothing to worry about, Andres. Theodore is not a threat to the family. It seems the boy has known about Bast for quite some time"—Gran sent Bastille a look that said *we'll talk later*—"and he hasn't done anything with the information. While we may not know his motives yet"—Gran paused in a way that said *but we will* before continuing—"His aura is mostly pure, even if it's a bit messed up. Nothing irreparable, though."

Theo whipped his head in Gran's direction, his eyes narrowed. "So you *can* see my aura. Who are you, really?"

Gran chuckled. Actually *chuckled*, breaking whatever tension there still was in the room. "Oh, you have so much of your grandfather in you. Well, your great-uncle, not that fool Esme married. I'm glad she couldn't spoil you like she did her children." Then, to my utter shock, she *patted Theo's cheek* like one would an adorable toddler.

Oh, to have my phone in hand so I could record this for Char. My girl would've *loved* to see this. Theo's speechless face was *priceless*.

I didn't know if he was about to bite her hand off or have a stroke, but the veins bulging on his neck and the flush on his cheeks were unnatural.

"Gran, stop playing with him and explain. We can't stay here much longer," Bast warned from beside me, and I dropped my arm, realizing I was still hanging on to him.

With a sigh, Gran let go of Theodore and stood to her full height—which wasn't much. She made a show out of straightening her dress, probably purposefully drawing attention to the ridiculous pattern of the day: a bunch of cat butts with their tails up and a clear focus on their assholes. While that was mild compared to some of her more ... graphic clothes, it was definitely nothing an eighty-year-old should be wearing, yet it was completely Gran.

"All right. You're right," Gran told Bast before turning to Theo, none of the previous mischief on her face. "I suppose I should apologize before we start over, but I couldn't resist messing with Esme's grandson for a bit. Now, I'll introduce myself and explain as much as possible, but you'll have to swear to listen to all I have to say before you start asking questions—because there *will* be questions. I'd also appreciate it if you could exercise a little more restraint over your magic. You're making the spirits antsy. They won't do you any harm, nor will I." She raised a hand when Theo opened his mouth to speak, and shockingly, he did shut up. "I'll answer your questions after, and then I'll give you a choice. If, after everything, you still struggle to believe me, then— and only then—will I allow you to see my aura. Just know, boy, I don't owe you anything. I'm doing this for Charisma and out of kindness to a friend. Nothing's stopping me from leaving you to drown in your misery for the rest of your days."

Harsh.

Theo's gaze jumped from Gran to something over her shoulder, his eyes widening before he nodded.

As if Gran and her posse weren't enough, now two people were listening to the dead in the room. I glanced at Bast to make sure my brother was as out of the loop as I was, slightly appeased when I noticed his attention was on Gran and not on whatever ghost—or ghosts—had shown up.

I didn't think I'd ever get used to the Soul Mages' power. Out of all of the branches of magic, including the Necromancers, a Soul Mage's ability to see the dead creeped me out the most. Probably because it always had me wondering if I was truly alone in a room or if I was unknowingly sharing the space with an army of ghosts.

I'd seen enough horror movies to firmly believe the souls of the dead should follow the light and not inhabit the same plane we did. But it wasn't like I made the decisions.

Theo ran a hand through his hair, sighing before he slumped back on the bed as if all the fight had left him.

"Okay. If Annie says I can trust you ...." Theo trailed off, and I did my best to pretend I hadn't frozen from shock. His *sister*? His very charming, very *dead* sister?

I shuddered.

"Why don't you sit down? All of you. It seems we have a lot to talk about."

I didn't want to sit down. I wanted to turn tail and run far, far away from the damn ghosts around here. For fuck's sake.

Before I could take Theo up on his offer to sit down, Gran was already shaking her head. "There's no need. I won't take long."

Bast snorted beside me, and I had to agree. She'd just made it sound like she was going to tell Theodore the entire freaking story, going back to her birth or something. And now she was saying we shouldn't sit because it wouldn't take long.

Contradictory much?

But then again, this was Gran. Of course she was going to contradict herself.

"You asked who I am, boy, and how I know so much. Well, you probably know me as Alma Siela. I used to be engaged to your great-uncle a long, long time ago."

Theo's eyes widened. "But you're dead," he accused, and Gran raised an eyebrow.

"I beg to fucking differ. As you can see, I'm very much alive." Gran shrugged like it was no big deal.

# 5

## THEO

"That's not possible," I protested, disregarding the fact that she was literally standing in front of me and, as she'd said, very much alive. Even Annie's confirmation didn't help me wrap my mind around this whole thing. "You *died*. Over fifty years ago. Your death broke Great-Uncle Lawrence. He had to step down because he went deep into mourning you. I can't believe you faked your own death. How could you do that to him? How could you just—"

She didn't let me finish my sentence.

Alma straightened her posture and sent me a look like I was no more than dirt under her boots. The milky, whitewashed gaze only made things more unnerving.

"How could I what, boy? Chase my own happiness? Marry the man I loved rather than someone my family had deemed appropriate? Lawrence and I were childhood friends, but that was it. We were never in love, and it wasn't my supposed death that broke him. It was your beloved grandmother and her thirst for power." She paced the room while cursing in another language.

"I don't understand," I said, even though I was starting to

understand just fine. Slowly but surely, little pieces were falling into place, and the picture Mrs. Alma Siela was painting was beginning to make more sense than the web of lies I'd always believed.

After all, the signs were all there.

I might not want to believe the worst about my own grandmother, but that had more to do with my family loyalty than anything else. I'd seen proof of it with my own eyes. Aunt Kate. My parents. And even me, apparently. Why would things have been any different when it came to my great-uncle? Why would the matriarch have some kind of mental, moral ground she wasn't willing to cross when she'd already done so fucking much?

It wasn't like anyone was stopping her. No one even knew about most of it, and no one was strong enough to oppose her, even if they'd known. Esme Soulbinder had made sure of that.

*Fuck.*

My whole life. Had it all been a lie? Had I been nothing more than yet another pawn?

Thank Goddess I'd been stubborn enough to go against the matriarch's wishes when it came to Char. Before, I'd thought her binding my Char's soul was a distant possibility, but now, I was immensely relieved I'd let her go.

Char had unknowingly dodged one hell of a bullet.

The realization didn't bring me any relief, however. Nothing ever would.

Bast walked to his grandmother and spoke to her in low, soothing tones while Andres sent me a murderous look, but I ignored it all.

I was too busy going through every interaction, every word my grandmother had ever said, trying to watch it all from outside, picking apart the undertones. And most of all, trying to remember the last time I'd read the matriarch's aura. Hers, or from any member of my family.

Years, maybe?

"I think that's why she prohibited us from reading the auras in the family, Theo," Annie said softly, as if she had a direct line to my thoughts.

My sister had always been able to tell what I was thinking, even though she was two years younger than me.

"It makes sense, don't you think? I mean, it was always weird how the rule only applied to family members, never to outsiders. And it wasn't like they knew that us using our powers would one day make us go blind if we abused them. It's what happened to Gran Alma, by the way. And something I was going to warn you about some other time. But anyway," Annie carried on as if she hadn't dropped yet *another* nuclear bomb on my lap.

The hits just kept on fucking coming. What the hell? I barely digested one thing; three others were thrown at me like some kind of pinball from hell.

Reading auras could make me *blind*?

One would think that would've been the first thing Annie would've told me the *second* she found out.

"Grandma Esme was probably afraid we'd notice something was up with our parents, or even that I might notice something was wrong with you. I mean, other than the usual, obviously. Goddess knows if she messed with my own aura, but I guess that's something we'll never know, huh? And that isn't the point right now. Weasley, you have to listen to Gran. Hear her out, and *believe* her. She has nothing to gain from lying to you, and she's the only one who can help."

"I'm not entirely sure he *deserves* my help anymore," Mrs. Alma protested from across the room.

"Gran!" Bast, Andres, and Annie said at the same time, making the elderly woman huff.

"What? He's an ungrateful, disrespectful, rude child. And he can't even blame that on that bitch Esme's meddling. That's all him. I have better things to do with my time than to stand here being insulted by someone who wasn't there to witness the things he's accusing me of. Let him be manipulated by his grandmother. It's none of my business." Mrs. Alma cast me one final dirty look and turned towards the door, the ghost of an older male hovering close to her and gently guiding her, whispering in her ear.

"Gran, please." Annie hovered in her direction, suddenly standing in Mrs. Alma's way and placing her hand on the other woman's arm. Mrs. Alma stopped before she went through Annie, and it was like she could feel my sister's hand on her arm. "He doesn't mean any harm. My brother is hardheaded and stubborn, but he's a good guy. He's just having trouble digesting our grandmother's betrayal. He didn't mean any offense, I swear. Please, Gran. Please help him. I know you think he doesn't deserve it, but please. He needs to stop her."

I was choosing not to be offended by all the insults Annie had thrown my way. Not like she was entirely wrong ... neither was Mrs. Alma. I had no idea how I felt knowing some random stranger knew more about me than most of my family.

"You've already come this far," Bast said when Mrs. Alma's gaze went to her grandson.

Andres, being Andres, just shrugged. "If you help him, you'll get to lord it over him until the day he dies."

For some reason, that was what had Mrs. Alma turning back to face me, her head tilted to the side, deep in thought.

Eventually, she sighed.

"Fine. But it'll cost you."

Of fucking course.

I opened my mouth to say something, but Annie's ghost fingers swiped at me, causing me to jump on the bed.

I hadn't even noticed her moving across the room.

Benefits of not having a physical body, I supposed.

Annie stared at me like a parent would a particularly unruly child, and I sighed, suddenly feeling exhausted.

This whole situation was shit. Worse than shit, really. I felt like I'd been forced to play Dungeons and Dragons with a particularly shitty character whose skill points had been attributed by a toddler throwing dice up in the air. Except the dice were cursed and always landed on ones or twos, and somehow the Dungeon Master was making me face the final boss with noob gear and zero strength.

The truth was that only one thing mattered to me right now. Even if Annie was wrong, even if this whole thing was some weird prank, Mrs. Alma had played the one card that would ensure my cooperation from the beginning, whether she knew it or not. Even so, I was starting to doubt this was a prank. The fact Mrs. Alma had known to hide her aura or have someone else do it was proof enough that she knew her stuff. Most mages didn't realize they had auras, let alone that some select few might be able to read them.

Her offhand comment about the matriarch having manipulated me to stay away from Char had hit home, and if nothing else, I wanted it gone.

Oh, I still wouldn't go after Char, not when that might put her right back in my grandmother's claws. However, I didn't like the idea that I'd been played without my knowledge.

The matriarch had overplayed her hand, and I'd do everything I could to make sure she paid for it, or die trying.

And if Mrs. Alma could help me make that happen, or at least give me complete control of my own fucking life, then so be it.

"Mrs. Alma, Annie is right. I apologize for what I said, I let my emotions and confusion get the better of me, and I lashed out. It's just been a lot of new information to process, a lot of things that go against what I've spent my entire life believing. I'm trying to make sense of it all, to process it. It's just a lot." Not to mention the enormity of my grandmother's betrayal, not only to me, but to our whole family. I was barely able to process everything, let alone react accordingly. "However, it's no excuse for what I said to you, and I apologize once more for that. I promise it won't happen again. I do, however, have a couple of questions, if you don't mind."

I might have imagined it, but I could've sworn Bast was regarding me with approval now, while Andres—being Andres—gave me a thumbs up.

Well, at least someone was on my side, *sort of.*

Mrs. Alma wasn't so easily appeased, though. Arms crossed in front of her; she stared me down while the ghosts around her assumed a very similar position.

Eerie as fuck.

"Alright. What do you want to know, boy?" All traces of friendliness were gone from her voice.

"Earlier you said my grandmother bound my soul to keep me away from Char, but she also did one to make me seek my soulmate, right?" I tried to phrase my next words carefully so I wouldn't accidentally offend her again and make an even bigger mess out of this whole thing. What I really wanted was to ask her if she was sure that these were the bindings Grandmother had placed on me, but there was no way I could ask that without coming across as an ass. So, instead, I tried a different approach. "Is it that ... easy to determine the objective of each binding? And if so, would you mind teaching me how?" In spite of the rules my grandmother had placed, I'd spent a long time studying Aunt Kate's aura. However, it wasn't like I'd been able to tell the bindings apart or know what they were supposed to do. All we knew was what we'd been told by the matriarch herself: that she'd had to bind Aunt Kate's soul in order to protect the family. Everything else we'd learned from eavesdropping when we weren't supposed to. It was how we found out about Aunt Kate's attempt to run away with her human lover.

Mrs. Alma smiled, and I didn't know whether to be scared or not. "That's three questions, boy, but fine. I suppose I volunteered to explain things to you." She approached my hospital bed, brushing off the ghosts who tried to help her maneuver around the room.

If I couldn't see the ghosts and how much they were helping her or gently guiding her, I never would've guessed Mrs. Alma had lost her vision. She did everything with so much confidence, probably trusting the souls helping her completely. It was nothing like I would've expected a blind person to behave. Although, even as the thought crossed my mind, I realized how prejudiced and narrow-minded I was probably being.

Man, I really was an asshole.

Mrs. Alma shocked me speechless when she sat at the foot of my hospital bed like it was no big deal.

"The first thing you must remember, boy, is that I've lived for a long, long time. I may not look it, but I'm older than your grandmother." Mrs. Alma winked at me, and honestly, now I'd seen it all.

Mrs. Alma took advantage of my shock. "Now, not only

am I old, but I also didn't know any better, and because of that, I constantly used my powers to read auras. Much like your sister said, the price for that was my eyesight, but that's neither here nor there. When you've lived as long as I have and relied on your aura reading skills for as long as I have, you learn a few things. So, to answer your initial question, no, it's not so easy to discern the intentions behind soul bindings, but it's not impossible. Lucky for us, Esme grew cocky. Which means she hasn't bothered to hide her dirty work as well as she used to."

I didn't know how *lucky* that was, but even I knew to keep my trap shut. So I stayed quiet and let her continue.

"If this had been forty years ago, it might've been harder for me to tell the intent behind each binding, but like I said, Esme grew cocky. Well, that, and I admit I already came up with my suspicions based on what Andres had told me. And before you ask," Mrs. Alma said, glancing at Annie, whose mouth was open as if she had been about to ask something.

Oh wow. Her skills were the real deal.

"There are multiple possibilities as to why you hadn't seen that Theodore's soul had been bound. The most simple being that yours could've been, too, with the sole intent of making sure you couldn't see his. After all, you two were the only Soul Mages able to read auras, right? Well, that Esme knew of, anyway. But there's no point in dwelling on that."

Mrs. Alma tilted her head so she would face me once more. "Now, you also asked me if I could teach you, and that will very much depend on your behavior and whether or not you'll be willing to make it worth my time. It won't be easy, and you'll have to be very careful about how you use your powers, too. Unless you don't mind ending up like me. Nothing we should concern ourselves with now, however.

After all, we have more pressing issues." She waggled her eyebrows, and it was super weird.

"Right. You said you could unbind my soul, right? And there would be a price. What do you want?"

Her milky white eyes glinted, and I braced myself.

I was for sure not going to like where this was going.

"Well, actually, I said I'd help *you*, not that I'd do it *for you*. You see, I'm too old, and as much as it hurts my pride to admit, I'm not strong enough to unbind your soul on my own. You'll have to do much of the work. I'll help, of course, both with my magic and by guiding you through the process. As a side benefit, you'll learn how to do something that only two people alive know how to do. In exchange, though, I want you to challenge your grandmother. I don't mean kill her. Confront her, and if necessary, challenge her so she'll step down. She can't be allowed to continue the way she has been, and she has to pay for all the shit she's done and gotten away with."

Holy fucking shit.

My eyes widened, and my heart started beating so fast, I could actually hear it.

There were protests all over the room, but my gaze was narrowed to one person and one person only. Everything else was nothing but background noises and blurry figures.

Treason. Mrs. Alma was willing to help me if I committed treason.

But was it any different than what I'd already considered? Mrs. Alma was right; Grandmother had to be stopped. I'd come to that conclusion myself, years ago, even before I'd known about all this shit.

There was only one flaw with her plan, though.

"I can try, but, ma'am, I don't know if I'm strong enough to face off against her," I admitted.

Mrs. Alma patted me on the cheek. "Boy, you're stronger than you know. Or did you really think someone like Esme would be satisfied just manipulating you on romantic matters? You're too naive for your own good. So, what's it going to be? You in, or have I wasted my time?"

# 6
## BAST

I didn't know what had surprised me the most: Gran's crazy plan or the fact it had taken very little convincing to get Theodore to agree to overthrow his grandmother. Even being disgusted by what the Soulbinder matriarch had done didn't mean I agreed with their solution. It wasn't that I didn't think Esme Soulbinder shouldn't have to face the severity of her crimes. I just didn't know if forcing Theodore to challenge his own family was the wisest move.

But when I'd tried voicing my concerns without offering a better alternative, Gran had done what she did best: ignored me.

Then they'd cast a circle, and Gran and Theo had held hands while they worked on fixing his soul. All we'd been able to see were the yellow and pink circles, and Gran's humming, nothing else. Until Gran had sagged against Theo's bed as the activation circles started to vanish. Theo had managed to catch her before he, too, slumped back on the hospital bed, unconscious, Gran on top of him.

It would've been a photo-worthy moment if we hadn't been so worried about their health. Andres and I had rushed to check on them, and then we'd had to carry a semi-conscious Gran back to the car and take her home so she could rest.

I'd called one of my cousins on the way, and Grant had met us at her place to watch over her while she recovered.

I'd have stayed, but Andres and I needed time to process shit before we met Char for game night.

Char. Goddess, I needed to figure out a way to explain all ... *this* to her.

I closed my eyes and pressed my forehead against the car's wheel.

I loved my grandmother. Really, I did. She may act crazy and have insane ideas, as well as a questionable sense of fashion, but her shenanigans never failed to make me laugh. Even though the amusement always came after, and more often than not, I ended up with a headache. But Gran was fiercely loyal. She'd helped raise both Blair and me after our mother died, and she'd always been there for us, no matter what we needed. She'd even helped me take on the mantle of head of the family when my parents had abdicated, taking on a lot of the responsibilities that should've been mine so I wouldn't be overwhelmed. All that, and she was always looking out for the Necromancers, always keeping an ear on the ground to make sure our people were safe.

So she liked to meddle with our lives sometimes and play a bit with the family when she got bored or she felt we needed to be kept on our toes—that was what made Gran, well, *Gran*.

She'd crossed a line today, though, and I didn't know how to fix it.

It wasn't even that she'd outed herself to Theodore Soulbinder, I'd kind of expected that when she'd dragged me and Andres to the hospital. It wasn't that she'd helped right a wrong that had been done to him, that was just how she worked. I'd have been disappointed in her if she hadn't offered to help him when there was something she could do —even if she had spent a long-ass time antagonizing Theodore before she'd gotten to the point. That, too, was an expected Gran behavior.

However, Gran had no business getting tangled in Soulbinder messes. She had no business demanding Theo challenge his own grandmother.

I understood she probably had some unknown ulterior motives. Or maybe she was just trying to look out for her people–because even though she'd been living as a Necromancer and hiding out, there was no denying she'd been born a Soul Mage, it wasn't something one would ever forget. Or maybe she felt like she owed Theo something, but she should've let him make his own fucking choices.

"Soooooo," Andres started beside me, probably having waited as long as he could for me to get my thoughts in order. "That was fun."

I snorted, raising my head to look at him. "It was a clusterfuck, is what you mean."

He just shrugged, but his lips were curled up at the corners. "I mean, I wouldn't say it's an ideal situation, but it sure is interesting. I always knew Mrs. Esme was a scary, manipulative woman, but even I did not expect this level of fucked-up from her. I thought my uncle was bad, but she has him beat by a *lot*."

"Not to be an ass, Andres, but I'm pretty sure if your uncle had the power, he would've done the same thing to you and your family," I said, causing Andres to shudder.

"Don't even. Can you imagine? Being used as a pawn without even knowing? Having your choices taken away and your free will violated like that? How fucked-up is it that right now I'm actually *glad* the only things Ricardo did to the family were try to poison my dad and challenge me? At least his attacks were out in the open, and we could do something about it. Less than ideal, obviously, but *fuck*, Esme Soulbinder makes Ricardo look well-adjusted. I never thought I'd see the day I'd actually feel bad for Theo."

Since I didn't have an answer for him, I turned the keys in the ignition and started the car, pulling out of the garage at Gran's building.

We didn't speak for a while, both of us lost in our thoughts.

"Hey, you think now that Theo's fixed, he's gonna try to win Char over again?" Andres asked, and I was glad we were both stuck in traffic because otherwise, I might've crashed.

"What!?" I turned to stare at Andres in shock, and it wasn't until someone laid on the horn behind us that I refocused on driving.

"I mean, I'm just saying. If he was being weird with her because of the powers-that-be, now that he's free ... it's not like he ever stopped loving her. Even when he was being an ass, he still followed her around like a puppy. At a distance, and sometimes it was kind of creepy, but still. Besides, Gran said they were soulmates, too, right? And if Theo can see auras, then he's always known. If I were him, the first thing I'd do once I woke up would be to crawl on my knees and beg Char for her forgiveness after I explained everything to her. Then I'd stay on my knees and eat her pussy until she forgave me because A) our girl is delicious, and B) multiple orgasms are the best way to get her to forget even her own name."

"You do realize you're talking about our girlfriend." My words were carefully blank, but if he'd stopped to pay attention, he'd see my hands were gripping the steering wheel tight enough to cut off my circulation.

Andres was oblivious like only Andres could be. "I know. I also know he hurt her a lot, and for a long-ass time. I'm not saying she should forget the last five years. But Bast, man, there's a reason she's still hurting about this whole thing. If she didn't love him anymore, after all this time, after everything, she wouldn't be hung up on him still. This is Char we're talking about. *Our* Char. I want her to be happy, and if putting up with Theo as a brother-husband is what she wants, then that's what I'll do. Besides, I'm pretty sure I can talk her into finding creative ways to punish him that will be great for me."

I grinned. I'd just bet he did.

"*There it is.* I was starting to worry you'd been body-snatched or something. For a while there, you almost sounded philosophical." I shook my head. Trust Andres to be all deep and emotional and shit and then ruin it with his kinky fantasies.

Besides, he was right. If taking Theo back and having him join her harem was what made Char happy, of course I'd agree to it. It didn't matter that I hated Theo's fucking guts for everything he did to her, Char's happiness was more important.

Although, I supposed, he hadn't been a jerk to Char on purpose, and we should take that into account. He'd been brainwashed, manipulated. He'd probably suffered more than we would ever know.

I should probably give Theodore some credit, even if I still wanted to see him grovel to earn Char back. If he survived his confrontation with his grandmother, that was.

I reached my building and maneuvered the car into the

private lot, wondering if Char had already gotten home, and how the hell we were going to tell her what we'd just done.

"Andres." At the mention of his name, he looked up from his phone.

"What?" he asked.

"How are we going to explain all this to Char?"

Eyes wide, he stared at me and then stared some more.

"Oh shit," he said under his breath. "Can we just not tell her?"

It was my turn to stare at him. "Are you for real? Is this a real question?"

He ran a hand through his hair, pulling at it and groaning. "No. I mean, yes but also no. It's not a real question. I know we have to tell her, but Bast," his eyes found mine, and under any other circumstance, the desperation in his gaze would be funny. "I don't want to."

"You think I want to be the one to poke at the still bleeding wound?"

This would hurt Char. It would make her doubt things and question herself, and I didn't want that for her. But I refused to keep secrets from my girl.

"We could rock-paper-scissors for it," Andres suggested, and it was the worst idea he could ever come up with.

"Best out of three?" I offered, holding my fist up.

"Fuck. Yeah. The loser gets to break Char's heart. The winner gets to grab the ice cream and spoon feed it to her through her tears."

Either way, we lost. And it wasn't even our fucking fault this time.

# 7

## CHARISMA

I lay in bed with Blaze, my head on his naked chest, enjoying the steady rhythm of his breathing as he dozed off.

Blaze had made good on his promise and made love to me until my eyes crossed and my toes curled. He'd made me come twice before he'd finally found his release, and then we'd both been a sweaty, breathless mess.

It had been amazing.

But the best part had been his declaration earlier. Blaze Futhark loved me, just like I loved him.

I smiled, listening to his heartbeat and inhaling his scent.

Blaze loved me, and I loved him. I probably shouldn't have been surprised by his revelation, but I had been. Hearing the words, knowing they were true, felt spectacular.

I sighed dreamily, careful not to make too much noise and wake Blaze. I felt good, *really* good, and after the workout I'd just had, I should be snoring alongside Blaze, but my brain was too damn wired to allow me to sleep.

Too much had happened, and I needed the time to process it all. I'd done this dance enough times to know there was no way around it. When things got overwhelming or a lot happened, I always needed to stop and just ... work through it.

At least what had started out as a shitty day had ended with a turn for the better.

And it was only getting started.

The guys would get home pretty soon, and game night would begin. I didn't know how Logan would fit in with my guys, or even if they'd like the intrusion. Bast had said I could invite anyone I wanted, and he and Andres had already teased me about Logan.

Granted, I'd thought they were out of their minds in implying Logan might be into me, let alone sharing me, but it seemed the guys had read Logan Nightshade better than I had.

I knew I was getting ahead of myself. Logan's interest might be more curiosity than anything. Hell, for all I knew, he could've just been trying to be nice after the traumatic experience we'd shared. Or he might just want to hire me to make him another MET.

That wasn't what my gut was telling me, though. And regardless of what really happened, there was one thing I'd have to address first.

Blaze.

He'd finally agreed to the idea of being one of my boyfriends, but it had cost him—which I completely understood, I really did. In his place, there was no fucking way I'd share him. Or any of them.

However, he loved me enough to compromise. We were building something good between us. He was even making an effort when it came to Andres and Bast.

And yet, he'd gotten all possessive and jealous at the mere thought of a guy I'd worked with, like, twice, while at AMIA.

But then, again, Andres had also gotten jealous and acted all possessive when I'd interacted with Daniel Mirare, and Andres was literally the guy who called Blaze and Bast his "brother-husbands" and teased me about Logan. So what the hell did I know?

Maybe there was some unspoken rule or guy code that could teach me which hot guy would make my men jealous and which ones wouldn't. It'd be handy if I could be clued in on it—not that I *wanted* to make them jealous, quite the contrary—so I would know where I stood.

I was so lost in thought, absently playing with Blaze's nipple while I spiraled, that I hadn't realized he'd woken up.

"Little Spitfire, if you keep doing that, I'll consider it an invitation."

I froze. My finger poised right above the snout of the wolf Blaze had tattooed on his chest. Whoever inked Blaze had taken the time to blend his nipple so it would be part of the wolf. Bet it had hurt like a bitch for Blaze, though, because there was no way the skin around wasn't crazy sensitive.

I'd know. I'd played with Blaze's body every chance I had.

"An invitation for what?" I asked innocently, raising my head so I could look at him.

I thought he would look sleepy, but Blaze looked completely awake. Despite the rumpled, messy hair, his mossy green eyes were open and alert. The heat in his gaze could only be described as *scorching hot*.

"Why don't you try it again and find out?" he challenged.

Damn him. He knew I couldn't resist the bait.

Biting my bottom lip, I held his gaze and did the only thing one possibly could in a situation like this.

I pinched his nipple, *hard*.

Blaze didn't disappoint. He didn't waste time. Blaze pounced on me so fast, I was on my back, with his mouth on my breast, sucking it before I could even blink.

As punishments went, I could live with this one.

I gripped his hair, not to push him away, but to draw him closer and encourage him. And then Blaze was doing that thing with his tongue that drove me wild.

I spread my legs wider, moving against him in search of friction, even as he moved between my breasts, intent on giving the other equal attention.

"Blaze," I said, unsure if it was a whine or a plea.

Probably a bit of both, honestly.

He adjusted our positions, never stopping his ministrations until I finally got the friction I wanted.

I rubbed against Blaze's cock, loving the way it was hitting my clit just *right*.

I knew I could come just from this. It had happened before, and I hoped it would happen many, many times in my future, but I was greedy, and I wanted *more*.

I should be sated from earlier, but instead, my body craved to reignite the connection between us. With him inside me, no barrier between us, as we both reached that peak together.

"Blaze, please, I need you inside me," I begged, reaching down to guide his dick home.

Blaze raised his head, looked at me, and *smirked*.

Fuck me sideways. Upwards. Downwards. Literally. Please. Anything.

So long as fucking was involved.

That smirk told me fucking might not be involved,

though, and if that was the case, then it was an unjust, unfair punishment.

"Not yet, Char. You'll get my cock eventually, but we're going to play a bit first," he said.

Blaze grabbed my hands and held them above my head on the bed, keeping me in place by my wrists.

My eyes widened when twin dark blue activation circles appeared right above my hands. Blaze let go of my wrists, but I stayed pinned in place.

"What the what?" I gaped at him, equal parts shocked and horny.

Blaze's smirk increased. "Been wanting to try that on you for a long time, Little Spitfire. Now I finally have the chance," he admitted, sounding smug as fuck. "If it gets to be too much, tell me, and I'll stop, okay?"

I nodded. "My safe word is apples." The Castle reference was out of my mouth before I could even think about it, but it didn't matter. Apples was as good a safe word as any.

Besides, I loved the glint in Blaze's eyes at my quick reply, and the implications behind it.

Then Blaze was kissing me, and nothing else mattered.

He kissed me until I was a squirming, breathless mess, shamelessly rubbing against him, unsuccessfully trying to find that perfect friction I'd had before.

Then he broke the kiss and started to move lower, nibbling on my earlobe, my neck, teasing my pert nipples, licking and kissing my belly. He nudged my legs apart and tongue-fucked my pussy until I screamed.

I had not seen my orgasm coming, and it had been mind-blowing.

Blaze didn't wait for me to calm down or lose the high; he lapped at me, licking me clean until I was on the verge of another orgasm. I tested the strength of my restraints, wanting to touch, needing to touch, but they held firm.

"You taste so fucking good, Little Spitfire. I can never get enough of you." Blaze spoke against my pussy, and my whole body vibrated along with it.

I opened my eyes to look at him and froze.

Andres and Bast stood in the bedroom door we'd forgotten to close.

Bast was holding Andres back by the arm, physically stopping him from joining us in bed.

"Char? You okay? Do you want me to stop?" Blaze asked, concern clear in his voice and eyes.

Damn, I loved this man.

"Yeah. It's just ... uh ... we're not alone anymore," I replied, nodding towards the door.

"Oh, don't stop on our account," Andres purred, smiling like the cat who got the canary. "We like to watch."

I knew all about Andres' predilection for watching, and I freaking loved it. Especially when he watched Bast fucking me and then ended up joining. Bast and I liked to play a little game to see how long Andres would be able to hold out before he finally caved and fucked me, and it was *glorious*.

Blaze, however, had tensed against me the second he'd heard Andres' voice. And while I loved playing games with Andres, I wasn't about to push Blaze out of his comfort zone. That wasn't how this relationship was going to work.

Blaze had made his boundaries very clear early on, and we were all going to respect that.

Consent worked both ways.

I opened my mouth to tell the guys to leave and close the door, but Bast beat me to it.

"Sorry, man. Sorry, Char. We came home and heard you

screaming, and we came to check. Since the door was open, Andres took it as an invitation. Anyway, you two can carry on. We were just leaving." In a show of strength that made me breathless, Bast grabbed Andres right below the shoulders and *lifted* him, *carrying* him out of the room like Andres weighed nothing.

If I'd been wet before, now I was *gushing*.

I may or may not have licked my lips in appreciation. Oh, I was *so* going to take advantage of that hot alpha male side of Bast later.

"Wait," Blaze called out, and I swore all three of us froze. All eyes went to Blaze, and I held my breath.

Was he about to ... ? No. There was no way. Right?

Blaze looked from me to the guys, then back to me.

"Do you like being watched, Little Spitfire?"

*Oh shit*. He totally was.

I started to nod, thought better of it, and cleared my throat.

Kind of an awkward time to have this conversation when I was naked, tied up, and my legs were over Blaze's shoulders, but there were things that had to be spoken out loud, and not just mumbled.

And this felt like it wasn't just a big moment but a huge one, for all of us.

"I like it when Andres watches, or Bast. But Blaze, what I like doesn't matter right now. I mean, obviously, it does in the sense that we wouldn't do anything I wasn't enjoying, but the point is, what *you* like matters too. If the idea of them watching makes you uncomfortable, then that's okay. It can be just you and me." I tugged against the restraints again, wanting to touch him, to cup his cheek so he'd know I meant it. But his damn magic was holding strong—literally.

"Seriously, Blaze, we can leave. I mean, don't get me

wrong, we'd love to watch. Love even more to participate, not going to lie, especially when Char is all spread open like the best damn buffet like that. But it's like she said. We all enjoy our alone time with our Char, and we didn't mean to intrude on yours. It was just that, well, you did leave the door open." Andres gave an awkward shrug—he was still being held up by Bast—and sent me a grin that showed those damn dimples. "Forgot you weren't aware of that rule, but it's cool. We'll go drive around the block or get dinner or something."

I could've kissed Andres right now.

He was totally getting a blowjob later, too.

Andres' words seemed to settle something in Blaze, though, because his next words surprised the hell out of me.

"I kind of like the idea of them seeing me claim you, though," Blaze admitted like he was saying something taboo.

Oh, my sweet, sweet Blaze.

Andres whooped, and Bast finally let go of him, but both of them stayed by the door.

"Are you sure about this?" I asked Blaze. "Remember, you're in charge here. We can do this any way you want."

"Yeah. I mean, I don't know if I'll be game for the other stuff, but if they want to stay and watch, I'm fine with it."

I glanced at Bast and Andres. "If Blaze changes his mind, will you two leave?" It felt awkward to ask them that, but I didn't want anyone to regret this tomorrow.

"Yeah. Don't worry, my love. It's like you said, Blaze is in charge here. Well, you are, too. We can take this as slow or as far as you two want."

Bast's words reassured Blaze even further, and without any warning, Blaze went back to feasting on my pussy like a starved man.

# 8

## ANDRES

Blaze Futhark had just earned my respect.

No, that wasn't true. He'd had my respect before. Right now, though, he had my gratitude.

I owed Blaze big time.

And it wasn't even just because he'd saved me from having to tell Char that her boy Theo had been brainwashed. It wasn't even that, thanks to him, we'd gotten home to the best sight: Char, naked, with her arms restrained above her head—though I couldn't see any cuffs or rope—and her mouth parted in pleasure, breathing labored, breasts arched, begging for me to taste, to take.

What had seriously struck me was that Blaze had pushed through his comfort zone to make an effort for Char.

Once I'd realized the open door to the bedroom hadn't been an invitation to join, I'd been prepared to leave with Bast. And it wasn't because Bast was trying to carry me out, either. I'd been prepared to leave of my own free will, being carried out had just amused me enough that I'd let Bast carry on with it.

My respect for Blaze wouldn't have changed even if he had wanted privacy with Char: not everybody was into exhibitionism, and I respected that. But Blaze had surprised me in the best of ways when he'd asked us to stay, offering a compromise.

Showing us he was more okay with the brother-husband thing than even he thought he was.

And for that, I was grateful. And I felt like I owed him because this *was* a gift he was giving us.

Deep down, I was sure he knew that while the whole group sex thing wasn't all that important to maintain the relationship with Char, it would strengthen our bond with her and each other.

He was leveling up as our brother-husband.

Char buckled against Blaze, calling out his name while using her legs to push him closer to her pussy.

Damn, that pussy. Char tasted freaking amazing. Just thinking about it made me hard.

Well, harder. My dick had been hard since I'd walked through that door and seen the buffet in front of me.

It was with herculean restraint that I simply watched without getting my fucking dick out of my pants and rubbing one out while I enjoyed the show.

Char would love it if I did. I knew that. My girl loved to see what her little breathy moans did to me. But I'd agreed to just watch.

I could be good every now and then.

"Blaze, please. I need ... I need you," Char begged.

*Fuck.*

"Tell him what you need, Char. Use your words," Bast's order caught me by surprise, and I stared at him, eyebrows raised.

Char moaned, bucking against Blaze.

Oh, we were testing the line, were we?

*Interesting.*

"His cock," Char said, but Bast shook his head.

"You aren't talking to me, Char. You're talking to him. Blaze is in charge here, remember? *Beg* him," Bast demanded.

I was watching Blaze, though, and it was with satisfaction I noticed he didn't seem to mind the interruption.

Especially when Char started begging with gusto.

"Please, Blaze. Fuck me. I need your cock inside of me. Please."

Something snapped in Blaze.

Blue activation circles shone on Char's arms, releasing them. Before I could even process the nifty trick, Blaze pulled Char by her legs, lifting her ass from the bed, and then he thrust into her.

I had no idea if he'd chosen this position for his benefit or ours, but from where Bast and I stood, we could see Char's delectable naked body, her tits bouncing with Blaze's every thrust.

Char moaned his name again, digging her heels into Blaze's ass to meet his thrusts, her half-lidded eyes never leaving him.

*Fuck.* I wanted to get in that damn bed and help Blaze take care of our girl. This was *torture*. The best kind of torture, but torture nonetheless.

Then Char's eyes met mine, and my balls felt like they'd burst.

"Eyes on Blaze, Char," Bast barked the order, and I didn't know whether I wanted to dick punch him or not. "It's only you and him."

I wanted to laugh. Trust Bast to say it was only them

when he was literally speaking and breaking their illusion of the moment.

Two could play this game, though.

"Tell him how good he feels inside of you, Char. Tell him how your tight pussy is going to milk his cock when he makes you come."

My words had Blaze grunting, and I watched with deep satisfaction as he started fucking Char even harder, his movements growing erratic. Knowing he was close to orgasm, he rubbed Char's clit with his hand. The sound of flesh hitting flesh and Char's throaty, breathless noises filled the room like music.

Then Char finally reached that peak, her eyes closing in bliss, and Blaze was right there with her.

*Lucky bastard.*

Blaze collapsed on top of Char, the two of them looking cozy as hell. Meanwhile, Bast went into the en suite, and I heard the sound of running water.

We could always count on Bast and his caretaking nature.

Though how he was able to walk when I felt like all the blood I had was in my dick, I had no damn clue.

So rather than risk making a fool of myself, I stayed where I was. I wanted to see how things would play out now, too, because I was pretty damn sure the post-sex moment was as important for the group dynamic as the sex itself had been.

I might never have been in this kind of relationship before, but I'd been familiarizing myself with the dynamics pretty much from the moment I'd met Blair. After all, when my sister had shown up at our doorstep, my father had explained a few things. Everything else, Blair and Bast had taught me over the years. I'd seen firsthand how their dads worked together and always kept the communication channel open. Well, before they'd retired from ... everything and became hermits of sorts.

Bast returned from the bathroom with a wet cloth and offered it to Blaze. Char smiled so brightly, she was beaming.

"Thanks," Blaze said, nodding to Bast and getting up so he could clean Char up.

Cue awkward silence.

I almost sighed. Now that the fun and games were over, it was pretty damn clear Blaze was unsure of where he stood —there was no way he needed to pay that much attention to cleaning Char up, as if he was working with some volatile magic or some shit. And yet, Char and Bast were trying to give him space to work through whatever was going on in his mind, probably in an attempt to respect his boundaries.

In trying to give him space, they were turning this whole thing into a bigger deal than it needed to be, though.

They were so lucky they had me.

I walked towards the bed. "That was so fucking hot," I complimented, pretending I didn't see the way Bast had tensed up or how Blaze had frozen.

I wanted to roll my eyes at the duo, but that would be counter-productive. Instead, I gave Char a chaste kiss on the lips. "Next time, though, it'll be my dick you're riding. I don't care who watches or participates, but it'll be my name you're screaming when you come."

Then I stood up, sent Blaze a wink, and sauntered off, whistling.

"Andres, wait," Char called out before I could leave the room.

I stopped and turned my head, watching as she sat on the bed. "Don't you guys think we should talk about this? Are we ... " Char bit her bottom lip, and dammit. I was only so strong. "Are we okay? Was this too much?" She asked Blaze, her eyes full of concern.

Of course we were okay, I wanted to say, but it wasn't my reassurance she needed.

Thankfully, though, Blaze wasn't as big an ass as he pretended to be at the Academy.

Blaze cupped Char's face, kissing her lightly. "It was pretty hot, actually," he admitted, and Goddess, the tips of his ears were red.

*As I live and breathe.*

Blaze Futhark was blushing. Now I'd seen it all.

"What about you guys?" Char looked at Bast and then me. "None of you erh … "

I smiled at her even as Bast shook his head. "This wasn't about us, my love. This was about the two of you."

"If Blaze ever decides he wants to be the one to watch, we can force him to stand on the sidelines to make up for it, though," I added, grinning.

Blaze surprised me by snorting. "Yeah, right. I don't think I'd ever be able to just watch without being able to touch our girl. Unless you asked me to, Little Spitfire. But you're too tempting for your own good."

It was Char's turn to blush, but she was grinning, and her eyes were shining with happiness.

Blaze talked a big game, but I was damn sure before the year was out, he'd be joining Bast, Char, and me for a foursome.

All our girl had to do was ask him to.

It was like he'd said. Char was too damn tempting. Keeping our hands away from her was nearly impossible.

And I wouldn't change a thing.

# 9

## CHARISMA

Blaze might be a sex wizard, but he *sucked* at Fall Guys.

I giggled as his jelly-bean-like avatar fell off the platform yet again, making Blaze curse up a storm while Andres goaded him, calling him a noob.

When Andres suggested we play Fall Guys for group bonding time, I'd been pretty confused. After all, while the game was online, it was single-player and short of each of us being on a different console or computer, there was no way we could all play together. Bast had been the one to suggest we take turns playing a few races while the rest watched—the parallel to our earliest, impromptu group activity hadn't escaped my mind.

As the girl currently lying on the couch with my head on Bast's lap while he ran his fingers through my hair, and my legs on Andres' lap, while Blaze sat on the floor in front of me so he could be close, I had zero complaints.

Besides, from this angle, I could watch the game *and* all the guys. Most of my attention, however, was on Blaze. Every time he had to make a jump that was particularly hard, he tensed up, and I'd even seen his legs moving a couple of times as if he could make his character jump further using sheer willpower.

It was adorable.

"Oh, c'mon! That guy just pushed me! Is that even allowed?" Blaze protested from the floor, whipping his head to look at us as we laughed.

I'd never actually played Fall Guys before. I'd seen videos and stuff, and it looked like fun, but I'd always thought it might not be for me. Kinda regretted that now, though, because my fingers were twitching to grab the controller from Blaze and help him.

Poor noob hadn't finished a single race so far, and it was his fifth attempt.

"There are no rules that say you can't, Blaze." I gave a weird shrug from my position, and his eyes narrowed on me. "You ready to rage quit, or will you keep trying?"

I was totally taunting him, but the resolve on his face made it worth it.

He turned back to the game just in time to see the timer run out and the big, blocky "eliminated" on screen.

"I'm going to fucking win the next race, you'll see," he promised.

Who knew Blaze was this damn competitive in video games? He sure was determined for a guy who'd claimed he hadn't played anything since he was a kid.

"Don't worry, man. Char's just jealous because she wants to play, too. I'm surprised she hasn't stolen the controllers from you."

"Hey!" I protested, staring at Bast. "Rude!"

He looked down at me, eyebrow raised. His dark eyes glinting with amusement. "Am I wrong?"

"That's beside the point," I grumbled.

Bast chuckled, and Andres tickled my toe.

I pulled my leg back, affronted. "The hell?"

Andres's smile was mischievous, his damn dimples showing. It was a damn conspiracy.

"You know, when I agreed to this whole relationship with all of you thing, I didn't expect you guys to gang up against *me*. If anything, you're supposed to gang up *with* me against one of the others." I was pouting, and I didn't care.

Andres pounced, pinning me to the couch. The fact my head was *still* on Bast's lap didn't bother him one bit. He laid right above me, every inch of us touching, except for our faces. He looked at me, and his smile was *wicked*. "Kitten, if you weren't sore from earlier, I'd show you just how good us ganging up on you could be."

It wasn't a threat. It was a promise. And so was the hard bulge pressed against my core.

Then Andres kissed me until I was breathless. Until I was clutching onto him, trying to draw him closer, ready to say "fuck it" to being sore. I could walk funny tomorrow; I didn't care.

Andres broke the kiss, biting my bottom lip one last time before he pulled away and resumed his position at the edge of the couch, my legs once again on his lap.

The fact he had to adjust his erection in his jeans and was just as breathless as I was gave me perverse satisfaction.

So did the fact my pillow had grown hard and kind of uncomfortable under me.

Blaze had completely abandoned the game and was now on the ground facing *me*.

There went my panties.

Goddess, there was no feeling more empowering than being the sole focus of three hot, amazing guys who wanted you just as much as you wanted them. Knowing that if I asked, they'd give me all the orgasms or let me give *them* all the orgasms. Knowing that no matter how much sex we had, it would never be enough.

I loved that they didn't try to hide it, either. They wanted me, and they made sure I knew it at all times.

And as tempting as it might be to take them up on the desire written all over their faces and, well, their bodies, our relationship was more than crazy hot sex.

So I had to break up the tension before I listened to the devil on my shoulder—or my vagina—and tried to see how many times I could have sex in a day and how many orgasms I could have before I spontaneously combusted or something.

I cleared my throat, *twice*, before I was able to actually form words.

"Sooo. Uh. Yeah."

I mentally cringed.

Eloquent as fuck. That was me. Always so good with the wording thing.

Thank Goddess for Bast, though. He went back to playing with my hair like nothing had happened, and spoke.

"Char, I've been meaning to ask, how did it go with your parents?"

Okay, so maybe I'd rather have jumped their bones and had all the sex, my vagina be damned, instead of having to answer this.

I exchanged a glance with Blaze and sighed.

But hey, at least this would for sure kill any residual sexual tension in the room, so there was that.

"That good, huh?"

Andres started massaging my feet, as if knowing I was going to need it.

"Oh, you have no idea. Or maybe you do, really. Now

that Cara is persona-non-grata in the family because of her involvement with the resistance and your uncle," I nodded to Andres, who grimaced, while Blaze actually shuddered.

Yeah, I was still trying to wrap my head around the fact my twenty-five-year-old cousin was having an affair with a guy who was about my father's age. I knew I shouldn't judge, but damn. Cara's *dad* was younger than Ricardo Illudere. Well, Ricardo No-Last-Name now, since he'd been shunned from the Illudere family line.

My cousin had already proven she was willing to sleep with whomever she wanted in order to use them. I hadn't forgotten she'd dated Blaze while also dating his brother in a weird power play Dean had orchestrated to fuck with Blaze's head. Dean had succeeded, too, at least up to a point. But Blaze had found out about the betrayal before Dean could fully accomplish his evil plans, which had put a damper on it.

Apparently, though, Cara had decided to level up on who she slept with because she'd gone from the heir generation straight to the family heads. Or whatever role Ricardo played in the family hierarchy before he'd overplayed his hand.

It was a whole, complicated mess I honestly did not want to think too hard about. The only thing I wanted to know when it came to Cara was where the hell she was and how soon we could arrest her so she could answer for her crimes. Same thing about Ricardo.

I just wanted them dealt with, so we could all carry on with our lives safely and without worrying about possible repercussions.

And since Blair was on Ricardo's tail, I had no doubt his days as a free, evil man were numbered. Blair put the bad in badass, and she was one of the best agents AMIA had. She'd find the bastard and tie up any loose ends when it came to the rebellion. I had complete faith in her abilities, and I'd help in whatever way I could.

"Anyway," I continued, realizing I'd dragged the silence a little too long. "Now that Cara's involvement and evil schemes have been revealed, the Silverstorms will have no choice but to—"

Bast groaned. "Please don't tell me—"

I didn't let him finish. "Oh yeah. They want me to be a placeholder heir. I'm supposed to get married to someone they find suitable and start ... procreating as soon as possible so I can make a magically strong baby who will then become the head of the Silverstorm family once my parents retire."

"I volunteer as a tribute to marry you and breed you real good and give you *all* the babies you want," Andres said, raising his hand in the air like a kid waiting to be called on in class.

I rolled my eyes at his antics, knowing he was trying to lighten the mood.

"Any children you might have would probably be Illusionists, Andres, and therefore wouldn't be able to assume the Silverstorm seat in the Council of Six," Blaze interjected, adding a "no offense" to me, which I brushed off.

He was just being the voice of reason. It wasn't like it was news. My magic was weak. I'd known it my whole life. And I was fine with it. I'd learned to accept it and embrace that side of myself. There was no point in stressing over it.

Goddess knew I'd already spent enough time wishing things were different. I was done, though. And I was happy with the life I led, with the power I had, and the skills I'd developed.

Andres pouted, and it was so unfair that even pouting he

looked hot rather than ridiculous. "But I wanted to be the one to give my Kitten magical babies."

I lightly kicked him. "No one is giving anyone any babies, magical or otherwise. Besides, we're missing the point here. As I was saying, they had this whole plan, and my mother was making a to-do list of all the things they'd do. Obviously, they expected to end my 'little relationships' and move back into the Silverstorm manor with the husband they'd picked out for me. Or the one they *were* picking out for me, because apparently there's a shortage of strong, single Elemental Mages who I could marry on short notice."

Bast snorted.

"Anyways. I said no thank you and basically gave a whole 'I'm Charisma Carter, bitches, I'm the boss of me' speech and left. Blaze picked me up, and the rest you guys know."

"I'm Charisma Carter, bitches?" Andres repeated, laughing.

I kicked him again. "Shut up. You weren't there. It was a pretty great speech. But yeah. Silverstorms are officially minus an heir, and I have no idea how my parents will find a new one fast enough to minimize the backlash from the scandal, but I don't really care. What about you two? Where did you go? You guys were gone a while."

I felt Andres and Bast both tense, and I braced myself. I'd asked the question lightly, not really expecting any big news. My whole intention had been to change the subject, and I'd thought I'd hear some new crazy shenanigan from Grandma Alma. However, it seemed I hadn't been the only one with an eventful day.

Bast and Andres exchanged a look that was *loaded* with unspoken things, until Andres sighed.

"Fine," he said, all traces of the earlier humor gone from his face.

Serious Andres? Shiiiit.

"You know how we said we were going to run some errands with Gran?" he asked me, waiting until I nodded so he could continue. "Right, so, Gran wanted to go to the hospital—"

"Is she okay? Did something happen?" I sprang from the couch, sitting up and reaching for Andres, worried about Gran.

"She's fine, my love. Gran's hospital visit had nothing to do with her health, or ours." Bast's words put me at ease, and I let him pull me back into his lap, though this time, I remained sitting up.

This actually made it easier for me to look at all three of them, which had probably been Bast's goal.

"Okay, so, then why did Gran want to go to the hospital if nobody was sick?"

Andres cleared his throat and rubbed the back of his neck. "Yeah, actually, she wanted to talk to Theo."

*What the what!?*

I opened my mouth, then closed it, then opened it once again, not really knowing what the fuck I was even going to say or do.

Gran had visited Theodore? Did Gran even *know* Theo?

I mean, obviously, she knew who he was. After all, Gran was Alma Siela-Tumba. She'd been engaged to Theo's great-uncle way back when. Even I knew that. But for all Theo and the Soulbinders knew, Gran had *died* a million years ago. Well, not actually a million, but like over sixty years ago or even longer? I had no idea how old Gran was, and it had felt rude to ask.

Bast's grandmother looked like she was in her early

seventies, though, which probably put her somewhere between seventy and five hundred years old. Maybe she'd found the philosopher stone and become immortal like Nicolas Flamel. How the hell should I know?

"How old is Gran?" I blurted out, and all three guys looked at me like I'd lost my mind.

I shrugged. "Just wondering."

Andres and Bast snorted.

"I'd love to be in your head, so I could see how you went from hearing Gran visited Theo to wondering how old Gran is," Andres teased, shaking his head at me.

Even I didn't know how things worked in my head most of the time. Stuff just made sense to me. And I'd always wondered about Gran's age.

"What did your grandmother want with Theo?" Blaze's question gently brought us back to the matter at hand, and I was grateful for him and his focus.

Before Andres could answer, the doorbell rang, and all three of us looked at Bast, eyes wide.

"Is this her? Does she *know* we were talking about her?" My voice was barely above a whisper.

Was Bast's grandmother like Beetlejuice? Say her name three times, and suddenly, she manifested? Because if so, it was equal parts freaky and cool. Undecided.

"Why are all of you looking at me?" Bast asked, eyes wide. "I'm not expecting visitors."

The doorbell rang again, and we were all still too freaked out to check the door.

"Well, this is your house," Andres pointed out in answer to his question, helpful as can be.

"Shouldn't one of you go see who's at the door instead of us just staring at each other?" Blaze suggested, and I didn't think he was grasping the importance of the moment.

But then, again, Blaze had only seen Gran like, once. He probably didn't know Alma Siela-Tumba could be terrifying while being completely awesome.

"You guys are being ridiculous," Bast complained, sighing, but he made no move to get off the couch. Granted, I was still sitting on his lap, but that was a mere detail.

My phone started to ring, and it wasn't until I saw Logan's name on the caller ID that I realized what was going on.

With everything that had happened, I'd completely forgotten I'd invited Logan over to hang out with us.

I'd meant to let the guys know and stuff, but then sex and post-orgasmic bliss and it'd just … slipped my mind.

I sprang from Bast's lap, running to the door so I could open it, rambling all the way there.

"So, funny story. Bast is correct. He's not expecting visitors. I sort-of kind-of invited Logan over for game night earlier today when I was at my parents. I meant to tell you guys, but then sex and then more sex and then Fall Guys and all the other stuff, and I … uh … so yeah. Hey, Logan is at the door, and he's going to hang out with us, and I hope that's okay, but if not, it's kind of too late, and I'm sorry, and let's please circle back to the Theo thing tomorrow, yeah? Thank you."

Then, before anyone could even say anything or I could think better of it, I opened the door to Logan Nightshade.

# 10

## LOGAN

"Logan, hi," Charisma opened the door, cheeks flushed and breathing hard.

I raised an eyebrow.

Charisma's pink hair was messy, making it seem like she'd just gotten out of bed—or been thoroughly fucked. She wore a man's blue shirt that was way too big for her, reaching her mid-thigh, and black leggings.

She looked at home, sexy, and *nervous*.

I ended the call and put my phone back in my pocket, relieved. I'd started to worry she had changed her mind or that I'd gotten the wrong address when the doorbell went unanswered.

"Good Evening, Charisma," I replied.

There was some scuffling, a yelp, and then suddenly, three men were looming behind her.

Blaze Futhark's blond hair was almost as messy as Char's. Despite being barefoot, he was tense, like he was bracing himself for an attack or to come to Charisma's defense.

As if I'd attack Charisma. For fuck's sake, I was trying to *court* her.

I kept a wary eye on Blaze, knowing that with the number of runes he had tattooed on his body, he could attack *me* faster than I could draw my MET–if I'd had one.

Next to Blaze, Andres Illudere was rubbing a spot on his head, mumbling under his breath. He grinned at me when he noticed he had my attention. Andres had none of Futhark's mistrust. In fact, he looked almost harmless. I'd seen his duel, though, and knew better. Most of Andres' easygoing nature was a front. He was as powerful as Futhark and me.

Last was the dark-skinned male I'd seen when Charisma, Theo, and I had escaped the resistance's headquarters and run into AMIA's rescue party though I doubted he was an agent. In fact, if there had been any doubt, the fact he was here now told me all I needed to know—Charisma's Necromancer boyfriend.

I waited to be invited in, but all four of them were just staring at me.

"Am I early?" I asked, even though I knew I wasn't. I was actually five minutes late. I'd forced myself to wait outside so Charisma wouldn't think I was too eager. It was embarrassing how much Charisma made me revert to acting like a teenager with a crush.

Actually, even as a teenager, I'd never acted this eager.

"Oh, no, no. You're right on time! Thank you for coming, and sorry for not getting the door earlier. We were ... well, anyway. Come on in!" Charisma rambled, stepping back and crashing into the wall of boyfriends behind her.

She cast me an apologetic look and turned to them, eyes narrowed and hands on her hips. "When did you guys even get here? Well. Anyway. Logan, you know

Andres and Blaze, right?" She didn't let me answer. "Of course you do. You're all heirs. Well, so the only one you don't know is Bast. Bastille that is. Bast, this is Logan Nightshade."

Bastille smiled and offered me his hand. "Nice to meet you." We shook hands, and he stepped back, too, making enough space that I could enter the apartment. "Come on in, and make yourself at home. We were just about to order dinner."

"We were?" Andres asked. "Oh. Right, yeah, we were," he added when Blaze elbowed him.

*Subtle.*

"Thank you. It's nice to meet you, too," I offered politely.

Bastille pushed Andres and Blaze further into the house, in the direction of the living room, leaving Charisma and me alone near the door.

Not awkward at all.

I'd clearly interrupted them mid-sex, or at least foreplay. But it was too late for that now.

Then Charisma smiled at me, and I was secretly glad I'd cock-blocked them.

"Sorry, I'm probably making this super awkward, right? It's just that, well, you're you, and you're here, and I don't know what that means or anything, and I'm glad you're here, but I'm also kind of freaking out. So, anyway. Please, come in. We can go to the living room and play video games or watch TV or something while we wait for the pizza, and I'll shut up now because I'm just rambling at this point and making things even worse."

Charisma grimaced, and I took a chance.

I closed the distance between us and cupped her cheek. "Charisma, I find you fascinating, and I'm deeply attracted to you. I want to date you if you're interested. However, for tonight, I just wanted to spend time with you. There's no pressure for anything else."

Charisma's lips parted, and I wanted to kiss her, but I didn't.

It wasn't that simple, and we weren't alone, either. Even if her boyfriends were being nice enough to give us the illusion of privacy. Probably Bastille's doing.

"Oh. Okay. Cool."

I chuckled. A lesser man would probably falter at her response, but I had enough self-confidence not to take offense. Besides, I was starting to get to know Charisma, and I'd learned that she never reacted quite as I expected her to. I'd also learned to read her body language. Like now, her pupils were blown wide, and her gaze was locked on my lips. Her head was tilted to the side slightly, towards my hand as if seeking more contact.

Charisma wanted me. Not that I'd ever doubted that. Even when we'd first started working together and she didn't like me very much, she was still attracted to me. She'd proven that when I'd kissed her.

Although, back then, my motivation had been less ... pure. Oh, I'd been as attracted to the pink-haired, confusing, chaotic girl as I was now, but the more I spent time with her, the more I'd realized it wasn't just her body I wanted.

I'd tried to deny it. I'd tried to bury the conflicting feelings she spurred in me, lying to myself that it was mere physical attraction. I'd tried to justify and analyze every single reaction I'd ever had to her, but that had only made things worse. I thought about her even more, at the oddest moments. In the end, I'd finally admitted the truth: I felt a connection to Charisma, one I had only felt once before, when I was no more than a child.

That, too, had terrified me. However, I'd be damned if I would allow fear to dictate how I led my life.

If Charisma agreed to it, I'd like to see where things with her would lead, even if it meant an unconventional arrangement. But I was done brushing off the connection and pretending I wasn't interested, which was why I was here.

Our moment was broken when Andres Illudere started singing "Kiss the girl". Or, rather, butchering the song my sister used to sing on repeat when she was a kid.

Charisma blushed and jumped back as if she'd just been caught doing something she shouldn't. I frowned at her reaction. We'd have to work on that later ... if she decided she wanted to pursue a relationship with me, that was.

For now, though, I followed her towards the living room where her boyfriends waited, amused in spite of myself that Andres was running in circles around the coffee table while singing, dodging random shit Bastille was throwing at him.

When Andres saw Charisma approaching, he ran to her, trying to hide behind her.

His mistake.

When Andres was within reach, Charisma sidestepped him, putting just her foot in his path.

Clearly, Andres hadn't expected it, because he tripped, his momentum sending him stumbling straight into me.

I had a split second to consider whether to help him or let him suffer for interrupting my moment with Charisma, but with a sigh, I decided that long-term, helping him would probably be best.

However, I was far from a nice guy. So, rather than using my own body to stop Andres' crash and thus injuring myself for his sake, I moved to the side, out of his path. Right when he was about to crash to the ground, I grabbed his arm and pulled him up.

If I'd had my MET, I could've used Elemental magic to soften his landing, but unfortunately, the resistance had destroyed my MET. Yet again.

Those fucking idiots.

Andres yelped in pain, but I was strong enough that I'd been able to pull him upright, and we both knew the pain was nothing compared to what might've happened if he'd crashed head-first on the ground.

"Nice catch," Bastille said from across the room, giving me a thumbs up.

Charisma and Blaze laughed, and Andres mumbled a "thanks" to me, rubbing his arm.

Then he turned to Charisma, making a show of grabbing his chest. "Kitten, your betrayal wounds me."

Charisma rolled her eyes at him. "Oh, please, you were about to use me as a human shield. You should've seen that coming." But she was smiling, and she walked closer and kissed his cheek in apology.

"I'm sorry about him," she told me. "Sometimes he can be a handful. Honestly, I don't know why we keep him around."

"Because I have a big dick and have crazy sex skills?" Andres teased, making Charisma blush.

Bastille cleared his throat. "Anyway. We were thinking about ordering pizza and then watching the newest Marvel movie."

And just like that, everyone started to pitch in about their pizza orders, as if none of the earlier chaos had even happened. Charisma grabbed my hand and led me to the couch, sitting beside me. The guys did their best to include me, not only on the food order, but asking my opinions on the movie and offering to change the choice when I'd admitted I wasn't a big fan of the genre.

Nobody questioned my presence; even Blaze was making an effort, despite his initial reticence.

Soon enough, I found myself letting my guard down and relaxing. There were no expectations, no walking on eggshells, no posturing. More than that, the people in this room grew up the same way I did, with most of the same expectations and responsibilities. They knew what it was like to be heirs to the Council of Six, and all the shit that came with it. Even Charisma had grown up the same way we did, and though I wasn't sure how things worked for the Necromancers, I doubted it was that different.

Here, we were simply five people enjoying each other's company. Four men vying for and wishing to spend time with the same girl.

Charisma was their center–our center–that was pretty clear, but there was a bond among the guys too. Andres and Bastille were more comfortable with each other than with Blaze, and that, too, was clear, but only if you paid close attention.

For her part, Charisma was pretty open about her affection for all of them. Whether it was a look, a touch, or a private smile, she paid equal attention to all of us, even me.

It was a completely new experience, but one I found myself enjoying more than I'd expected.

*I could get used to this.*

## 11

## CHARISMA

I scrolled through the archives I'd managed to dig out of the resistance hard drives, frowning. I hated this kind of work. I knew it was important, which was why I did it, but it was so freaking boring.

Give me a MET to code, or even ask me to come up with some handy new gadget that might help AMIA or their agents, and I was the right girl for the job. But this?

It wasn't that the information I was finding was boring, exactly, but I had a big aversion to sitting down and reading through page after page of contracts with legal gibberish, restaurant receipts, and failed plans.

I didn't really care to read through a twenty-page document on resistance members who we'd already arrested—though I'd read every single word, bribing myself with a cookie for every page read—or five pages worth of coding that looked like it had been written by a toddler with no knowledge on the subject.

Even as I diligently took notes of everything I found and organized it into folders so the right parties could receive the information and do whatever they were going to do with it, what I really wanted was a clue regarding Ricardo's whereabouts.

*That* was my job now.

AMIA successfully captured most of the resistance members, destroying and discrediting the movement. The news that Ricardo Illudere had been the person in charge of the rebellion helped with that. It was ironic, really, that while the resistance's goal and Ricardo's had aligned—to stage a coup that would overthrow the Council of Six—their endgame was different, and that was something Ricardo hadn't made known. The foot soldiers, the rebels, wanted a different type of ruling body. They wanted people without much magical power to get a say on things regardless of their power level. It was commendable, really, and I could sympathize with that. In fact, I completely understood where they were coming from.

However, Ricardo had sold them that idea while manipulating things from the background so that, once the council was overruled, *he* could take charge. Alone. Like some kind of king of all things magical.

Once that had gotten out, the resistance had *not* been happy. People tended not to take kindly to being used and lied to, which had worked in AMIA's favor in the end—probably the reason the news had "accidentally been leaked" in the first place.

However, Ricardo was still out there, and he was too big a threat to be allowed to roam free. He had to answer for his crimes, and while Blair was leading a team to hunt him down, my role was to give her any useful information that might help her catch him.

Easier said than done, though. Still, after the past few months and the hellish mess that my life had become, I was glad to be mostly sitting this one out and helping from the shadows.

I'd had more adventures in the past few months than most people had in a lifetime, and I was more than ready to live a peaceful, quiet life in my mailbox with my men.

Just thinking about them made me smile.

Last night had been amazing. I'd never expected Logan Nightshade would fit in with my guys, but he'd surprised me. Although, maybe "fit in" wasn't the right way to call it. He'd stood out, alright, but in a very Logan way.

Logan had observed the dynamics and the shenanigans more than taken part in them, not because he was judging us or because he felt he was better than us, but simply because the activities we'd picked weren't his cup of tea. He'd made an effort, though—I mean, the man had shown up wearing *jeans*, for Goddess' sake—and so had the guys.

I'd worried about how Blaze would react to Logan's presence, especially because I'd fucked up and forgotten to give him a warning that Logan would come. Blaze had surprised me once again, though. It was like having someone else who wasn't overly familiar with Bast had put Blaze at ease or something.

The reason didn't matter, though. What mattered was that group bonding time had been a success, even with the new addition, and the guys were planning on making it a weekly thing. To think these were the same men who used to compete about everything and been unable to stay in the same room together without arguing. Oh, when it came to council matters, they'd made an effort, but there had always been insane tension among them.

Now, though, they acted like buddies. Logan had even offered his house for the next one! Apparently, he had a cinema-worthy TV room.

Their talk about the future and the planning made me anxious, though. I couldn't help but wonder when the guys would realize this whole sharing me thing wasn't what they wanted. When they'd grow bored with the novelty and think that the difficulties we would face—because there were always difficulties—weren't worth the rewards. After all, how would any of this even work? Blaze and Andres were heirs to their houses. They would be expected to get married one day and make magically powerful babies. Andres might've joked about it yesterday when I'd told them what my parents had planned, but Blaze's words had basically hit the nail on the head.

Bast had been the one to push me into dating all of them. Or, rather, into dating more than one guy and following my heart, and he'd always done everything to reassure me that this was for the long run. After all, his parents had a similar relationship, though I'd never actually met his dads.

The more time passed, the more I grew attached to them. Hell, who was I kidding? I loved them. Bast, Andres, and Blaze. Not to mention the pretty big crush I had on Logan, which had only grown when he'd opened up about his past during our little stint in the resistance's dungeon.

I just ... I had no idea what I'd do with myself when they realized they were better off having their own wives without having to share me.

"Char? Love, what's wrong?" Bast's hand on my shoulder startled me so badly that I jumped from the chair, bumping my knee against the office desk.

I may also have screamed a little.

Bringing a hand to my racing heart, I turned to stare at him.

He raised his hands in the air, palms facing me as if

surrendering. "Sorry, sorry, I didn't mean to startle you. I called you twice."

"Oh. Sorry. I didn't hear you." I'd been too busy drowning in self-pity.

"I'm the one who's sorry, Char. That was my bad." He shrugged, then cupped my face, forcing me to look at him and the concern in his eyes.

"Are you okay? You looked lost there for a second, and I don't just mean lost in your thoughts. Are the resistance files giving you trouble? Do you want me to help?"

How was Bast real? How the hell had I gotten so lucky as to have a guy like him in my life? He was hot, funny, caring, *and* he could cook. The whole freaking package.

Unable to stop myself, I hugged him. Well, I hugged his waist, breathing in his scent. Bast ran his fingers through my hair, soothing me and letting me draw comfort from his presence.

We stayed just like that for a while until I finally felt steady enough.

I let go of him and straightened on my chair. "Thanks, Bast. I needed that."

Bast bent over and brushed his lips against mine. "Anytime, Char. Anytime. Why don't you tell me what had you feeling all lost, and we can find a way to fix it?"

"I was just being silly," I admitted. I was kind of embarrassed that Bast had caught me when I'd been spiraling with self-doubt. Neither he nor the guys had done anything to justify my questioning our relationship, yet here I was. Doing just that.

"Char, don't brush off what you're feeling. If something made you sad or upset, then it's not silly. Your feelings are *always* valid."

My vision blurred with tears.

All my life I'd been a nuisance, a disappointment. I'd lost count of the times I'd heard my parents tell me I was being ridiculous if I was upset over something.

Yet, here was Bast, knowing exactly what to say and how to reassure me. Reminding me that I had every right to simply ... feel. Simply be.

I got up from the chair and jumped in his arms, clinging to him.

"I love you. A whole lot. More than pizza, more than video games or the internet. Thank you for being you."

"Woah, that's a lot of love there, Char." Bast chuckled, holding me tight against him. "I love you just as much. You know that, right?"

Yeah.

Whatever the future held, we would be okay. Bast would make sure of it.

## 12

## BLAZE

Fucking Dean.

I unlocked the door to my apartment, not bothering to turn on the lights or anything, and headed straight to the kitchen. I needed an ice pack to put on my eye to hopefully decrease the swelling before it got worse.

It was inconvenient that I couldn't use my rune magic to speed up the healing process, but if I got rid of the evidence, my asshole of a brother would try to make it seem like I was the one in the wrong.

Not that our parents would give a shit, either way. All they cared about was who had won the fight and whether there had been any witnesses that would need to be dealt with.

Such a healthy parenting style. Really set up the groundwork for some major sibling love and friendship.

Only one of the reasons why Bastille's relationship with Andres baffled the hell out of me. And they weren't even brothers, not really. They just had a sister in common. Stepbrothers would be the best word for it, but even that wasn't quite right.

Well, not that it mattered now.

I opened the freezer and grabbed the only thing I had inside: one of those gel packs I kept frozen for this type of occurrence.

I wished I could say I hardly ever needed the ice pack or that I'd only bought it as a precaution, but the truth was, I was no stranger to fights with my brother.

Whenever Dean's latest manipulative scheme went wrong, he tended to get physical. While that had worked when we were kids because he was a few years older, and stronger, I'd quickly learned that the best way not to get the shit beat out of me was to learn to fight back. Over the past ten years, Dean hadn't won a single fight, but it hadn't stopped him from trying.

I wrapped the frozen packet in some cloth and placed it on my eye, wincing at the cold.

Unfortunately, though, just because I tended to win, it didn't mean I came out of it unscathed. Fucking Dean fought dirty, and he didn't give a shit.

I wanted to go to Bast's house to be with Char, not be alone in my apartment in the middle of the day, preparing to clean up yet another one of Dean's messes.

Thank Goddess I'd listened to my instincts yesterday and hadn't gone to our parents' mansion for the so-called meeting. I'd have walked straight into a trap set by Dean.

When would my brother learn that the underhanded tactics and schemes were not the way for him to take my place as the Futhark heir? If anything, his attempts only served to further confirm that he wasn't fit for a position of power. Dean was reckless, immature, spoiled, and self-centered. He thought that because he was the firstborn, the right to the Futhark seat in the Council of Six should go to him. However, not only was that not how our society was structured, but our parents had always made it very clear that the heir would be the strongest child. We'd had to duel enough times—inside, with no witnesses outside the family—that Dean should've accepted his fate. Instead, he was a constant thorn in my life.

My father had called me, confused about the text I'd sent him apologizing for missing the meeting, and explained that both he and my mother were overseeing the reconstruction of the family home the rebellion had blown apart.

I probably shouldn't have gone to Dean's house this morning to pay him a little visit, but I'd wanted to try to get him to stop with the stupid underhanded shenanigans once and for all.

I went to the couch and laid down with the ice pack still over my eye. I needed to shower and then head to AMIA. There were a million things I needed to do and take care of before I could get back to Char. With all the chaos from the past few weeks, I'd neglected most of my duties as a Futhark, not only when it came to family but as a voice to all Rune Mages. I'd prioritized my girlfriend over my responsibilities, and I didn't regret that. However, things were turning dire.

AMIA's Director of Operations had called in a meeting with the heads of the Council of Six in order to determine how we would deal with the rebels that had handed themselves in. The whole thing was a shitshow, and my father was supposed to be the one to attend the meeting, but this morning he'd informed me it was about time I took on more responsibilities as a Futhark. He'd also said some bullshit about showing a united front when half the other families were on the verge of collapse. Though how we were supposed to show a united front when I was attending the meeting alone, I had no fucking clue. He should be the one attending, not me—or at least we should be going together.

I had no idea what he was thinking, sending me off alone, but I knew better than to question a direct order. He was the family head, after all.

Besides, he was right about one thing. There was a ton of internal conflict, and three of the six families were on the verge of ruin.

First, there was the Manteis family, who was dealing with the backlash of Michael's betrayal and his attempt to murder his sisters. Second, the Illuderes were going to have to answer for Ricardo's actions, even if it wasn't their fault. Nobody gave a shit. In the eyes of the council, Diego Illudere had failed to police a member of his clan, hell, a member of his family. Not only that, but Diego hadn't stopped Ricardo, allowing him to escape. I had no doubt the Soulbinder matriarch would attempt to pin the responsibility for the entire rebellion on Diego Illudere's shoulders.

And last but not least, there was the problem with the Silverstorms. Not only the scandal caused by Cara's involvement with the resistance but the fact that, as of yesterday, they no longer had an heir. And I'd be damned if I'd allow Ian and Elizabeth Silverstorm to drag my Char into their mess.

Especially when their little plan involved forcing her to marry a random stranger and start making babies. There was no fucking way. They better find an alternative to their little problem that didn't involve my girl.

The irony was that the Futhark family, with all its internal conflict and messed-up relationships, was one of the few who still had a good reputation. My parents wanted me to take advantage of that to amass more power for the Rune Mages.

Little did they know, my loyalties were not with the Futhark name but with Char and the rest of her harem.

My phone vibrated in my pocket, and I smiled, thinking Char had been conjured by my thoughts, and decided to text me.

My smile vanished when I noticed the text wasn't from her.

*Logan Nightshade: We need to talk.*

I frowned, wincing when that made the pain in my face worse.

I had mixed feelings when it came to Logan Nightshade. Yesterday, I'd been surprised by his arrival at Bast's, even though neither Andres nor Bast had seemed particularly shocked. Even when all three of us had eavesdropped on Logan's conversation with Char—if one could call that a conversation—it'd been clear I'd been the only one who hadn't been expecting his words.

It wasn't that I was surprised he was romantically interested in Char. My girl was pretty spectacular in every way. She was smart, hot, and had a heart of gold. However, all my previous interactions with Logan had led me to believe the guy was basically an unfeeling robot.

Apparently, he was as bewitched by Char as the rest of us, which he'd proved yesterday. I'd also had to begrudgingly respect the fact while Logan wanted to pursue Char. Although I was holding judgment on my feelings towards that. He'd known she was already in a poly relationship and had made an effort to make sure his intentions were clear to all of us, without trying to steal her or do shit behind our backs.

For someone like me, who had never expected to share a girlfriend with others, the fact Logan knew how to act in such a situation put my guard up even more.

However, I doubted Logan was texting me about Char.

Before I could come up with a reply, I got another text from him.

*Logan Nightshade: There are things you should know before the meeting today.*

Bastard really did know how to get someone's attention.

*Blaze: Where do you want to meet? I can be there in ten.*

I could rush through a shower and use my MET to put up some illusions that would mask the black eye. Short of making me go all the way to the Nightshade mansion, I could see Logan and be at AMIA before the meeting started.

*Logan Nightshade: If you have no objections, I can be at your apartment in five.*

Talk about overachiever.

*Blaze: That's fine. I'll see you soon.*

Looked like I wouldn't be having that shower after all.

## 13

## THEO

*Free at last*, I thought, as I dragged myself into my home.

I felt like I'd been put through a meat grinder not once but twice, spit out, and then stepped on by a herd of elephants.

It had been a tough few days, and yet, even after I'd used up all my magic to free the ghosts at the resistance's compound Logan and I had broken into, I hadn't felt this bad. Not even when I'd woken up at the hospital the day after we'd been rescued did I feel this shitty, and back then, I'd been fighting off starvation, dehydration, *and* being struck by literal lightning.

Apparently, unraveling multiple bindings on your soul was worse. Mrs. Alma *had* warned me, but I thought she'd been trying to scare me. Now I knew that, if anything, she'd underplayed how much it fucking sucked.

*Should've listened to her from the start.*

On the plus side, because I'd had to stay another night at the hospital, the matriarch had been unable to "pick me up" —which I'd been against even before Mrs. Alma's visit—and sent a car instead.

That had bought me a little time to work through everything that had happened, sort my emotions, and brace myself for what I'd have to do.

I was so screwed, even Annie was looking at me with pity.

She'd been awkwardly hovering beside me, looking at me like I was a dead man walking. Ironic, considering she was a ghost.

Just my luck.

I placed the keys on the table and bypassed the living room, going straight to the liquor cabinet I kept well stocked even though I hardly ever drank.

A good host should always have a variety of beverages—alcoholic or otherwise—of the highest quality to offer guests.

Just one of the lessons that had been drilled into me from a young age.

Well, today I was about to put the fucking booze to good use. The fact I chose the matriarch's favorite whiskey as my drink of choice was a small, petty rebellion that wouldn't even matter long term.

Still, I was feeling petty.

"Theo," Annie started, eyes wide, when she saw me opening the bottle and taking a swig straight from it.

"Don't, Annie. Seriously. Not now. I'm sorry, but I deserve this, don't you think? Besides, I'm celebrating! And what better way to do it than to drink a whiskey that costs more than most cars?"

I raised the bottle in silent cheers to her and drank some more. It burned all the way down and tasted no different than any other whiskey to me. But then, again, I hated the stuff.

Pettiness knew no bounds, though.

I headed to the bathroom. I wanted a shower to wash the hospital stay away, and then I was going to drink myself numb. I didn't want to think about everything that had happened, everything I'd learned. I didn't want to face the fact I'd have to challenge my grandmother.

My only regret was that I'd never be able to make things right with Char, but she was better off without me anyway. Now more than ever.

Besides, if things went south tomorrow, I'd be nothing more than another puppet at my grandmother's beck and call, just like Aunt Kate. Trying to make amends with Char now for my sake would be even more selfish than anything I'd done this far.

"Theo, you can't use alcohol to numb your feelings away."

I stopped walking to stare at my sister. "Fucking watch me, Annie."

I knew I was being an asshole to her, too, and she didn't deserve this, but dammit. I was tired. So fucking tired.

Annie passed through me on purpose, making me shudder.

I supposed I deserved that, too.

"Theo, c'mon. We should talk about this. We should come up with a plan. There's got to be something we can do to make Grandma see reason. I don't know what yet, but we're smart. We should be able to figure this out. We could even call Char and—"

"We're not going to drag Charisma into this, Annie. She's suffered enough, don't you think?"

Annie flinched, and I sighed. I rubbed a hand against my face.

Goddess, I was so damn *tired*.

"Listen, Annie, I know you mean well. And I love you.

You know that, right? You're the best sister I could've ever asked for, even if I never told you that when you were alive. But, the matriarch has been playing Goddess for years. Now that I've seen reason and been given the tools to fix this mess, I'm not going to waste the opportunity. You think talking to Grandmother will make any difference?" I laughed bitterly. "Sis, if I give her so much as an inch, she'll bind me for eternity. Forget free will. She'll probably break me worse than she did Aunt Kate. I can't risk it, Annie. I'm also not going to run away from my responsibilities. But for now, please, just let me have this."

Annie's green eyes were sad, but she nodded.

"I know I won't be of much help tomorrow, but know I'll be with you every step of the way. I won't let you carry this burden alone," she vowed.

"Thanks, sis."

My sister had my back; I didn't need anything else.

And who knew? Maybe if I told myself that enough times, I'd eventually manage to make it true.

There was nothing I could do today, though. Not when my magic was still recovering. All I could do was wait and hope for the best.

Mrs. Alma believed I could do this, and since she'd been right about everything else, I might as well entrust my fate to her. If I survived this, I'd find a way to apologize to Char and to fix my family—fix Aunt Kate, my parents, and any other Soul Mages who Grandmother might've bound.

If not, well...it wasn't like anyone would miss me, anyway.

## 14

## LOGAN

Another day, another pointless meeting that did nothing but waste my time.

I admired the fact that the director of the Arcane Mage Intelligence Agency wanted to give the Council of Six the illusion that they were included in the big decisions but wished he hadn't bothered.

Rather than discussing what should be done about the members of the resistance—at least those whose main crime had been to put their trust in the wrong person—and trying to come up with a solution that would prevent a movement like that from ever gaining as much force, we were wasting precious time with finger-pointing.

It was honestly baffling how the people representing the main Arcane families in our city could behave like squabbling children.

Although, in fairness, most of the childish behavior came from the Silverstorms and my own parents—who had no business being in this meeting, but my father had decided to be present to show the Nightshades' strength. Unfortunately, my father was still the head of the Nightshades, even if in name only, and therefore I had been unable to stop him from attending.

I was, however, glad that Blaze's parents hadn't come; otherwise, the fighting would've been worse.

I looked around the conference room, wishing I could be anywhere else but here.

While my parents made fools of themselves arguing with the Silverstorms—who were in ruin and trying to drag anyone they could with them—I'd taken the time to gauge where the rest of the council stood.

All four Manteis members had come. Mark and Diane Manteis, the current heads of the Divinator family, sat side by side, with their twin daughters, Danica and Onyka, sitting to their father's left. They hadn't spoken much since arriving, but that wasn't surprising. The Manteis family tended to avoid conflict, and calling attention to themselves might make things worse right now, considering their family had dealt with Michael Manteis' betrayal not that long ago.

Still, I knew I could count on them to be reasonable.

Next to the Manteis family were the Silverstorms. I was just grateful they'd sat across the table from my parents because if they'd ended up side by side, I feared the altercation might've ended up turning physical.

As it stood, they just made everyone else uncomfortable.

AMIA's Director sat at the head of the table, jaw twitching, but he didn't say anything. He probably knew trying to interfere would be just a waste of breath.

Near the Director, on my side of the table, were Diego and Serena Illudere. The couple held their heads high and didn't take the bait or bother trying to defend themselves against the insane accusations thrown their way.

Blaze and I acted as a physical barrier between the Illuderes and my parents.

The final member of the council, who'd also come alone, was Esme Soulbinder. The Soulbinder matriarch sat at the end of the table, looking at all of us with superiority. As if the fact she was directly across from the Director meant she was better than us.

The woman was delusional. What was worse, though, was that while she wasn't joining the argument, she'd made enough snide comments to encourage the chaos.

Two hours of my life I'd never get back had already passed, and nothing had been decided.

I pulled my phone from my pocket, ignoring Blaze's alarmed gaze.

Ah. Right. He wasn't used to attending these things. While it was true the heirs were supposed to accompany the family heads to all manner of events and meetings, most of the Council of Six's inner conflicts were kept behind closed doors and between the actual heads. However, since my parents had basically abdicated and given me all the responsibilities, I'd been attending meetings like this since I'd graduated from the Academy.

It had been one of the reasons I'd asked to meet with him before this circus. I'd wanted to warn him not only of how pointless it would be but also make sure his parents wouldn't attend.

I'd felt like I owed him one after yesterday.

I unlocked my phone and texted Charisma.

**Logan:** *I had fun last night.*

I wondered if I could convince her to go out with me tonight. Just the two of us. I wanted to spend more time with her. Get to know her better. Have a chance to ... seduce her.

I didn't know what it was about Charisma Carter that had me so enamored, but I wanted to find out. And the more time I spent with her, the more I wanted her.

Charisma's reply was almost instant.

*Charisma: So did I.*

*Charisma: Thanks for coming!*

*Charisma: Sorry if things were a little overwhelming.*

*Charisma: We're not usually that crazy, I promise.*

*Charisma: Well. Actually. Maybe we are. But the good kind of crazy.*

I smiled at the rapid-fire texts. Things had been a little overwhelming, but I wasn't lying when I said I'd had fun. Hanging out with Charisma, Andres, Blaze, and Bast had been surprisingly easy.

*Logan: Want to have dinner with me tonight?*

*Logan: Just us?*

I added the second part to ensure there would be no confusion. After all, I wanted to date Charisma, not her boyfriends. No matter how friendly they might've been.

"Enough." Esme Soulbinder didn't yell, but she put enough power behind her voice that it carried around the room, shutting everyone up.

*About damn time.*

I'd started to worry I'd have to be the one to interfere rather than just cut in with my idea.

All eyes went to her. "This is getting nowhere. Were we called here to chit-chat?"

She directed her question at the Director, effectively dismissing everyone else in the room.

Her choice of words was almost amusing, however.

Christian, AMIA's Director of Operations, raised a bushy eyebrow.

I had to give it to him, he was good. If I hadn't been looking for it, I might've missed the way the vein ticked on his neck or the way he clenched and unclenched his jaw.

"Ma'am, as I said at the beginning of the meeting, I was

hoping the Council of Six would have suggestions on the best way to deal with the minor players in the resistance. I currently have more than a hundred people in holding cells and a lot more under a temporary arrangement, but I'm afraid we do not have the manpower or the holding space for so many. Not only that, but if we arrest every single person who had dealings with the resistance, there will be even bigger unrest."

In other words, if AMIA arrested every single miserable bastard who had empathized with the resistance, most of the mages would need to be locked up and that was ridiculous.

The only rebels who needed to be brought to justice were the ones who actually *committed* a crime. And those were few and far between.

Blaze and I shared a look.

This was the moment I'd been waiting for, and the reason I'd visited him before the meeting. I'd wanted to gauge where he stood on the subject so I could determine whether he'd back me up or not. I already knew the Manteis and Illudere families would. Even if Esme Soulbinder and the Silverstorms opposed, we'd still have the majority vote.

That was all I needed.

"Actually, about that," I said, cutting in before anyone else could. "I have a suggestion."

## 15

## CHARISMA

The guys weren't back yet, and it was starting to make me anxious.

I drummed my fingers against the table, staring blankly at the screen in front of me. I'd lost focus on the job about half an hour ago, and I knew I wouldn't be able to start over. Not today. Not when my eyes felt blurry and my gaze continuously drifted to the little clock on the screen.

Well, at least I'd been incredibly productive after working all day, which was something, I supposed.

But it was almost six pm, and none of the guys had returned from their errands. I knew I was probably acting paranoid, but I couldn't help but worry.

I knew the guys could take care of themselves. They were, after all, Battle Mages. Some of the best in our society, not only because they were crazy powerful, but because they knew how to *use* said power.

It wasn't just a happy circumstance that they would one day be the heads of their magical families. I was proof of that. Being born an heir to the most powerful families didn't mean much if you didn't have the power and skill to back it up. My guys were the whole package.

However, I liked it better when they were with me, or at least together. Then at least they could have each other's back.

I sighed and rubbed my eyes.

Well, I might not be able to protect them right now or help them if they needed me, but there were other ways I could be useful.

I closed the tabs on the files I'd been reading and opened the software I used to program METs. This morning, I'd gotten a text from my ironsmith that the stuff I'd commissioned would be delivered either later today or early tomorrow—knowing him, it would most likely arrive tomorrow afternoon, but that worked just fine. Since I had some time to spare, I might as well finish the coding I'd been working on for a while.

Logan's new MET would be a replica of the last one I'd done—not that he'd asked me to do it, but I felt I owed him after he'd saved my life and Theo's. However, I'd been able to make some minor tweaks on the program now that I knew him better and had seen him in action. Nothing major, just bug fixes and a couple of added spells I thought might one day be handy.

Then there was my new MET. Well, I thought, placing a hand on my earring, my official new MET. I'd learned my lesson and finally gotten a backup option to what I'd been using. Andres had laughed when I'd called my earrings the "oh shit" MET, but it was a pretty accurate description. Even though I hoped I'd never need it, I'd decided never to be caught in a position where I wouldn't have a MET again.

After the resistance had broken two of my METs— once when they blew up my apartment with me inside, the other when they'd kidnapped and imprisoned me—I was done leaving things to chance. My main MET would still be like my previous two: a sleek phone-like mini computer that allowed me to code spell combinations on the go, as well as pre-programmed ready-to-go with the press of a button. The earrings had a simple design and very few spells programmed, but it should be enough to get me out of a pinch.

The third piece arriving tomorrow would be Bast's MET—finally. Because it was a surprise, I hadn't been able to customize the coding as much as I would've liked, but he'd at least be able to do basic spells from other magic branches. With time, I'd be able to add or change stuff based on his preferences or desires, but for now, this would do. I just hoped he liked the hardware design, too. Since we'd met through gaming, I'd figured that a gaming controller would be a cute but unique MET for my Necromancer.

Plus, even if just in my imagination, I'd giggled once or twice over the idea of Bast using a joystick to control a literal zombie—not that he'd use his powers to bring back the dead nor anything. I'd quizzed him on it enough times that I'd finally accepted the "no zombie making" rule.

Laaame.

Well. Actually. I had no idea how I'd feel if I saw a reanimated dead body in real life, but it was always pretty cool in movies and anime.

But I digressed.

The final MET was the one I was most nervous about. Honestly, I had no business designing Theo a new MET, but the resistance had destroyed his, and, well ... it hadn't escaped my notice he'd been using the same MET I'd made him all those years ago. I didn't know what it meant, and I'd finally decided not to think too hard about it, but

Theodore Soulbinder *had* saved my life. The least I could do was make him a new MET. If he used it or not was up to him.

My fingers flew over the keyboard as I fixed and wrote new lines of code, all the while keeping an eye on the time. I'd give it another two hours, and if the guys didn't get home, text, or call me, *then* I'd do something about it.

I didn't know what I'd do exactly, but actions would definitely be taken. By me.

I heard the front door opening and sprang from my chair, running to see who'd arrived.

Bast barely had time to brace himself before I was on him, colliding against his chest and clinging to him.

"Hey, are you okay? Did you have another panic attack?" he asked, picking me up and carrying me to the couch, where he sat with me on his lap.

He had some crazy maneuvering skills we would need to explore someday.

I had my face pressed against the crook of his neck and was busily inhaling his scent.

"Yeah. I mean, no. I was just worried. You're the first one home," I admitted, still pressed against him.

Bast rubbed my back in soothing circles, and I melted against him.

"I'm sorry, love. I didn't think I'd be out so late, but since Blair is busy with AMIA business, I was on Gran duty, and she made me drive her all over town. Did you know that in the past two weeks, three new bakeries opened that offer adult-themed sweets? I know because Gran made me take her to every single one."

I snorted against his neck. I could just imagine Bastille's face as he had to watch his grandmother eat dick-shaped pastries.

Bast raised my hand to his mouth and playfully bit my wrist in punishment.

"I'm glad you think this is funny because I told Gran that you'd be the one taking her next time. She was delighted my girlfriend was also an adult-pastry connoisseur."

I groaned, raising my head to glare at him. "You didn't!"

His grin told me everything I needed to know. Damn him.

Then he grew serious. "Sorry you were alone for this long, Char. Where is everyone?"

"Blaze had that meeting to go to, and Andres got a call from his dad a few hours ago and had to leave, too." I knew I sounded like a sulky kid, but I couldn't help myself.

Bast frowned. "Why didn't you go with him? Andres, I mean. Pretty sure Diego would've loved to have you."

I shrugged. "It was Illudere business. I didn't want to intrude. I'm not going to lie; he was the one I worried about the most, what with Ricardo being out there still. But Andres was just going to his parents, and I felt I could be of more help if I stayed here, going through the resistance files."

"And you didn't want him to feel like you didn't trust his skills or power when he'd already proved he could win against his uncle if it came down to it," Bast added.

He really did know me too well.

"Pretty much, yeah." I played with Bast's beard, feeling a little embarrassed. I shouldn't have overreacted. I'd known I was being paranoid, but I couldn't shake off the feeling that something big was going to happen, and it was driving me crazy.

Waiting was the worst.

Bast kissed me. "Well, I'm back, and Andres should be home soon. How about you sit in the kitchen while I make dinner? Then you can tell me about your day, and I can entertain you with a vivid description of people's reactions when they saw Gran eating pussy-shaped eclairs at the bakery."

Oh, man. I'd have paid to see that, not going to lie. Even if I'd have kept my gaze averted from Bast's gran the whole time and only focused on the people around us.

After all, some things could not be unseen.

I got up from Bast's lap. "Sounds good."

"Is Blaze joining us?" Bast asked when we reached the kitchen.

"Yeah, he said he'd be back tonight. There's some meeting going on among the family heads, and based on the texts I got from him and Logan, it went on for hours. It's why Andres had to leave, too. His parents called him once the meeting was over to fill him in. Blaze said he had some stuff to do and needed to update his parents before he could be here. That was … three hours ago?"

I shrugged once again, taking a seat on one of the stools at the kitchen counter while Bast rummaged through the fridge for the ingredients he'd need to make us dinner.

"Logan, huh?" Bast teased, without looking at me.

I blushed. "Yeah. Uh. He texted to say he had fun yesterday."

It didn't matter how many times Bast said it wasn't a big deal; it still felt odd to discuss a guy I was crushing on with the guy I was in love with and in a relationship with.

"He didn't ask you out?" Now Bast turned, frowning.

I blinked at him. "How did you know?"

His face cleared with a smile. "Ah. Good. I worried I'd misread him for a second. But if you're here and he's not, that means you said no, right? Why didn't you go out with him?"

I stared at him, taking longer to answer than I probably should've, but my brain was glitching harder than an Internet Explorer browser.

Bast carried on with the dinner prep, giving me time to gather my thoughts.

"I ... I don't know. I realized I hadn't spoken to the three of you about him, not properly, not how we did before Blaze joined the mix. I wanted to make sure all three of you were okay with the possibility of me dating Logan. I didn't say no, though. I just tentatively scheduled for tomorrow."

"Ah. This way, you'd have time to gauge how Blaze really felt about the possibility of adding another male to the group dynamic. You know Andres and I are okay with it, right? You don't have to worry about us. All we want is for you to be happy, Char. Besides, we spoke about Logan before, remember?" Bast came close enough to give me another kiss, then pressed his forehead against mine. "I'm so proud of you. You're navigating this relationship really well. Thank you for always taking our feelings into consideration and making sure you check with us before you do anything. It's how I know we'll be able to make this work and have the type of relationship my parents did. I love you, Char."

Seriously, this man.

We heard the front door opening and Andres yelling, "Honey, I'm home."

Bast kissed me once more and went back to his food prep while I sighed dreamily. I was nothing more than a pile of feels, and I knew for a fact I was the luckiest girl in the whole world.

# 16

## CHARISMA

My phone's incessant buzzing woke me up. I tried to see who was calling me at this ungodly hour, but the second I raised the screen to try to look at it, the light burned my eyes.

Motherfucker.

*This better be important.*

"'Ello?" I whispered, causing Andres to stir beside me. He opened one eye to check on me, but I shook my head, and he went back to sleep.

"Char."

It took me a moment to recognize the voice, but when I did, I only grew more confused.

"Theo? Hang on." I made my way out of the bedroom, doing my best not to wake the guys up.

I had no fucking clue what time it was, and I really didn't care. Still, if Theo was calling me at the ass crack of dawn, it could only mean trouble.

The second the bedroom door closed behind me, I headed to the kitchen, mindful to keep my voice down so as not to wake Blaze up. He'd arrived pretty late yesterday and taken the couch to let Bast, Andres, and I share the bed.

We really needed to sit down and consider some long-term solutions for our sleeping arrangement because I hated the idea of at least one of them always sleeping on the couch. Maybe I should just buy a new apartment with extra bedrooms. Even without the insurance money from my old apartment, I still had enough saved from my work as Onyx that I could afford a nice place. One that would not only have extra bedrooms and bathrooms but a brand new office for me to engineer to my heart's desire. I missed my old setup so bad.

Bast's setup was ... well. For someone who made video games for a living, he didn't even have an office. He'd converted the dining table into a weird computer haven, but there were too many distractions. I needed a place just for work, where I could just hide in my cave and do stuff with as little outside stimuli as possible.

"Theo," I asked and frowned when there was no answer. "Theo? Did something happen? Are you okay?" I was starting to sound panicked. But was there even another way to react when your ex called you drunk as a skunk at the ass crack of dawn?

There was a crash, but then he finally answered.

"No, I'm not. Char, baby, I haven't been okay since I had to give you up."

My breath hitched, but he kept talking. His words were slurred like he was drunk—or on drugs. Not that I'd ever seen him doing either, but there was no faking this kind of thing.

What the fuck was going on with Theodore?

I closed my eyes, wishing I knew what to say in this situation, but his words were opening some pretty deep wounds that had never really healed.

"You don't mean that," I said at last.

I had no idea if Theo heard me or not, but he started talking again. Or rather, drunkenly rambling. "I'm sorry, Char. I'm an asshole. I've been an asshole to you this whole time. I know that."

At least he'd become self-aware. *How marvelous.*

"It was on purpose, you see? Had to be an asshole to you. Had to make you hate me. Had to make you move on from me, from us. Hated myself for it, but I knew you could do better and be happy. All I ever wanted was for you to be happy. You're happy now, aren't you, Char baby? Now that you have them. The family you always wanted."

*Goddess, I'm too tired for this. I should be sleeping.*

"Theo, what are you talking about?" He wasn't making any freaking sense.

"Your—" there was a weird gulping sound. "—mates."

I gripped the phone tighter.

There were a lot of things I wanted to ask, and I was probably going to spend a long, *long* time analyzing this conversation later, but for now, I was more worried about his drunken state and the fact he didn't seem to be stopping.

Plus, the microwave in the kitchen confirmed that it was stupidly late. Or early.

Wasn't three in the morning the witching hour or something?

"Theo, are you drinking?"

"Yup." He popped the p. "I'm *celebrating*. Never been drunk before. Don't like the room spinning but needed to talk to you. Needed to apologize for being an ass...a hole. Ass-hole."

I should hang up. I one hundred percent should hang up

on him and leave him to his celebration. Nothing good ever came out of drunk dialing people. Even I knew that.

I also knew better than to listen to the ramblings of a drunk.

And yet ...

"Why were you an asshole to me, then? If you didn't want to be?"

I already knew I was going to regret asking. Goddess knew I'd regretted it when I visited him at the hospital. But I was a glutton for punishment, apparently, and I had a list of insecurities a mile long that had started and ended with the way Theo had treated me. I deserved to know, even if only to close that chapter of my life.

And that was what I'd keep telling myself until the day I died.

"Thought I was protecting you. You didn't want to keep living with that heir stuff. You told me time and time again you didn't want that life." He paused, and I could hear him drinking some more on the other side of the line. "You hated it, how it made you feel. I hated it too, for you, and for us. But if I didn't, Annie would have to, and she'd hate it more. So I had to. You had your way out, and I wasn't going to trap you with me. Didn't want you to be miserable because of me. Couldn't live with it if you hated me for it. Now you hate me anyway."

Theo laughed, but there was no humor to it. Just a deep bitterness that chilled my blood.

"Theo, I don't understand." It wasn't true.

I had the terrible feeling I was starting to understand, and I didn't like it one bit.

Oh, the next time I saw this drunken idiot, I'd give him a piece of my mind he would never forget.

"She wanted me to marry you. Propose at eighteen.

Make you a Soulbinder. Have you work for us and only us. And then make babies with you. Always wanted to make babies with you, but not like that, not because we *had* to. Didn't want her to mess with your head too. Didn't know she'd messed with mine. 'Is why I couldn't stay away, even though I tried. I tried, Char baby. I tried. But I had to see you. Had to." Then the rambling became actual rambles that made no sense, but I'd heard enough.

"Who wanted you to marry me, Theo?"

"The *matriarch*," he whispered the word like he was afraid someone would overhear. "She saw the MET you made me for my birthday. Said it was about time I made it official with you. She wanted to use you, like you were *less* or something because of your magic, but how it wouldn't matter because our babies would be Soulbinders through and thru ... thrugh ... through."

Goddess, I was getting really fucking tired of this whole pressure on my womb. Like, for real. Why was it that all of a sudden, everyone wanted me to make fucking babies or talk to me about children? I knew I was a woman, so, obviously, the only thing I might be good for was to breed the next generation—at least in some archaic, misogynistic mentality—but if one more person mentioned my name and babies in the same sentence, I was going to lose my damned mind.

Drunk Theo was clueless about my mental torment and just kept rambling.

"So I *lied*. I lied to Grandmother. At first, she didn't believe me, but when she saw we weren't together anymore, and nobody was seeing us together, she finally believed it."

I rubbed my chest. None of this should surprise me or hurt me, and yet ...

"Why didn't you tell me, Theo? Why did you wait until now?" If I sounded tired, it was because I *was*. Physically and mentally, I was completely and utterly exhausted, feeling like I was a hundred rather than twenty-three.

"Couldn't. Thought it was 'cause I was protecting you from her. Knew if I told you back then, you would've chosen me. Couldn't, though."

I wanted to laugh. Motherfucker knew I'd have chosen him, so he took away my choice?

"Of course you could've told me, Theo. In fact, you should've told me. It was my choice to make, not yours. I asked you time and time again, and you refused to tell me why."

"No, no, Char baby," Theo spoke, sounding almost desperate. "I *couldn't* couldn't. Even if I'd tried."

He wasn't making any fucking sense.

I was done, though. I'd heard all this shit a million times before, and if he was going to refuse to take responsibility for his actions and his mistakes, then we had nothing to talk about. I'd mail him his new MET tomorrow and be done with Theodore Soulbinder for good.

"Listen, Theo, it's late, and I'm tired. I appreciate you telling me this now, even if it took you getting drunk to do it, but it doesn't change anything. I'm tired of the games and the second-guessing. Get some sleep."

I pulled the phone from my ear, ready to hang up, when his next words had me bringing the phone back to my ear so fast, I hit my cheekbone with it.

"She bound me, Char."

"*What?*"

"That's why we are the Soulbinders. We can bind souls. Technically. We shouldn't use the power, like, ever, and nobody is supposed to even know how to do it, but the matriarch has always known. It's why Aunt Kate acts so weird and never leaves the house. Thought it was only her, and my parents. But noooo. Crazy Alma lady said it was me, too. Helped me fix it, but it hurt a lot. *A lot* a lot."

Shit. So this was what Gran had been up to with Bast and Andres when she'd visited them at the hospital. That was probably what Andres had been about to tell me when Logan arrived, and then it kind of slipped my mind to ask.

I'd be fucking damned.

"Yup. She was scary and crazy."

*Sounds about right,* I thought, knowing that under other circumstances, I'd have laughed at the way Theo said that.

"Came to visit me at the hospital and said a lot of things that confused me. Your Necro…manner…Necro. *Mancer.* boyfriend came too. And freaking Andres. Didn't know how to react. But Annie said I should trust her and hear her out, so I did. Then she fixed me. Mrs. Alma did, not Annie. I mean. Well, actually, I fixed myself, but Mrs. Alma taught me how to do it and helped me 'cause I couldn't do it alone. Then I slept for a whole day after, scared the Healers. Now I'm home, and I'm celebrating. Wanted you here celebrating with me, but you can't because you have them now. And they make you happy. And you hate me. But it's okay because I love you enough for the both of us."

"Theo, honey, you should stop drinking and get some sleep." Goddess knew tomorrow I'd have to sit Andres, Bast, and Gran down and have a serious talk with them.

"'Kay. Just wanted to 'pologize to you and talk to you before tomorrow."

I did not like the way he said that.

"Why tomorrow? What's happening tomorrow, Theo?"

"Gotta make it right. Gonna confront Grandmother. Promised Scary Alma that I would. Don't wanna challenge the matriarch. I mean, even if she's evil, she's my grandmother, but might have to. It's okay, though, 'cause nobody would miss me anyway."

I swore I could hear my heart breaking all over again into a thousand pieces.

"Theo, don't say that. Lots of people would miss you. *I* would miss you."

I might just have to miss him from jail, though, because I might end up murdering two of my guys for being dumbasses, and their grandmother to go with them.

"Nuh-huh. It's okay, though. You have them, and you're happy. Don't worry about me or tomorrow, Char. It's okay."

"Theodore. Listen to me." I gripped the phone tightly, wishing I could somehow magically teleport through the phone to give that drunken idiot a hug and then talk some sense into him. "Don't challenge your grandmother to a duel tomorrow. Please, Theo. Think it through. *Please*. I can help you. *We* can help you. We can come up with a plan. Don't just go all in, guns blazing. You only just left the hospital after the resistance tried to kill us," I sounded desperate, but I didn't give a shit.

I *was* desperate.

The matriarch was one scary, powerful foe, and it was clear that Theo wasn't acting like his usual self. And even if he were ... I had my doubts about whether or not he'd win. Even if he were stronger than Mrs. Esme, his grandmother had years of experience and was a lot more cunning than he was. Theo may have been an asshole to me and gone about it all wrong, but deep down, he was a good guy and had a gentle heart. I doubted he had the kind of stomach it would take to gain the upper hand against his own family, no matter what they'd done.

"'Tis okay, Char baby. I'll make it right. I love you."

And then he hung up before I could stop him.

I didn't realize I was crying until I lowered the phone and stared at it, intending to call him back, and noticed the tears falling on the screen.

I had to stop Theo before that lovable idiot got himself killed.

But first, I had to wake the guys up so I could yell at them.

# 17

## THEO

Morning light filtered through the window in my bedroom, and I groaned, pulling my pillow over my head to block it out.

My mouth was so dry, it felt like some desert creature had crawled up and died in there, leaving sand and ashes behind. My head hurt worse than when I'd woken up after being struck by fucking lightning, and that was saying something.

My whole body was stiff and hurting, and for some reason, my bed was more uncomfortable than I remembered it ever being.

Colder, too.

Waking up feeling like shit for the second day in a row must be some record for me. The first time, at least, it had been for a noble cause.

I tried to open my eyes so I could drag myself to the bathroom, knowing that, just like yesterday, a shower would go a long way toward making me feel better, but my eyelashes were sticky, and the brightness in the room made my head throb worse.

I closed my eyes again.

Maybe I could go back to sleep. Who knew? Perhaps if I rested a bit more, I wouldn't feel nearly as bad.

I turned on my cold, hard bed—wait, the ground? Well, it didn't matter; the floor would do just fine.

I had a vague recollection of drunkenly passing out on the couch after drinking a whole bottle of whiskey. The memories from last night were fuzzy, but drunk me had at least had the foresight of stripping out of my pants before I collapsed. Somehow, I must've fallen from the couch during the night and ended up on the floor. At least I'd brought the throw pillows along with me.

Definitely going to invest in a fluffy carpet once I felt like a human being again.

"Theo, wake up."

Huh. That was so weird. I was probably still pretty freaking drunk because, for a second there, I could've sworn Char's voice was calling me.

But of course it couldn't be. Char was probably all snuggled up in bed with her guys. The men who weren't mind-controlled dicks and had been smart enough to know the treasure they had in their arms.

I hated the bastards, but not nearly as much as I hated myself or the matriarch.

The ghosts got louder, their voices muffled by the pillow I had over my head. I wished they would just shut the hell up and let me wallow in peace. I'd earned this hangover, and I fully intended to suffer through it ... alone.

Suddenly, the pillow was pulled out of my hands. Cursing, I tried to shield my eyes with my hands, but someone stopped me.

"Oh no, you don't," Char said, and I forced my eyes open, blinking fast to try to clear my vision.

Was I hallucinating? Was I dead? Actually, I didn't give a shit. Char was here. My Char.

"Char, baby," I murmured, my voice coming out all croaky and weird.

Goddess, I needed water. Did all ghosts feel like they were talking around sandpaper? I should find Annie and ask her.

Later, though. Right now, all I wanted was to look at my Char.

She looked like a Goddess. Just as beautiful as the first time I'd seen her. No, even *more* beautiful. My Char had grown up, and not just in the way she filled out her clothes or how her face had matured. No, Char'd become self-confident, sure of her place in the world. She'd grown to accept and love herself, and it showed not only in the way she carried herself but in her *aura*.

Char's aura shone like the sun. All pure and beautiful, all the colors blending and twirling in a way I'd never seen on another living person. I knew that, if given the chance, I'd spend the rest of my life just staring at her and her aura until I went blind.

My Char baby was so, so beautiful it hurt to look at her.

"Goddess, Theo, are you still drunk?" Char's tone was disapproving, but her cheeks were turning a pretty pink, just like her hair.

Someone snorted. "Damn right she's beautiful. It's a pity you're such a fool, Theo, but at least you have good taste."

I frowned at the male's voice. That hadn't sounded like a ghost at all. That had sounded like someone I knew. *Andres*?

But why would Andres Illudere be at my house? In fact, how had Char even gotten in?

I may have been drunk as fuck, but I didn't think I'd

actually leave the house. Pretty sure Annie would've stopped me if I'd tried.

"Annie?" I called out and felt an answering chill on my forehead.

"I'm here, Weasley. And before you go all crazy again, you're neither dead nor hallucinating. Char really is here, and she isn't alone. You really, really should make an effort to wake the fuck up. Or get up. Whatever."

My sister sounded pissed at me. Had I done something to set her off again?

*Oh. Right.*

I remembered how Annie had tried to stop me from drinking when I'd gotten home and how I'd been an ass to her. I groaned again.

"I'm sorry, sis. I didn't mean any of what I said."

"What the hell is he talking about? Fucking Soul Mages and their creepy ghost-talking abilities. I'm never going to get used to this. Goddess."

I ignored the voice. It was nothing I hadn't heard before and nothing I could do about it. I saw dead people and spoke to them. So what? It was just another layer to myself. Like how Char could control the elements. At least my power wasn't destructive like the Nightshades'. Dark matter was painful and deadly. All *we* did was try to help the departed cross over. Though that was a lot harder and took a lot more time than they made it seem like on TV.

Wait.

Hadn't Annie just said Char was here? At my house?

I opened my eyes once again, not realizing I'd closed them in the first place. Then I just ... stared.

Char was here. In my house. Staring at me with concern and ... pity?

Dammit, I didn't want her pity.

I tried to sit up, but the world spun like crazy.

"Woah there, tiger. Calm down," Char said, holding me up and helping me sit even though the world was spinning.

"Blaze, can you get a glass of water? And Andres, would you mind helping me get him into the shower?"

# 18

## CHARISMA

I worried my bottom lip, leaving Theo's bedroom door open and making my way back to the disaster that was his living room.

Bast, bless him, was puttering around the kitchen, looking for the necessary ingredients to make Theo coffee and, by the sounds of it, some actual breakfast.

Blaze was carefully picking up the glass shards on the fancy, wooden floor and putting it all in a plastic bag he'd found only the Goddess knew where. Sometime during the night, Theo must've dropped the bottle of whiskey he'd been drinking. Based on the scene we'd walked in on, Theo had been sleeping dangerously close to the broken glass. While Blaze was on cleanup duty, Andres, being Andres, simply snooped, whistling and making happy noises at whatever he was finding.

It was stupidly early, not even seven in the morning, but after Theo's drunken call last night—early this morning?—I hadn't been able to go back to sleep. Instead, I'd woken the guys up in a panic, and they had to calm me down and talk some sense into me.

They'd been right. Theo hadn't gone off while drunk and tried to challenge his grandmother, which was a relief. Still, I hadn't expected to find Theo the way we had.

I stared at the throw pillows on the floor and the blanket, my heart hurting just thinking he'd been so far gone he'd passed out on the hard floor. It was a miracle he hadn't hurt himself with the glass shards.

When I heard the water running in the bathroom, I sighed and went to help Blaze clear up the living room.

Theo had been awake enough that he'd refused Andres' help in the shower—much to Andres' relief—and locked himself inside. That was a good sign, right?

Once he was clean and had a clear head, we could all sit down and talk like actual human beings. And since my guys had finally filled me in on everything that had happened between Theo and Gran, at least now I knew what was going on.

Oh, I was furious. Pissed right the fuck off at all three goons and Gran, too. But most of all, incredibly freaking angry at Esme Soulbinder. The woman had always given me the chills, but what she'd done? And to her own family?

How the hell had she managed to get away with so much for so long? It was pure insanity, that's what it was.

And while I agreed that Mrs. Soulbinder had to answer for her crimes, that didn't mean Theo had to shoulder that weight alone. It wasn't his fault his grandmother was a psychopath, and he shouldn't have to go up against her alone. It was reckless, dangerous, and more than a little bit insane.

All I wanted to do was curl up into a ball and rock back and forth while I pulled my hair out. Was that too much to ask? Seriously, it just felt like it was one thing after another lately, and right when I was getting settled, boom! Another freaking hurricane.

It was exhausting.

I knew, though, that unless I wanted to have a mental breakdown, I needed to get my shit together and deal with one thing at a time. That meant, for right now, I had to put all my feelings aside and focus on Theo.

Well. Helping Theo, anyway. Not focusing on the way his hungover self had stared up at me like I hung the moon and stars when I'd woken him up. Or the way he'd been in nothing but boxers and how he'd grown to fill them out just *fine* in the years since I'd last seen him naked.

If I ignored the bloodshot green eyes, the shadows underneath them, and the way he'd smelled like a distillery.

Andres appeared back in the living room just as we stopped hearing the shower. He picked me up and sat on the cozy gray couch with me on his lap.

"You're frowning, Kitten," he teased, and I wanted to snort.

"No shit, Sherlock."

Andres flicked my nose, punishing me for my sass. "Stop stressing. It's going to be fine. We'll figure something out."

"I'm still mad at you, and this isn't helping it."

Maybe mad wasn't the right word for it, but I was definitely unhappy that he and Bast had kept this whole thing from me. Their only saving grace was that they *had* tried to tell me, and we'd gotten interrupted, and then it had slipped my mind. However, for something this big? They should've made more of an effort.

Andres just hugged me insanely tight. "Aww, c'mon. We're sorry, Char. Don't be mad." he coaxed, giving me puppy dog eyes. "It was a sensitive topic. You can't really be mad at us for not wanting to open that can of worms when you had a guest over. We were basically between a rock and a hard place."

I conceded, and Andres rewarded me with a kiss on the forehead.

"Besides," he said, voice growing serious. "As much as the way it happened was crappy, wasn't it better to have heard it from him? I was going to tell you, sure, because we didn't want to keep secrets. But it had felt weird. Like it was his story to tell, you know?"

We heard the bathroom door open, and Andres and I turned in time to watch as Theo walked out of it.

Theo wore jeans and a black shirt that contrasted with his pale skin. His red hair was a wet mess, and he was walking while toweling it off. He must've heard something because he jerked his head up and stared at us from the open bedroom door.

I gave him a little finger wave.

Yup. I'd just gone and made this whole thing even more awkward.

I had mad skills.

Theo's mouth opened and closed again a few times as if he was trying to think of something to say.

"Nice place," Andres complimented, sounding smug as fuck.

I jabbed him with my elbow.

Theo just looked at him, bewildered. "Thanks?" He threw the wet towel on his bed and came out, putting his hands in his pockets and just staring at us.

"Uh. I don't mean to be ungrateful or act like an ass, but what are all of you doing here?" He paused for a second, tilting his head. "Actually, how did you even get *in* here? I thought I'd locked the door."

Theo sounded adorably confused.

I averted my gaze, jabbing Andres again when he snickered. I could hear Bast chuckling from the kitchen, and even Blaze was doing this weird cough-hacking thing as if trying to cover up his laughter.

"The door was locked," Bast confirmed, coming from the kitchen with a cup of coffee in his hand and offering it to Theo.

"Uh. Then how did you ... ?" Theo stared down at the coffee in his hands as if trying to reassure himself he wasn't drunk anymore.

Knowing I was blushing, I averted my gaze, suddenly *very* fascinated by the shape of my nails.

"Char knew where you kept your spare keys."

Andres was a rat bastard who was going to wake up one day and discover all his boxers had magically vanished. He'd have to go commando until he bought new ones. I'd make sure of it.

He was also not going to be allowed to participate in the next sex-a-thon. He wasn't even going to get to watch.

While I was busy plotting my revenge, I didn't notice the room had gone quiet. That was, until Theo spoke again.

"The plastic figurines?" he asked, and I was so surprised that I raised my head.

His green eyes were wide as saucers, and his mouth was hanging open.

"That was you?"

"What? No. Of course not! I'd never."

I wasn't fooling anyone.

"Wait, what? What are you guys talking about?" Andres asked, but we ignored him.

Theo was staring at me with a mix of shock and respect. "Seriously? This whole time, I thought it was Annie. She never said otherwise, not even when I retaliated."

Embarrassed, I shrugged. "I was feeling petty, and Annie was kinda mad at you, too, as my best friend. So she helped me."

Five years ago, a few months after Theo had started ghosting me, he'd moved into this apartment. A gift from his family. Theo's apartment was close enough to the Academy that he could walk there if he wanted to, which he did, according to Annie.

One day, when I'd been feeling particularly miserable about the shitty way he'd been treating me—or not treating me, since he'd just ghosted me—I'd talked Annie into helping me with my revenge. Egging his home or car had felt too easy, so instead, I'd dragged her into a dollar store, and I'd spent my whole paycheck there. I'd bought hundreds, if not thousands, of plastic Pokemon figurines. And then Annie and I had snuck into his brand new, recently furnished apartment, and we'd hidden them *everywhere*.

It had just been childish behavior that caused minor inconvenience, but it had made me feel better. I'd wanted him to find the damn things for weeks, months, even, in the oddest places. And even if he'd never known it had been me, I'd know I did it, and I was annoying him forever.

Annie had never mentioned she'd taken the blame for it. But then, I probably should've guessed.

"I can't believe this. Fucking hell, Char, I'm still finding the damn things around the house. It's been years."

If he wanted me to feel bad about it, I didn't. In fact, now that the embarrassment was over, I was feeling kind of smug.

"You should've thought of that before you ghosted me." I regretted the words the second they left my mouth, but it was too late.

Theo's face crumbled. "I'm sorry, Char."

I didn't know whether I wanted to punch myself or just give up and cry. "Yeah. I'm sorry, too. Not about the prank but ... the whole thing."

I was trying so damn hard not to think about myself right now. To not dwell on all the confusing, messy feelings that were making me feel all over the place. I was trying so, so very hard not to analyze or think too hard about the fact that Theo's behavior all these years hadn't been of his own doing. Still ... five years. Five years of being ghosted and ignored, and then he'd suddenly popped back into my life again, with the weird, stalkerish behavior. I didn't know what had been his doing or what had been his grandmother's. I didn't know what had been real and what wasn't.

It would be so much easier if I could forget the last five years and start things over, like deleting a few lines of code or starting a new save in a game. But life was never easy, and it was certainly never simple.

None of this would help Theo now, though. Which was why I needed to fucking focus. Stay in the present.

Be selfless and shit.

I blew out a breath. "Okay. Well. I'm sorry for barging in here, but since we're here and all, why don't we talk? It seems we have some catching up to do."

# 19

## THEO

Char had wanted to talk, so talk we did.

For hours.

By the time the four of them had left, I'd felt exhausted. Exhausted ... but hopeful.

Hope was a dangerous, dangerous thing for a guy like me to feel, but dammit.

Annie had been right. Oh, she was going to be smug as fuck when I admitted that—which I would because I needed to make some amends with her too. But damn. My sister had been right in trying to convince me to get help. It was just that I'd felt like I didn't *deserve* Char's help. I still thought that, actually, not that I'd told her that. She probably would've dick punched me or something.

Char could be ruthless when she wanted to be. I didn't know if it was because of the way she grew up, but she was so damn strong. And I didn't mean just physical strength. Char had risen to every challenge thrown her way and kicked its ass. Even as kids, despite the way her parents treated her and the kids who bullied her at school, she'd never cowered, never skipped class. It was what had made me fall for her in the first place, all those years ago.

Was it any wonder I had never stopped?

Having her here, in my home, had felt so right. I'd never thought the day would come when I'd have her *here*. Granted, she hadn't come as my girlfriend or to hang out with me because she loved me, but she'd come nonetheless. Even after everything I did, everything I'd put her through, Char was willing to help me.

Because that was just the kind of person she was.

What was even better, however, was the fact Char's presence here had served as confirmation that the unraveling had worked. For the first time in years, I hadn't felt any of the conflicting, obsessive, confusing feelings that battled for dominance inside of me. There hadn't been the red haze of jealousy when I saw her interacting with her men or the impulse to keep her away, followed by the compulsion to follow her the second she left my sight. It had been … like it used to be when we'd dated. Peaceful, easy. Well, not easy, because there had been a lot of awkwardness and walking on eggshells. I couldn't erase the past or the way my actions had affected her, and I wouldn't even if I could. Not because I wanted Char to have suffered, but because now more than ever, I knew that I'd been right to fear what my grandmother might've done to Char.

How had I not noticed something had been wrong with me, though? It seemed so clear now that my thoughts weren't filled with the haze.

Annie appeared, arms crossed in front of her, looking smug as fuck, and I smiled at her.

I felt … lighter somehow. Not completely free, but not as weighted down by things as I used to. I mean, I still felt like trash because of the hangover, but I deserved that. In fact, I should probably be feeling much, much worse.

"Go ahead, say it. I know you're *dying* to."

Annie threw her hair over her shoulder, all smug. "I have no idea what you're talking about," she replied.

I snorted. "Go on. You've earned it. You can say it. I'm a big man. I'll survive."

As if that was all Annie had been waiting for, she stared at me with a Cheshire grin. "I told you."

Yup. There it was.

"Yes, you did. You were right, and I was wrong. I'm a worthless, worthless worm who should've listened to you." Annie had forced me to use this speech every time she was proven right about something, and it was mandatory. Still, it was better than the shirt she'd tried to get me to wear once, that said I was a dumbass who served her Royal Rightness Annie. "Am I forgiven?"

She placed her hands on her hips. "That depends."

"Depends on what?"

Annie was enjoying this way too much. I drew the line at having to wear the Royal Rightness shirt, though. I'd thrown it in the trash the first chance I'd gotten back when we'd been teenagers.

She waited until I wiped my sweaty palms on my jeans, just because she could.

"Are you going to finally get your head out of your ass and grovel to try to get Char back, or will you grow old as a stubborn, bitter, lonely man? Because, I have to say, I don't know if I'll want to keep your grumpy ass company for eternity. I got ghost business and stuff."

I closed my eyes, groaning. I should've known Annie would ask that. I knew how my sister's mind worked.

Anxiety churned in my stomach, making me feel

queasy, while a shit ton of thoughts raced through my head. The idea of trying to win Char back after everything I'd done to her, everything I'd put her through...I didn't deserve her.

But if our plan worked—and Char was sure it would—then Annie was right. I'd have a long, long life ahead of me, and there was only one person in the world I wanted to spend it with.

I opened my eyes so I could look at Annie when I answered. "Yeah. If the plan works, if the matriarch stops being a threat ... then I'll grovel and beg Char to take me back. Even if I have to share her with the others, so long as she wants me and is ready to forgive me, then yeah. Whether or not that happens, I'll do everything I can to make sure she's happy."

I was also pretty positive that even if Char never forgave me, Annie would go back on her word and haunt me forever so I wouldn't have to be a lonely, grumpy, old man. So there was that.

Annie patted me on the head slightly like one would a dog. "Good boy, Weasley. Then yes, you're forgiven." Then she floated back until she was hovering over the couch. "So, drunk dialing, huh?"

I groaned.

Fuck my freaking life.

When Char had admitted that was why she'd barged in here, I'd racked my brain trying to remember the conversation but came up blank. When I'd asked her, Char had refused to tell me.

So had Annie. The second I'd tried to get her to tell me—when Char had still been here—Annie had conveniently lost hold of her ghostly form and vanished.

And while I was grateful that my drunk self had been

brave enough to do what I hadn't had the balls to, not knowing what I'd actually said would haunt me forever.

"You should've stopped me. Why didn't you stop me?"

"Why on earth would I have stopped you when drunk you agreed with me?" Then she looked down at her nails. "Besides, if anything, I did try to talk you out of getting shit-faced, remember? And what was it you said? Oh right. You were *celebrating*."

Urgh. Annie would never let me live this down.

I ran a hand through my hair, stomping towards the kitchen. I had a pile of dirty dishes in the sink since I hadn't let Char and her guys clean up after us. They were already doing enough; the least I could do was feed them—well, I ordered food, but it worked just the same—and not give them extra work. Besides, the menial task allowed me the freedom to think.

"Listen, sis, I'm sorry. I just realized I haven't said this before, and in the spirit of groveling and shit, I just wanted to make sure I apologized to you too. Sorry for being a dick. And thanks for having my back."

She smiled, floating until she was beside me. "Don't worry, Weasley. That's what family's for."

Then she paused, and we both grimaced. "Well. I mean."

"Yeah, I know what you meant. It's what we should be for, anyway. It'll be okay, Annie. You'll see." I was starting to believe it, too. Not because I had some crazy illusion of grandeur, but because Char's plan had been simple enough —at least in theory—that it might work.

"It better, or I'll make Bast bring you back to life so I can possess someone's body and kill you myself."

I snorted. "Oh, I'm so scared."

She blew a raspberry at me. "You should be! I'm badass."

"Well, alright, badass, are you sure you're okay with your

part in the plan? If I'm going to set the scene and put cameras all over her study for the confrontation, you'll have to keep an eye on Grandmother and be careful not to be seen. Not only by her but the rest of our family." We had no way of knowing who was under the matriarch's control and who wasn't, and when in doubt ... trust no one.

"Puh-lease. I got this. I have crazy ninja ghost skills. I'm more worried about you. I mean, it sucks that I'm dead, but the good thing is that she can't actually hurt me."

We both knew Grandmother could control her as a ghost just as easily as she had controlled our family. In fact, any Soul Mage could control a ghost, even if only temporarily. But I didn't bother bringing that up. Annie knew the risks. Besides, if our roles had been reversed, I'd want in on the plan, too. No matter the cost.

"I'll be okay. I won't be going in alone, remember?"

The idea was to set the stage, so to speak, with cameras beforehand so that when I confronted my grandmother, even if she got to me and bound my soul again, we'd have proof of it. If not, then her admission would be on tape. Or so we hoped. Regardless, the risk that the matriarch might still try to bind me was too big, which brought us to the second stage of the plan. When I went to talk to her, I wouldn't be going alone. Char, Andres, Blaze, and even Bast were going to go with me. This way, Grandmother would be outnumbered, and it would be harder for her to do her dirty work. None of this meant the matriarch would admit to her evil deeds, though, which was where Mrs. Alma came in.

It was going to be risky, but I was pretty damn sure that if my Grandmother saw Mrs. Alma was alive and well, the matriarch would fuck up.

Sure, I could risk challenging my grandmother to a duel

in front of them as witnesses, but I knew that forcing her to step down would be worse for her.

And she'd have to choose between giving up her position of power or the end of the Soulbinders. Because if she disagreed? Char was going to make sure the video and the truth were turned over to the public, and then there would be a *riot*. Grandmother was powerful, and she was good, but she couldn't win against every single Soul Mage. She may have played Goddess, but she wasn't all-powerful.

Me? I didn't give a shit about being the family head or having a seat in the council. I'd been groomed for it, and it was expected of me, but I'd give it up in a heartbeat if it meant someone better suited for the job showed up.

All I wanted was Char.

However, the matriarch would never allow our family's name to be sullied, and that was what we were all counting on.

Worst case scenario, I'd duel her and take the title by force. Whatever it took, so long as it meant Esme Soulbinder would no longer have the control she did.

## 20

# CHARISMA

"You're fidgeting."

I blinked at Blaze's words, tilting my chin far back to try to look at him. I was lying on the couch, using one of its arms as a pillow, and since Blaze had just come from behind me, that meant I had to go all Spiderman to be able to see him.

Even upside-down, Blaze was hot.

"Huh?"

He shook his head, smiling, and walked closer until he grabbed my phone from my hands. The same phone I'd been spinning like an expensive, oversized fidget spinner while I spaced out on the couch.

*Oops?*

"I'm not fidgeting," I lied blatantly, raising my hands to grab my phone back, but Blaze stepped out of reach. Damn him. "I'm just ... " I tried to come up with a good excuse, and my brain latched onto the one thing that could explain any and all weirdness. "Doing a scientific experiment."

Blaze's chuckle called to my very soul, warming me up

inside. Blaze was good looking, there was no denying that. But when he laughed or he smiled? He was breathtaking.

And *mine*. Completely and utterly mine. I'd licked him *all over* to make sure of it. Those were them rules.

"Why are you so nervous?" he asked, coming around the couch–thank fuck, because my neck was starting to hurt from the awkward angle–and standing in front of the TV.

"Is this about Theo or your date with Logan?"

*Both? Both.* Both was good. Both was the answer I wanted to give Blaze, but ...

I sighed, staring into his pretty mossy green eyes. Already, Blaze knew me too damn well. Which wasn't a problem, really. I was damn lucky to have him in my life, loving me as much as I loved him, but ...

I bit my bottom lip. "It's not ... I'm not nervous, exactly," I admitted, trying to organize my inner turmoil in a way that made sense. "More like ... anxiously excited? I'm looking forward to this date with Logan. Goddess, this feels weird to say out loud, especially to you." Blaze had surprised me time and time again, and when I'd told the three of them Logan had asked me on a proper date, I thought he'd balk at the idea or be against it. But Blaze had been surprisingly okay with it. I'd known all three of them had eavesdropped on Logan's admission that he wanted to date me properly and see where things went, but I'd been worried Blaze would be against that. His reaction to the mere idea of the stranger my parents had wanted to force me to marry was proof of how jealous he could get.

It was confusing as hell.

This whole multiple relationships thing was pretty damn great in theory—and in real life, too, not going to lie —but trying to navigate everyone's feelings and knowing where the lines were drawn was pretty freaking hard.

Not that I was complaining. I wouldn't dare complain. I was the one having all the benefits here, so zero complaints from me.

"Char, it's okay," Blaze said soothingly. He grabbed my legs and lifted them gently so he could sit on the couch before pulling my legs over his lap.

I blinked at him a couple of times to make sure that had really happened, and yup.

"Uh. I could've made way for you on the couch. You didn't have to—" I flailed my hands around like a weird jazz dancer to encompass his maneuver, but he just winked.

And damn that wink. Blaze winking was the ultimate hotness form. He hardly ever showed that side of him, but when he did, it made me want to do ... things. Naughty, kinky things. Like jumping him on the couch and asking him to fuck me until I couldn't walk for a week.

He gripped my toe, pulling it slightly to get me back to the here and now.

"Huh?"

I was so good at this wording shit. Someone give me a typewriter or computer so I could write the next bestselling novel. It would be about an opossum who hissed at anyone who came close to her trash. Literary masterpiece right there.

"Char, listen to me; I know I was against sharing you, and I won't lie and pretend there will be moments where I won't feel jealous or need you to be patient with me. However, when I agreed to this, I knew there might be others you would be interested in." He started massaging my feet, loosening the knots or whatever kind of wizardry it was that made me feel all relaxed and *good*. It took more effort than I wanted to admit to keep my focus on him and his words and not start moaning at the unexpected wave of heat building inside me.

"But, Char, when I said I was all in, I meant it. Besides, the biggest fear I had regarding this relationship was that you'd favor one over another, and you don't. You're always so careful of all of us. You pay each of us equal attention because you really do love all of us equally. And you always take the time to talk about things, even the hard things, with us before you do something, because you're mindful of our feelings. Not only did you wait to ask us about going out with Logan—even though you don't technically need our permission—you did it multiple times, just to make sure we hadn't changed our minds."

"Well, I mean, yeah. I don't want you to feel obligated to something you said in the heat of the moment or because the others were okay with it. I'd never do anything to hurt you guys."

Blaze smiled. "And that's why I know it'll work out."

"You're awesome. Did you know that?" I told him, my eyes watering. Damn those imaginary onions someone must be cutting right about now, making me teary.

I got up and went to Blaze, sitting beside him, my legs slung over his. Then I laid my head on the crook of his shoulder, sniffing him. Blaze smelled good. All my guys did, really. I'd chosen them well.

"Thank you for being mine."

Blaze's arm tightened around me. "No, Little Spitfire. Thank *you* for being ours. Now, come on, tell me what it is about the date with Logan that's making you anxious. Maybe I can help?"

"You want to help put my mind at ease about a date with another man? Who are you, and what did you do to my

Blaze?" I jokingly asked, feeling awesome when he rewarded me with a snort.

"Maybe I'm trying to be a great boyfriend and shit. You know, one up Andres and how he helped you dress for my date with you."

I whipped my head so fast, I accidentally head-butted his chin. But I was too shocked to apologize. "Wait, you know about that?" My voice was a tiny smidge high, but I did not care.

I covered Blaze's ears. "Andres!" I yelled, knowing he was somewhere in the house, probably eavesdropping on this conversation too. Bast was the only one who wasn't home. He'd gone to try to bribe his grandmother into agreeing to our plan to help Theo. "Come here!"

Andres magically—literally magically—appeared right in front of us, and I gave a horror-movie-worthy scream.

Motherfucker had been using his illusions to hide while he snooped and just managed to scare five years off my life.

My heart was beating faster than the one time I'd been stupid enough to play Amnesia at night—I'd wanted to see what the fuss had been all about when the game had become a hit, and been even more stupid as to think playing it at night wouldn't make a difference. Boy, had I learned my lesson.

"What the fuck, Andres? Goddess, give a girl a fucking warning or something next time," I complained, even as I raised a hand over my beating heart. Pretty soon, the poor thing would try to come out of my throat or something. Was I getting gray hair? I pulled one of my strands and breathed a little sigh of relief when I noticed it was still pink.

I didn't care that it was dyed and not the natural color. Logic didn't matter when one's ghost had left one's body and was surveying the scene from above.

Andres started to laugh, and I wished I could say I was mature enough to be the bigger person, but I was not. I was salty and petty, and Andres should've really seen this coming.

One second, Andres was laughing. The next, I had my brand new MET in hand. I quickly keyed in commands, and before Andres could say, "Forgive me, Char, for I have sinned," an orange activation circle appeared in front of him. Andres had just enough time to widen his eyes and look up—he really should've closed his eyes instead—and then there was about a gallon of water falling over him, drenching him.

I watched with evil satisfaction as he sputtered. Blaze's laughter filled the room like music to my ears.

But then, because I loved Andres and feared retribution, I keyed in another command on my MET, making all the water evaporate from both Andres and the surrounding area —Bast would've totally been grumpy about the state of his apartment otherwise, and I didn't want to put his love to the test.

Andres just stared at me like a wounded puppy. The effect, however, was ruined by the messy hair and clothes. I might've gotten rid of the water, but that didn't mean he hadn't been left with the aftermath of being drenched.

Before he could say anything, though, my phone started buzzing in my pocket.

Shit! My alarm!

I jumped from the couch and was already halfway to the bedroom when I turned the alarm off.

"Char? What is it?" Blaze asked, coming after me.

"Sorry. No time! I have to get ready. Logan's picking me up in half an hour, and I'm not ready. I'm not dressed. I need to shower and shave and, like, pick something amazing.

There's no time." By the time I'd finished answering, I was already in the bathroom, wiggling out of my shorts. I took off my shirt next, my head whipping around when I heard a wolf whistle.

Andres and Blaze stood at the open bathroom door, eyes heated and roaming over my underwear-clad body.

I wasted precious seconds staring back at them, seriously considering taking them up on their unspoken offer. However, if I let them in, if I let them help me shower, there would be a lot of sexing-up and not enough showering, which would be amazing and feel super good, but ... there was no way I'd be ready on time.

Andres unbuttoned his jeans, and I gulped.

Maybe we could make this super quick? Goddess knew just the idea of being the filling in a yummy Blaze-Andres sandwich already had me plenty wet.

*No! Must focus!* I covered my eyes with my hands, making the guys laugh.

"Out. Both of you. I need to get ready, and we all know that won't happen if you're here with me. Besides, it wouldn't be fair to Logan for me to be late because I was having some crazy amazing sex." Then I turned, finished stripping, entered the shower stall, and turned on the cold water tap before I could change my mind.

# 21

# CHARISMA

The limousine stopped, and I looked out of the window, confused.

"Uh. Where are we?" I asked Logan, who just gave me a knowing smirk.

"You'll see," he replied enigmatically before he got out of the car and crossed to open my door.

Logan had been oddly mysterious about where he'd be taking us on our date. It had been yet another reason I'd been freaking out a little. How was a girl supposed to know what to wear when she didn't know where she was going? Preparing for all occasions was great in theory, but when it came down to it, it was hard to find an outfit that was sexy, practical, dressy, and relaxed. Like, the holy grail of clothing. And since I was yet to discover the magical clothes that would work for everything, I'd ended up having to get creative.

In the end, I'd gone for a dark burgundy romper that looked like a dress but gave me the added confidence of shorts. I'd paired it with my brand-new black boots—courtesy of Andres—that reached just below my knees.

Maybe this could be my One Outfit To Rule Them All.

Logan offered me his hand to help me out of the car, and I smiled at him. He was such a gentleman.

When I got out of the car, rather than let go of me, he pulled me closer, caging me in. My pulse increased with the proximity and the emotions I could see in his gaze. We were so, so close. Logan's head was bent over, and I knew I could steal a kiss from him if I just got up on my tiptoes. Just thinking about that had me licking my lips.

We'd only kissed once before, right after we'd officially met, and even though he'd done it to shut me up—which wasn't exactly a great reason—it had been mind-blowing. Unforgettable.

I closed my eyes in anticipation, but when nothing happened, I opened them again.

Logan's lips were tilted up the slightest bit as he let go of me. "Later," he growled. It was a promise, and damn.

*Shut up and take my panties.*

My knees felt weak, but I did my best to stand, blinking and finally looking around us. We were in the middle of a busy street, but Logan had me pinned between him and the open car door, so nobody bumped into us. It took me a while to calm my raging libido, and when I did, I was finally able to recognize where we were.

Behind Logan, the words "Observation Deck" shone in gold on a black background. I glanced from the golden doors back to Logan, back to it, excitement blooming inside me and making me want to do a little dance.

"Let's go. We don't want to be late," he said, offering me his hand.

Okay, so, I was a big girl. Well, mostly, anyway. I was twenty-three years old. I had not one, not two, but *three* boyfriends. And yet, walking hand in hand with Logan

Nightshade while we entered one of the tallest buildings in the city—which, thanks to Logan, was empty except for the staff—made me feel like I was on cloud nine.

Then we were entering the elevator and going all the way up to the top floor.

The doors opened to let us out, but Logan held me back, keeping me inside. I looked at him questioningly, surprised when I saw the worry in his gaze.

"I forgot to ask, but you're not afraid of heights, are you?"

The question made me smile.

"Nah. I actually really like the view from above."

He flashed me an adorably boyish smirk that made my heart pitter-patter like crazy.

Who knew Logan had a side like that? He gave off so many strong Dom vibes, just learning he had a softer side had been a welcome surprise. But boyish Logan? It was my Achilles heel.

"Good," he said, pulling on my hand gently and leading me onto the shiny marble floor. "Then you'll love this."

I wanted to point out that I was already loving this, but then I actually saw what lay behind the huge glass panels, and I couldn't say anything at all.

Without conscious thought, I walked closer until I was right at the edge, looking down at the city above. All that life, all those people. From this high up, I felt like I could see the entire city, and it was *lively*. It was a good thing I wasn't afraid of heights or didn't suffer from vertigo because the experience was *intense*.

"Wow, it's so beautiful!" I exclaimed, unable to take my eyes away.

I wanted to put my hands against the glass so I could be even closer, but I didn't want to smudge the surface.

So glad I'd chosen a romper over a dress, though, because if anyone looked up, they would've seen my underwear. Well, probably not from this high up, but one could never be too sure.

"I don't get the chance to come here often, but whenever I'm struggling with a decision or want time with my thoughts, I like to come here. Seeing things from this far up helps put your problems in perspective."

Logan's quiet admission was surprising enough that I was able to tear my gaze from the view and stare at him instead.

From this angle, all I could see was his profile. The dark hair, the strong jaw. The well-fitting slacks and the dressy shirt that was the same icy blue color as his eyes—no suit this time either. Logan looked relaxed. Not like the acting head of the Nightshade family or the guy I'd met weeks ago who'd thought he was better than me, even if he did acknowledge my skills. Not like the tormented man who'd been starving, with sunken eyes, full of righteous anger at being imprisoned by the resistance. Not like the guy who'd awkwardly sat on Bast's couch, trying to fit in but being just a little out of it. This Logan was ... different. Happier, maybe. Definitely more relaxed.

All sides of him were equally as sexy, though.

"I've never been here before," I admitted, still more fascinated by him than the view—and that was saying a hell of a lot. "It's wonderful. I can see why you like to come here. Though, I have to ask, how on Earth did you manage to get rid of all the tourists?" My tone was teasing, but the question was legit.

This place should've been packed. It was one of the reasons I'd never visited. Just thinking about sharing the same space with a bazillion strangers made my introverted little heart twitchy.

Logan shrugged as if it was no big deal, but I was watching him. And because of it, I saw the cocky smile.

"I just asked them nicely."

"Ha! Yeah, right." Who did he think he was kidding? "I mean, no offense, I'm sure when you want to, you can be crazy nice, but people don't just vacate a main tourist spot during peak tourist hour just because you ask them *nicely*." Unless the asking nicely involved a shit ton of money.

Which, I wasn't complaining, but damn.

Logan turned to me then, his eyes full of mischief. "They do when you tell them you want to impress a girl."

"Is that—" I had to stop and clear my throat. I was feeling so many things. I didn't even know where to start or how to identify them. "Is that what you're doing? Trying to impress me?" Did he not see himself in the mirror? He was plenty impressive already. And it wasn't even just because he was so damn hot. Or because he was crazy-powerful. Or because he made my panties wet every time he raised an eyebrow and just stared at me.

He drew me closer, and I went willingly, pulled by his gravity. "I thought that was obvious."

"Oh, Logan." I placed my hand on his cheek and rose on my tiptoes. "You don't have to impress me. You just have to be yourself." And then I kissed him. Just a gentle whisper of a kiss, really. A test, a promise.

Logan chased when I started to draw back, his lips pressing against mine with certainty, hunger even.

*Finally*, I thought and opened my mouth to allow him entrance.

Our kiss was better than that first time, better than I remembered or could've imagined. I clung to him, forgetting time and place as our tongues tangled. Logan's fingers trailed over my hair, and he pulled the strands just enough to hurt.

Then *I* was the one pulling *his* hair, and the sound he made had me rubbing my legs together.

Logan's hand slid down to my ass and he gripped me, pulling me closer until his erection was digging into me. I moaned against his mouth, and grabbed *his* ass.

And holy shit, Logan's ass was *prime* stuff.

He rewarded me by biting my lower lip, hard, and then soothing the pain away before possessing my mouth in a dominating kiss.

I wanted to jump up so he could grab me and I could dry hump him. Or maybe have him pin me against the glass and fuck me, uncaring of who might be watching.

I blamed Andres for my newly found exhibitionist streak.

"Logan," I murmured his name when he started to trail kisses down my neck. I could feel his hard cock pressed against my stomach, and he was *hung*.

No wonder Logan was all sexy confidence. He could definitely back it up.

Oh, I'd love it if he backed *me* up.

Logan nibbled on my earlobe, and I was lost.

"Okay," I said, panting as if I'd just run a marathon. "That's it. We're going." I drew a step back, pulling my arms from him and letting them drop at my sides.

Logan's hair was all mussed from my hands, his lips red from our kisses, and good Goddess, I wanted to just jump him so *bad*. Just climb him until my legs were over his head and he was eating me out. I'd read that in a book once and had been wanting to try it out. At least in my fantasies, because I'd probably fall backward when I came or something equally stupid.

However, we were in a public space with cameras around, and I didn't care how much my exhibitionist trait was begging for it; I wasn't going to get naked and do the deed where anyone might walk in. I was also not going to have sex in a sort of public bathroom. Too damn gross, and I'd be wondering about the germs the whole time.

Logan seemed to be having a hard time keeping his hands away from me, though, and when he went to grab me, I stepped back once again.

"No, sir. I mean, yes, but not here. We're going to the car so we can make out all the way to your place, or Bast's. Or anywhere that's nearby and doesn't have cameras, I don't care. I *really* need your dick inside me, but we're not going to do that here. Anywhere will work, so long as we have privacy."

"You're right. I suppose we both got a little carried away." Logan took some deep breaths looking anywhere but at me while he adjusted the anaconda in his pants. Then he raised his hands to fix his hair, but I stopped him.

"Don't. I like knowing I was the one who messed it up," I admitted.

The look Logan sent me was ... there were just no words to describe it. Maybe center-of-the-Earth hot.

Was it possible to spontaneously combust from a look? Because I was pretty sure I was halfway there already. Forget drenched underwear, mine was seconds away from being completely useless.

I power-walked to the elevator—so the people watching the security footage wouldn't think I was desperate—and pushed the button. Then I pushed it a couple more times because that would obviously make it open faster.

Then Logan was there, pressed against my back, his arms wrapped around me, and he was kissed my ear. My neck.

I gasped.

"Logan." I wasn't sure if it was a protest or a demand.

"Just helping you relax while we wait," he teased, his breath against my ear.

*Fuck.*

We made it to the car. Barely.

We totally made out in the elevator, too. After all, it was a seventy-floor ride. The second the doors closed on us, Logan had pinned me against the wall and kissed me until we were both panting.

But we managed to keep our clothes on. Well. Maybe a few buttons on Logan's shirt were open, and his shirt was definitely no longer tucked in his pants, but he had his body covered, and so did I. Rompers had awesome space on the leg area, so Logan had managed to touch me without even having to unzip me.

I sat on the furthest corner of the limousine, and when Logan tried to sit beside me, I raised my hands to stop him.

"Nope. This is not happening here. I need you to sit right over there—" I pointed to the opposite end of the seat "—and keep your hands to yourself. Seriously. We can't ... not here." I gave a pointed look in the driver's direction just in case Logan was not catching my drift.

Despite my protests, I was one raised eyebrow away from saying to hell with everything and just fucking him on the first convenient surface. Giving his driver a show? Well, not really in my bucket list, but right now, I could definitely be talked into it. Hell, we'd already given the whole Observatory staff something to think about late at night.

Logan didn't say anything, he just smirked. His gaze locked on mine, and he pressed a button that made a little dark thing cover the window between the backseat and the driver.

"It's called a *privacy* window," he informed me, putting extra emphasis on the word.

Well. I *had* told him anywhere would work so long as we had privacy.

I bit my bottom lip, torn between my hormones and my brain, knowing fully well that my pussy was fighting to take charge.

As if Logan could see my struggle, which he probably could, he grabbed his brand new MET—I'd given him the gift when he'd picked me up—and used it to put up wards around us.

Now, not only was there a privacy window separating us from the driver, but we were inside a black bubble—well, square—of dark matter.

"That'll keep anyone outside from seeing or hearing us," he told me.

*Sold*!

That was all the reassurance I needed.

If only I could say I was all sultry with what I did next, but unfortunately, if there was one thing I was not, it was femme fatale material. I launched myself at him like a starved woman, landing awkwardly on his lap and fusing our mouths together to stop Logan's chuckle.

He filled his hands with my ass, his grip just short of bruising, and thrust his hips.

It wasn't enough. It might never be enough. There were too many layers between us.

That didn't stop me from moving against him, in search of more friction while my fingers unbuttoned his shirt.

My eyes bugged out when I realized Logan had chest hair. I'd seen him bare shirted—wait, no, chested, bare chested—once before, and I had not noticed his chest hair. I'd probably have taken more time admiring it otherwise. In fact, I might've launched myself at him and had my way with him sooner.

I broke the kiss, looking down as my fingers explored his chest. It wasn't like a whole lot of it to the point it would be disturbing, just enough to make me wonder if it'd tickle if I tried to kiss him there.

"Charisma."

"Huh?"

"What the fuck are you wearing and how do I get it off? If I don't get a taste of your tits soon, I might die. I'd have torn it off, but I didn't want you to get annoyed about it."

I giggled, unprepared for the deep frustration in Logan's voice, even while I seriously considered the idea of just letting him rip my clothes apart.

That was definitely one of my fantasies, but maybe we could circle back to it when we weren't in the back of a car.

"There's a zipper, here," I twisted slightly on his lap, raising my left arm awkwardly to let him work down the hidden zipper. Logan made quick work of it, and soon enough, I was naked from the waist up.

One thing about this romper was that it did not work with a bra.

"Beautiful," Logan murmured, taking his time to admire the view.

I squirmed on top of him. He could look at me naked some other time; right now, I needed to fucking come.

I must've said that out loud because he chuckled.

"Needy little thing, aren't you?" And then he was sucking on my breast. Logan snuck his hand between us, his finger rubbing against my clit.

I closed my eyes, thrusting my hips forward to get him to do it again.

"Goddess, Charisma, you're drenched," he praised when he spread my lower lips, circling my clit until I was nothing but a squirming mess. When I thought there could be nothing better, Logan started to finger fuck me.

I whimpered, tugging him by the hair so I could kiss him again while I rode his hand.

"That's it, baby, I can't wait to have my cock inside of you. You're so fucking tight, I bet you feel so damn good."

Almost desperately, I held onto Logan's shoulders as I rode his hand. I could feel my orgasm approaching, but somehow, for some reason, I wasn't able to get there just yet. Logan's filthy words were music to my ears, and he was playing my body just right, but my pussy was spasming on his fingers, greedy for more.

"Logan, *please*." I didn't know what I was asking for, and I didn't really care.

Logan increased the rhythm, the palm of his hand rubbing against my clit as his fingers kept hitting that spot inside of me that made my toes curl.

Something pinched both my nipples, and I exploded.

## 22

## LOGAN

"Did you just ... did you just use Dark Matter on my nipples to make me come?" Charisma panted the second she finished riding the wave of her orgasm.

I had, in fact, done exactly that, and based on the way her cunt had pulsed around my fingers, I knew she hadn't minded.

"Trust me, Charisma, I'm just getting started." I lazily stroked inside her, enjoying how she rocked forward, seeking more even though she had just come. "One day, I'll make you come using just my magic and nothing else. I'll make you come over and over again, and it still won't be enough. You'll be begging for my cock to fill this greedy pussy of yours." Charisma rocked on my hand as I spoke, making the most adorable noises. "And once you've begged me enough, I'll wrap my hand in your hair just like this—" I illustrated my point by gripping the pink strands, careful not to pull on them enough that it would hurt her. "And I'll fuck this smart mouth of yours the way I've been fantasizing about doing since we met. I'll give you my cock until you're choking on my come, and then, and only then, will I let one of your other boyfriends fuck this pussy. You'll be so needy, so high strung, that the second you feel their cock inside of you, you'll come over and over again, milking them dry."

I could see it all so clearly in my head, how good she'd look, how beautiful her little cries of pleasure would be.

Charisma, spread open on my bed, small orbs of dark matter working on her nipples and clit. I'd show her just how amazing my magic truly was, how great straddling that line between pain and pleasure could be.

But that was something for later; right now, I had Charisma half-naked from the waist up on top of me, rocking and trying to get off once more.

I waited until she was close, and then I pulled my fingers out and licked them clean.

Charisma's whimper of protest became a moan when she saw I was tasting her.

She tasted amazing, too. I almost switched our positions so I could eat her out.

Unfortunately, though, we'd arrived at my building a few minutes ago. If Charisma had been uncomfortable with the idea of people seeing us in the security cameras of the tower, she'd probably frown knowing the car had been parked for the past five minutes.

More than anything, though, I wanted to be inside of her. I was so damn hard, I felt I might come from the dry humping alone, like some eager teenager. And while I had no problem with the idea of continuing this exactly where we were, I wanted to see Charisma in my bed. I wanted her in my apartment again, and this time, doing something far more enjoyable than discussing business.

"Wait. Did you just say you've been fantasizing about fucking my mouth since we met?" Charisma asked, biting her bottom lip and looking at me with hooded eyes.

She had no idea just how much she was testing my control.

"The day we met, while we were still on Academy grounds. You had red lipstick on, and you were acting all flustered and submissive. I wanted you to get down on your knees and suck me off until your lipstick was all smudged from my cock," I admitted, my voice husky.

Back then, I'd only wanted her for her body, not expecting there to be so much more beyond the exterior.

"Oh? Like this?"

Before I could so much as blink, Charisma was kneeling between my legs and freeing my erection from my pants.

She stared at my dick as if she'd just been served her favorite dessert. She licked her lips, and I had to close my eyes.

Big mistake.

Charisma took me in her mouth without warning, swallowing around me until I was hitting the back of her throat.

*Fuck.*

I opened my eyes. I wanted to savor every second of this.

"You look so pretty with my dick in your throat, baby."

Charisma hummed at my compliment, the vibration making my balls tighten even more. I needed to take control. Otherwise, I was about to embarrass myself.

I gripped her hair. "I'm going to fuck this mouth of yours now. If it's too much, or if you need me to stop, I want you to tap my leg twice, okay?"

She nodded the smallest bit, my dick sliding between her lips.

I wrapped one hand on the base of my cock, the part she hadn't been able to fit so I'd know how far I could go without hurting her, and then I started to thrust in and out, slowly at first, so she could get used to the pace.

Charisma's hand grabbed my balls, and she gently played with them.

"Next time, we'll do this in front of a mirror so I can see how much you're enjoying this. I bet your pussy is dripping right now, desperate for my cock, isn't it, Charisma? Contracting on nothing while your mouth takes it all."

Charisma hummed against me, whether in pleasure or agreement, I didn't know, but I was too far gone.

When I felt I was right on the edge, I started to pull out.

For our first time together, I wanted to come inside her tight little cunt while she screamed my name. And once we'd both caught our breaths, I'd fuck her all over again.

When just my tip was inside Charisma's mouth, she sucked, hard, hollowing her cheeks and gripping my balls.

I came with a curse, forgetting time and place, thrusting erratically into her until I was spent.

The little minx gave me a smug smile, cum dripping from her mouth. For a minute, I was worried about how rough I'd gotten, but she didn't look upset.

And more beautiful than ever.

Then, proving she wasn't done surprising me and trying to bring me to my knees, Charisma, eyes still on me, licked her lips, catching the cum she hadn't been able to swallow.

I was pretty sure that was when I fell for her.

No, I fell for her when I'd gone to pick her up for our date, and she'd answered the door looking beautiful and happy, a gift in her hands. She'd put a little red bow on top of the brand new MET she'd designed and programmed to replace the old one. A replica of the MET she'd made me. And she'd done it because she wanted to, because that was the type of person she was. Charisma was attentive and caring, and she'd given something priceless simply because she knew it was something I needed. I couldn't even remember the last time anyone had given me a present, let alone one without any strings attached, for no other reason than they wanted to.

Half-crazed and out of control, I pulled her up, kissing her, claiming her, *branding* her.

The fact I could still taste myself in her mouth only made this whole thing filthier, hotter.

Charisma was mine, and I'd spend all night showing her just that.

## 23

## CHARISMA

I'd made Logan lose control. *Me.*
And it was *glorious*.

After our kiss, Logan had helped me fix my clothes and his, and we'd taken his private elevator straight to the penthouse. The second he'd closed the door to his apartment, we were all over each other like we couldn't get enough.

I knew I couldn't.

I was one horny, needy mess, and I wanted *more*.

We kissed and touched everywhere, making quick work of stripping each other, uncaring where the clothing ended up. By the time Logan laid me on the bed, we were both naked and *wanting*.

And yet, it wasn't enough. I knew what I wanted, though, and how to get it.

I opened my legs, grabbing his hard length and trying to guide him where I needed him most.

Logan stopped me before I could. "Oh no, you don't." Logan chuckled against my ear. "I know you think you're in charge here, especially after what you did in my car, but make no mistake, Charisma, in this bedroom, I'm the one calling the shots. And it's about time I showed you that, don't you think? Besides, now that you were so nice as to finish me off in the car, I can last *much* longer."

I did not, in fact, think that. What I did think was that it was about time his dick filled my pussy, hammering me until I could no longer walk.

"But—" I started to protest, but when Logan suddenly flipped me over, words failed me. He pinned me against the bed, my back to his front, his cock nestled against my ass.

"No butt stuff," I blurted out, almost in a panic. "I mean, I'm all for butt stuff, really, but you're too damn thick. I don't think I could take it without seeing the Goddess in person, and I kind of have a whole sex bucket list I want to get through before it's my time to meet the Goddess for real."

I wasn't entirely sure there was enough prep in the world that would help me take a dick like Logan's.

"Relax, Charisma. That's not what we'll be doing. Not today, at least. Not without the proper care. Get on your hands and knees for me, baby. Yes, just like that," he said when I obeyed his command.

Logan helped me find a position I was comfortable with, then he was behind me, spreading my cheeks and eating me out from behind like a starved man. I gripped his sheets, pushing against him, always greedy for more, and he rewarded me by rubbing my clit while he tongue fucked me over and over again.

"I'm so close. Please, Logan. I need you inside of me. All of you."

I turned my head as far as I could to look at him.

"Eyes up front, Charisma. You don't get to watch. Not today," he ordered, and I obeyed.

I was willing to do just about anything if it meant his dick would be inside me in the next five seconds.

"Good girl," he complimented. I grew even wetter, my pussy *begging* to be filled, spasming on fucking *nothing*. Pretty sure my brain synapses short-circuited, too.

Yup, I definitely had a thing for being praised. Especially when Logan used that alpha-male voice of his.

There was a moment when Logan wasn't touching me, and then I felt the bed move, and Logan was ramming into me without warning. He thrust hard, deep, not giving me time to get used to his length, but I loved it.

I felt so full, stretched out to my limits, and it was so, so *good*. I closed my eyes, giving myself fully to the sensation of him. Logan pulled out almost completely, and then he was ramming into me again, somehow going even deeper. The bed creaked every time he filled me, the continuous noise like a symphony that muffled my breathy noises.

"Faster," I begged.

Logan gripped me by the hips and fucked me even faster. I clung to the bed for dear life and enjoyed the ride. I matched his rhythm, encouraging him to keep going until he was hitting that perfect spot with every. Single. Thrust.

Logan's hand rubbed my over-sensitive clit, and I came, shouting his name. He fucked me even faster as I rode my orgasm, his rhythm faltering, and I knew he was close, too. Then he was shouting my name, grunting against me as he came, taking me close to the edge one last time.

I lost the strength in my arms and fell head-first on the bed, happy and utterly spent.

"You know," Logan said, his fingers trailing down my naked back. "This was not how I expected today to go."

"Oh?" I asked, not moving from my spot. I was lying beside Logan on his bed, my head on his chest. He was a pretty great pillow. After we'd had sex, Logan had carried me to the bathroom so we could both clean up—all my limbs had been doing their best jello resemblance—which had ended up with a little more dirtying up before we'd both finally collapsed on the bed, exhausted.

I hadn't expected Logan to be into snuggles, but he'd pulled me in his arms and seemed content petting my hair and back. I had zero complaints. In fact, I'd been almost drifting off to sleep when he'd spoken, and now I was trying to fight the drowsiness.

"And what did you expect?" I prompted when he didn't immediately answer.

Logan's fingers never stopped their lazy exploration as he talked. "We were supposed to watch the sunset. Then I'd take you to dinner in a nice restaurant, seduce you, and invite you here for a nightcap. Then I'd convince you to stay the night. Instead, *you* seduced *me*. I didn't even have a chance to feed you before I all but mauled you."

I giggled. "Well, you did feed me." My reminder had him groaning.

"And you took my cock beautifully, Charisma. However, I feel like I failed you tonight for this date."

"You seem to have put a lot of thought into it," I teased, raising my head to look at him. Inside, my heart fluttered like crazy, and it only got worse when I saw his satisfied smile and rumpled hair. Logan's eyes were closed, too, and he seemed completely relaxed. Happy, even.

I'd done that. I'd taken down his defenses to see the real man behind the icy exterior.

"Hmmm ... that's because I did," he admitted, and my breath caught. He opened his eyes, and it was like they were laughing at me. "I had a lot of time to think about it with the number of times a certain someone postponed our date."

My cheeks burned with embarrassment. "I'm sorry about that. Things have just been so crazy, and I felt like I had to make sure the others were okay with this. With us. I didn't want to sneak behind their backs, and I definitely don't want to keep secrets from them, not when they're already giving up so much for me. I love them, you know? I wouldn't be here with you right now if this was going to hurt them."

Then I bit my bottom lip, gathering the courage to ask the question I'd been meaning to for a while now. "Does it bother you?"

Logan's hand paused its exploration of my back. "Does what bother me?"

"Them. Us. This." Honestly, I could be so freaking eloquent sometimes.

I let out a frustrated breath and tried again. "The fact I'm dating them, in love with them, but dating you too." Or, at least, I thought we were now dating. I mean. He *had* explicitly asked me out on a date, knowing I had multiple boyfriends. And he'd met the guys for game night and made his intentions clear to all of us.

"Oh. That." Logan shrugged slightly, and his fingers went back to tracing the mindless patterns on my skin. "No, it doesn't. I wouldn't have asked you out otherwise, Charisma."

That was the thing I didn't understand, though. Bast had grown up with multiple dads, and Andres had known Bast and his family for a while, so it made sense for the two of them. Blaze had dated me first, before the guys, and we'd sort of broken up before I'd started dating Bast. Still, when

Blaze had tried to win me back, he'd struggled with the idea of multiple relationships for a long time—not that I blamed him. Blaze's reaction had made sense and been comprehensible, all things considered. Still, I thought our relationship was stronger because of it. But Logan ... he'd asked me out knowing I was dating others, and he wasn't familiar with the lifestyle—I didn't think—nor was he aware of soulmates. So why?

Logan must've seen the questions on my face because his smile vanished. "Ask what you want to ask." He sounded more resigned than anything.

I didn't want to doubt him or make it seem like I didn't trust him, but ... I also didn't want to get too involved and end up being hurt. As it were, I was already dangerously close.

"Why doesn't it bother you? You're Logan Nightshade. One of the most handsome, most influential, and powerful men in Arcane Society. You could have anyone. Why me?"

I hadn't meant to voice that last bit, but even though I'd grown and become stronger, even though Bast and the guys had proved time and time again that they loved me, I was, deep down, still insecure about some things. I knew I had to work on that, and with time, I was sure I would. But that little voice in my head existed, and it would pop up at inconvenient times. Like this one.

Logan was suddenly on top of me, my arms pinned to the bed, his face dangerously close to mine. His eyes had a dangerous glint that I hadn't seen yet.

"What do you mean by that? Why *not* you?" he growled, sounding *pissed*.

My eyes widened in shock, and I tried to speak over the blood that was traveling south dangerously fast at his caveman display.

"Answer me, Charisma. Tell me. *Why. Not. You?*"

I bit my tongue. I didn't understand why he was so freaking furious right now. It was a completely reasonable question, but he was acting like I'd offended him or crossed some line.

Then, before I could make sense of it, it was like a switch was flipped inside him, and Logan sighed. He kissed my forehead and then laid back down, bringing me over him once again. We resumed our earlier position on the bed as if nothing had happened.

"I'm sorry, I just don't like you diminishing yourself like that. Clearly, I'll need to have a talk with your other boyfriends so we can work on your sense of worth." It did not escape my notice that he'd said my "other" boyfriends. As if he were adding himself to the category.

"For now, though, I did say I'd answer your questions, though I can't promise you'll like the answer. The truth is, Charisma, I'm not a nice man." Even as he talked, his fingers found their way into my hair, and he was petting me absently, an almost direct contrast to his words. "I'm possessive, selfish, and I like to win. More than anything, though, I like control. However, whenever I'm with you, you threaten my control and my sense of order, and yet, I can't get enough. You refuse to be locked and categorized in a box inside my head like all the other things in my life, and it baffled me at first."

I should probably be offended at his admission, but it was kind of funny. To think I'd unknowingly brought a man like Logan to his knees just by being myself. I smiled. *Just like I snapped his control earlier. I knew he was planning on pulling out of my mouth before he came. To prolong the moment. But I'd wanted to surprise him. That's why I did my best hoover impersonation. The reward? Seeing Logan looking at me in total awe. A girl could really get used to that.* No regrets.

"You know, I'd all but given up on ever feeling like this again. As a teenager, I loved Zoey, and I wanted to marry her. When she died, when she was murdered by Ricardo and his minions, I let grief take me, and I gave up on the idea of ever finding someone again. I'd always assumed I'd take my place as head of the Nightshades, do my job, seek my revenge on Ricardo, and then when the time came, train one of Marcella's children to take my place."

My heart broke for Logan. It was no wonder he'd been a grumpy, icy control freak when I'd met him. He'd grieved for his lost love and buried himself in the only thing he thought would give him pleasure—work. Condemning himself to a lonely existence. It wasn't the fact he'd never expected to have children that made my heart bleed for him, but that he never even considered he might be happy again.

"Until you."

At his admission, I pushed up on my elbow so I could look at him once more. He waited until I was settled, mouth gaping like a fish, which made him smile before he continued. "You brought chaos and color into my life." He put some of the strands of my hair behind my ear. "And you challenged me and put me in my place time and time again. You're full of life and spirit, Charisma, even with everything that you've been through. I may be selfish and greedy, but I won't be responsible for snuffing your light. So, if that means I have to share you with men who were smart enough to recognize how utterly amazing you are before I did, then that's what I'll do."

He brushed his lips against mine. "And if they can take orders? Then I'll make sure we work together to bring you so much pleasure you'll be soaring in bliss for weeks."

His words, his promise, they did things to me. Unable to speak, to form a coherent sentence, I kissed him, moving on top of him. If I couldn't say it yet, I'd at least show him just what his words had done to me.

## 24

## BAST

"Gran, remember what we talked about." I stood in front of the locked door to my apartment, key in hand, staring at my grandmother, waiting for her to nod in agreement.

Gran pouted like a kid being denied their favorite toy. It probably would've been effective on someone else, but I'd grown up with her shenanigans. Not only that, but my eighty-year-old grandmother was wearing one of her crazy dresses with pornographic prints on them. Today's eyesore print might trick people into thinking they were flowers, but they were, in fact, dicks—ballsack and all—springing out of leaves. When I'd gone to pick her up, I'd seen she'd bought matching throw pillows for her room of horrors. The depths she went to in order to traumatize us all was honestly impressive.

So yeah, my grandmother was a lot of things, but innocent was not one of them.

"Gran," I warned when she just kept pouting and didn't answer.

Gran rolled her eyes. "Fine. Whatever. I'll behave." She

crossed her arms in front of herself, sulking, but I wasn't falling for it.

"You know, *you* came to *me* for help. The least you could do is not to be such a buzzkill. You used to be fun, Bastille."

Oh yeah, back when I'd been a teenager and had helped her with the shenanigans. Gran, Blair, and I used to have a shit ton of fun tormenting the rest of the family. But as my sister and I got older, we'd had to take on more responsibilities, and Gran's brand of chaos tended to give us more trouble than we could deal with. I loved my grandmother with all my heart, but the number of times we'd gotten in trouble because of her? I'd lost count.

"Gran, you know damn well you're the sole reason we're even doing this in the first place." She opened her mouth to complain, but I was faster. "Now, before you say anything, I know why you did it, and I agree with you. Maybe not with the way you got around to it, and I wish like hell we didn't have to get involved with Soulbinder business or to reveal the fact you're alive, but there's no way around it now. Esme needs to be stopped, and you were the one who gave her grandson this task."

Gran closed her mouth with a "humph".

But I wasn't done. "You knew we'd need your help for it. In fact, you probably formed a plan the second you confirmed your suspicions about Theodore. You can fool just about anyone, Gran, but you can't fool me. So we'll go in there, and you'll behave."

"Fine, but one of you better take me to that bakery again. The one we went to the other day. Their eclairs were orgasmic."

I tried very, very hard not to relive the memory of my grandmother eating all those adult pastries while making the most embarrassing noises. I'd tried hard not to react to it or make eye contact. Gran would've only gone at it with even more gusto.

"I'm sure Theo will take you there as a way to thank you. And buy any and all the pastries you want." I didn't really give a shit who I was throwing under the bus so long as I didn't have to go back there with her. Besides, Gran and Theo would need to bond if he wanted her to teach him more about auras.

Gran grinned. "Alright. Let's get on with it, then. Why are we standing here like cat burglars? Let's go inside. I'm dying to meet the girl's new boy-toy. Word on the street is that his ass is *tight*."

Giving up on her, I unlocked the door and let her inside. Logan was a big guy. I was sure he could fend off Gran and protect his virtue—if he even had any.

And if not, well. I supposed Gran groping Char's newest boyfriends could be some weird rite of passage. If nothing else, Char would enjoy the shenanigans. My girl could be just as prone to mischief as Gran if it suited her.

Gran had a crush on Logan.

At first, I thought Gran was just keeping her end of the bargain and behaving as she'd promised. However, the longer I watched them interacting, the more I realized the reason for Gran's good behavior was another one entirely.

We were all in my living room—which was becoming a little too crowded—waiting for Theo to arrive. Char was sitting on Blaze's lap on the couch, Andres and me on either side of them. Logan had been on the lone armchair, but when Gran had arrived, he'd offered her his seat.

Then he'd complimented her dress.

That smooth motherfucker.

"Is she ... is she *blushing?*" Andres whispered in our direction, and Char squeezed his arm to keep him quiet.

None of us wanted to miss the show. Even Blaze, who barely knew Gran, was watching in fascination.

Logan was sitting beside Gran in a chair he'd created out of dark matter—actually, Char had said it was the gooey stuff he could use to make a shield out of, but she hadn't known whether it was another side of the dark matter or not.

I watched with fascination as Gran brushed Logan's arm over something he'd said, batting her lashes at him. Then she said something that had *him* throwing his head back and laughing, and I was pretty fucking sure hell had just frozen over.

I turned my head, and sure enough, Char was gaping at them, eyes wide.

"Someone please tell me you're seeing what I'm seeing. Seriously, you guys, is this an illusion? I mean, as an Illudere, I should at least be able to feel if there was an illusion, even one too strong for me to break past, but this isn't one, is it? I've checked twice." Andres kept rambling, but none of us bothered to answer him. We were too afraid we'd break the spell and find out the apocalypse was here.

Then, a smiling Logan caught Char's eye and winked at her before carrying on with his conversation with Gran.

"I think this is the greatest moment of my life," Char whispered in awe.

"The greatest moment?" Blaze asked in Char's ear, wrapping his arms around her. "Greater than when you had my dick inside you while your other boyfriends watched?" His voice was low enough that I didn't think Gran or Logan could hear, but Andres and I definitely could.

"Or that time Bast and I tag-teamed you? When Bast took your pussy, and I took your ass, and you came so many times you prayed to the Goddess, thinking you were going to die?"

At Andres' words, Char squirmed on Blaze's lap.

I remembered that day. It had been amazing. Char had been on top, riding my dick when Andres had taken her ass. Her already tight cunt had been even tighter because of it, and I'd gotten a great view of her tits bouncing up and down while we drove our girl wild. We should definitely do that again, and soon.

"Excuse me, children," Gran's words were more effective in ruining the mood than if she'd doused us with cold water. Char jumped on Blaze's lap and based on his grunt, I was pretty sure she hit him right in the dick.

"The adults are talking. If you could please behave? I don't want to see the lot of you getting frisky. It'll ruin my appetite."

I didn't bother pointing out she couldn't actually see anything. There would be no point; besides, my dick had already deflated like a balloon. How had I forgotten, even for a second, that Gran was here?

Fucking Blaze and Andres.

"Frisky? No. No one is getting frisky, Mrs. Alma. We were just. Uh. We were all just ... Goddess, what time is it? Shouldn't Theo have arrived already?" Charisma got up and started pacing around the living room while she rambled, looking at her wrist as if expecting to see a watch, and then frowning at it as if wondering where it had gone.

As far as I knew, Char had never actually worn a watch.

When she passed near Logan, he grabbed her hand and pulled her in his lap.

Gran whistled. "Char, you better not let go of that one. If

only I were a few decades younger, I'd definitely put up a fight to steal him from right under your nose. I'd even call him Daddy Logan if he asked me to."

We all groaned at the mental image. Except for Logan, who chuckled. Bastard was enjoying himself.

Char whipped her head around on his lap, staring wide-eyed at him. "Daddy Logan?" She choked the words out, her voice high-pitched.

"Mrs. Alma, if that were the case, *I* would have stolen *you* from your husband. Make no mistake."

Gran blushed. Actually blushed bright red.

I didn't even know she could do that at her age.

"But I'm afraid someone else found me first, and I'm quite taken by her," he said, wrapping his arms around Char, who all but melted against him at his admission.

I had to give it to Logan; he was smooth. The guys had made it seem like Logan was some unfeeling robot, and he'd seemed pretty stiff in my first few interactions with him, but now? It was like he'd finally learned to relax.

There was no doubt in my mind that the person responsible for that change in him was currently smiling dreamily on his lap.

Good for them.

I checked the time on my phone and cleared my throat. "Listen, not wanting to ruin the mood, but Theo is going to be here soon, and we were ... distracted and haven't really talked about things. Logan, has Char filled you in on the situation?" They'd gone out on their date a couple of nights ago, and Char had spent most of yesterday with him. Andres had played the chorus of "Walk of Shame" by P!nk as a joke when she'd arrived last night, making her turn scarlet. Then she'd chased after him to try to make the music stop while he ran from her. They'd ended up tangled on the couch, laughing.

At times like that, I was incredibly glad Char had chosen Andres to join our relationship. He always knew how to crack a joke or defuse an awkward situation. Playing the song to tease Char had been his way of reminding her she had nothing to worry about and that we were okay with her growing relationship with Logan.

Logan nodded. "Yes, Charisma filled me in yesterday. I'm willing to help, though I doubt Esme Soulbinder will be an easy foe. I've also asked my PIs to dig up dirt on her, just in case they can find something we can use."

"See?" Gran said, turning to Char. "I told you he's a keeper. Gotta love the strong, controlling type. He'll take good care of you, Char dear."

"What are we, chopped liver?" Andres protested, and all three of us were glaring at Gran.

Just because she had a crush on Logan, that didn't mean she had to make it seem like Char had to *choose* Logan over us. Char could have us all, dammit.

"Of course not, Andres dear. You're one of my beloved grandchildren. But have you seen his ass? I thought Blaze's was nice, but Logan here is the real deal."

The fact Andres even considered arguing with our *grandmother* about who had the best ass was enough to tell me it was time to put a stop to it.

I cleared my throat *again*, and everyone stared at me expectantly, but the doorbell rang, saving me from having to come up with another change of subject.

Thank fuck.

## 25

## THEO

I stood awkwardly at the edge of the living room, unsure of where I should sit or what, exactly, I was supposed to be doing here.

No, that wasn't true. I did know what I was doing here. Char had invited me over—to her Necromancer boyfriend's house—so we could go over the plan one more time. It's not like we could've just talked about it over the phone; it was too risky. Just like I had Annie shadowing Grandmother for us, we had no way of knowing if the matriarch had a ghost or two keeping tabs on me.

However, Char and her guys had recently put some powerful wards on Bast's house that should keep any uninvited guests out, including ghosts–most of them, anyway. That was just one more thing I had to learn from Mrs. Alma once this was finally over.

Still, as I looked around the living room, it was obvious I was the odd man out.

Bastille's living room was packed with people. On the couch, Bastille himself, Andres, and Blaze were sitting side by side, with just enough space between Andres and the arm of the sofa for Charisma to fit, which I assumed was where she'd been sitting before she opened the door for me. In front of the guys, there was a coffee table filled with remote controls, video game controllers, and an assortment of other stuff. Mrs. Alma was sitting on an armchair closer to the TV, and beside her, sitting on a weird chair that didn't match the rest of the furniture, was Logan Nightshade.

"Uh. So. Theo, you know everyone, right? Everyone, Theo's here," Char said, wringing her hands together.

She had been acting odd since she'd opened the door for me. Char had been blushing and breathless, and I thought I'd interrupted something, but now that I saw Logan and Mrs. Alma were here, I doubted it.

Unless Char and Logan were now together too? But even then, Mrs. Alma's presence would probably be a major cockblock.

Annie whistled. "Oh wow. It's like the next generation of the Council of Six is all here. All Char needs is a Manteis now, and she'd be set. Hell, she could even make it the Council of Seven again. Way to go, girl!"

Annie raised her hand for a high-five in Char's direction, but since Char couldn't actually see ghosts, Annie raised her other hand and high-fived herself.

Mrs. Alma laughed. "Right you are, kid, right you are. I'm afraid a Manteis isn't in the cards for her, though. So she'll have to settle for the six, not seven."

Everyone in the room stared at Mrs. Alma in confusion, having missed half the conversation.

"Uh ... riiight," Char dragged the word, looking from Mrs. Alma to me, a question clear in her silver eyes. "Well, I'm going to agree with Gran since I have no idea what she's talking about. Unless one of you would like to translate it for us?"

Mrs. Alma smirked, raising an eyebrow at me in clear challenge.

"Oh, c'mon, Weasley. Char is my best friend, and she's been missing out on my amazing quips. Part of your job as a Soulbinder is to pass the messages from beyond. Well. This was my message. Now pass it on!" Annie started to swipe her hand back and forth over my arm, annoyingly giving me chills over and over every time she did it.

"Stop doing that." I pulled my arm away from her, then sighed at the triumph in her eyes.

Everyone in the room was already staring at me like I was insane, except for Mrs. Alma, who was biting her bottom lip to keep from laughing.

Such a great way to make a good impression and start my road to redemption so Char would forgive me and take me back.

"My sister Annie is here." Annie did a finger wave that nobody could see.

"Wait, I thought the wards were supposed to keep the ghosts out?" Blaze asked, frowning and looking at Mrs. Alma for confirmation.

Mrs. Alma hummed. "They are. But there's a way around that, like most things," she admitted.

By "a way around that" she meant Annie had to hold onto me the whole time I was crossing the wards, and that was the only way a ghost would be able to get in or out of here right now. Apparently, Mrs. Alma had explained that to Annie when she knew we would be here too. Mrs. Alma wanted a way for her "seeing-eye ghosts" to be able to go wherever she went, and no soul sent to spy on us would be able to foresee the little loophole.

"Don't worry about it," Mrs. Alma brushed the subject off and the questions that she would probably have been bombarded with otherwise. "Theodore wasn't done. So, what did Annie say, Theo?"

Thrown under the bus yet again. Great.

Annie made the shape of an L on her forehead in sibling support, and I sighed, running a hand through my hair. "Right. Annie made a comment about how this is basically a meeting between the Council of Six's next generation." I left out the part about Char missing a Manteis to complete her collection, and Mrs. Alma gave me a knowing smirk.

She was too damn amused by this whole thing.

"Oh." Char looked around, and her eyes widened. It was like she'd only just come to that conclusion too. "Annie is right." Then she blushed. "Well, mostly, anyway. I'm not the Elemental heir. And we're missing the twins. But if we swapped the Elementals with the Necromancers, then it could count as the Council of Six, I guess."

"Way to go, Kitten, attracting all the powerful people. We should go out on a group date somewhere your parents could see you. They'd probably have a stroke and regret ever casting you out," Andres sing-songed, getting up from the couch and grabbing Char so he could carry her back and sit with her on his lap. "Now, that's better, isn't it? My lap was feeling rather lonely, Kitten. You gave Blaze and Logan attention, and now it's my turn." Then he started to nuzzle against her cheek like a cat scent-marking his mate, not giving a shit we were all watching.

Good thing, too, because I needed a second to process what Andres had just hinted at.

Char and Logan really *had* gotten together. Even though I knew they were soulmates, that all of them were her soulmates—minus Mrs. Alma, of course—I hadn't expected they'd actually all agree to share her. I'd challenged them over it a couple of months ago when I'd called a meeting and laid a claim to Char in one of my most confusing moments.

I'd given up on the idea that Char and I could ever be together, but I'd seen the other heirs sniffing around her and finally showing an interest in her. Knowing they were her soulmates, too, I'd done a little meddling. It stood to reason that the more of an ass I was about the situation, the more it would piss the others off and make them do exactly the opposite of what I demanded. I'd called the meeting to stake a claim I had no right to, and even though I hadn't expected the stupid bet, it had worked—sort of.

Now I knew I'd been a dumbass to try to manipulate things from the shadows, and I probably wasn't much better than my own grandmother, but if my meddling had helped Char and her men even a little bit? I'd take it.

My heart hurt to know I might've missed my chance with her, even if I fully intended on begging for another one, but I was happy for her. Seeing the way she smiled, basking in the love and touches from her men.

There were none of the bags under her eyes that used to be there all the time, none of the darkness in her aura that made my heart break, especially knowing I'd had a part in putting it there. Now her aura was so bright, so beautiful, it hurt my eyes just looking.

Mrs. Alma must've sensed what I was doing because she raised an eyebrow at me. Another challenge.

I couldn't answer her, though, not when there were so many people looking.

Thankfully, Annie answered for me. "He's going to try, Gran. We talked about it. He's going to try to make things right. I think I finally got him to realize that he deserves to be happy, too, not just her."

Mrs. Alma nodded approvingly at Annie's words, then turned her attention back to the others.

"Alright, let's get this meeting started already. All your lovey-dovey crap is making the ghosts uncomfortable. You lot brought me here to talk about taking down the evil witch, right? So far, there's been a lot of cuddling and petting and not enough plotting. It's disgusting."

I hid my smile by turning my face. The only ghosts in the room were Annie and the elder male who always seemed to be around Mrs. Alma, neither of which were uncomfortable in the least.

"Alright, yeah. Sorry. So, Theo, did you guys manage to set up the spy cameras?"

I nodded at Char's question. "Yeah. We're all set," I said, even as Annie gave a thumbs up beside me.

It had taken a while and a lot of sneaking around our own family home, but we'd managed to set up all the spy cameras. Thank fuck those things were crazy small and could be camouflaged in almost anything—which was really creepy if you thought too hard about it, but we were using them for good, not evil. Mainly, though, it helped that Grandmother didn't suspect anything. She thought I was still soul-bound, and I was avoiding her as much as possible. It helped that she was busy with council business and trying to discover which Soul Mage had imprisoned the ghosts at the warehouse Logan and I had visited.

So far, none of the Soul Mages with known ties to the resistance had enough power to do something like that, which had only worried Grandmother further. After all, whoever it was might be powerful enough to threaten her position, and she couldn't allow that.

"Cool. So, how are we going to do this? Are we just going to barge into her office and demand an explanation? Should you call her for a meeting and check if she notices the changes?"

"I think Theo should go in alone," Andres suggested. Char was still on his lap, and she tried to turn to look at him, a frown on her face. "No, I don't mean *alone* alone. We'll be with him. I'll just be hiding us with my illusions. There's no way Mrs. Esme would admit to anything if she saw us there, even with Gran throwing her off."

"I agree with Andres," Logan said, sitting back on his chair and crossing his hands together. "Esme is cunning, and she's careful. Otherwise, she wouldn't be where she is now. Based on everything you said and my own impressions, if Theodore goes in with Charisma, or if Esme even sees Mrs. Alma—"

"Alma, dear. I told you to call me Alma," Mrs. Alma cut in, smiling at him. Mrs. Alma's late husband—or at least that was who I thought the ghost was—glared at Logan, but didn't say anything.

Logan nodded. "Even if Esme sees Alma, I doubt she'd be so careless as to say something incriminating. If anything, she'll be on her guard even more. Your best bet is for Theodore to go in alone or, at least, for it to seem like he's alone." Then he looked at me. "Don't mention your soul binding either. Not at first. When you talk to her, confront her about your aunt or your parents' bindings. If you play your cards right, she'll admit it or try to justify it before attempting to bind your soul again to keep you from talking. She's grooming you to take her place one day, so she'll want to ensure she has your cooperation. If I understand correctly, she knows that the bindings will break if she dies, so she'll need you to be there and willing to renew when the time comes."

Shit, I hadn't even thought about that.

"Esme will probably try to bind you regardless to ensure your cooperation whether you agree to it or not, but we can make our presence known before she does. That's where you come in, Alma." Honest to the Goddess, Mrs. Alma flipped her hair back when Logan said that and sent him a saucy wink saying, "Gotcha."

Logan's smirk came quickly and vanished just as quickly. Then he was all business once again. "And then, only once your grandmother is already cornered will you confront her about your own bindings, if you want. Then it'll be pointless for her to deny it. Your grandmother will have no choice but to choose between stepping down or having the Soulbinder name ruined, and I can assure you she'll see more value in stepping down than in having her legacy destroyed."

"He's right," Mrs. Alma agreed. "I've known your grandmother for a long time. She'll put up a fight, but once it's clear what her choices are, she'll step down. Not because she wants to, but because she would do anything to make sure the Soulbinder name stays strong. It's how she was raised. She's old, and knows she won't live forever. In fact, she should've stepped down already and given the mantle to your parents years ago. The longer she refuses to step down, the more likely it is that some outsider will try to challenge her for her place in the council, and she knows that, too. Unfortunately, this will mean she'll never be arrested for the shit she's done, but at least you'll be able to make things right."

I'd be able to finally set my family free. That hardly

made up for years of being controlled, but it had to be better than nothing.

And while a part of me wished I could see her arrested for the ways she abused her authority and her place in the family, she was still my grandmother. Even knowing everything she'd done to me, my parents, and the rest of the family, I still felt something for her. I didn't want her dead or behind bars. I just wanted to hold her accountable and make sure she never made the same mistakes again.

# 26

# CHARISMA

"Char, would you mind going with me to the car? I was hoping we could talk." Theo stood awkwardly near the door, looking at me expectantly, his green eyes full of hope and nerves.

I didn't have to look around to know that every one of my guys—and Gran—were paying close attention to everything we said or did.

Theo had the right idea in suggesting we go outside to talk, but if I left the wards with him, our entire plan might go up in smoke.

"I don't think we should be seen together right now," I admitted. Then, realizing how it sounded and noticing how Theo's shoulders slumped as if resigned, I was quick to add. "But we could talk inside? In the bedroom, I mean. I'll put up a couple of extra wards to ensure we have privacy."

I gave Andres a pointed look, and he grinned, unashamed.

Theo gave me a little smile. "Sure. That works. If you don't mind."

I turned to lead Theo to the bedroom, and my eyes

landed on the box with his MET that was sitting forgotten near my laptop. I grabbed it, then bypassed the living room and took Theo straight to Bast's bedroom.

Once inside, I played some really loud music, grabbed my MET, and put up a couple of extra wards—one could never be too careful with this crowd.

By the time I was done, Theo was staring at me as if I'd grown a second head.

"What? Between Mrs. Alma's ghost network, Andres' illusions, and Bast and Blaze's general snoopiness, you can never be too careful." Seriously. And they gossiped, too. If Blair had been here and not off chasing Ricardo's elusive trail, it would be even worse.

"It's good to see you happy, Char."

I was surprised to see Theo smiling at me. I couldn't remember the last time we'd been alone in a room together, and I hadn't been overwhelmed by hurt. When he hadn't looked angry or sad.

Even though he looked kind of tense and had his hands in his pockets, this Theo looked more like the one I'd grown up with rather than the ragey or standoffish stranger he'd become. The hot-and-cold attitude had given me multiple whiplashes.

"Thanks, I ..." I trailed off, looking around the bedroom, trying to gather my thoughts together. Theo was right in front of the bed, and I was still awkwardly by the door, so I circled around him to sit on the unmade bed.

Damn, Andres was supposed to have made the bed this morning. Oh well. Too late for that now.

"Sorry, why don't you sit down? Goddess, this is awkward, isn't it? Why is it so awkward?"

"Uh. I don't think sitting down is a good idea, Char." Theo said, staring at the unmade bed and blushing.

I jumped out of the bed like someone had set it on fire, blushing too. "Yeah. Sorry. Right. Bad idea."

I couldn't believe I'd just asked my ex to sit with me on my current boyfriend's bed. The same one I shared with him and two of my other boyfriends.

Huh. I had four boyfriends now. I wondered where Logan would sleep.

*In his own apartment, Char. He has like, a million bedrooms. You really should bite the bullet and buy your own place so everyone can have space and be comfortable and not piled on top of each other like sardines.*

"It's okay. Listen, I don't mean to make things awkward or anything. I'm sorry for that. In fact, I'm sorry for a lot of things. That's why I wanted to talk to you. You didn't deserve to be treated the way I treated you all those years. I was an ass, worse than that, really. I just wanted to apologize for that. Now. When I'm sober and fully aware of what I'm doing. I know just apologizing isn't enough, and probably never will be, but ... I'm sorry, Char. For everything."

Five years. I'd waited five years to hear these words. My eyes filled with tears, and I tried to hold them back by sinking my nails into my palms, but it was an impossible fight.

"It wasn't your fault, Theo. You were brainwashed."

Theo shook his head. "No, Char. I'm not going to chalk up five years of hurting you to my grandmother having bound my soul. That would be the easy way out, and you deserve better."

Fuck, I was ugly crying now. There was no stopping the waterworks. My heart felt tight and full and broken and mended all at the same time, and I just couldn't stop the tears.

"Hey, hey, don't cry." Theo pulled me into his arms,

hugging me and letting me cry on his shirt while he ran his fingers through my hair, trying to soothe me.

"I'm sorry, Char. I really, really am. I'll probably never stop saying it. I'm sorry for making you hurt back then, the last five years, and even now. I'm sorry for never having told you why I was an asshole, and for all the suffering I caused you directly or indirectly. But, Char, even without the soul binding, even if Grandmother hadn't prevented me from telling you and from being near you, the truth is I still would've broken your heart. I probably would've tried to find a better way to do it, not just ghosted you and acted like an idiot, but that's one thing I don't regret."

"Why, Theo?" I clung to his shirt, to him, even as I cried harder.

"To protect you, Char baby. From her. Don't you see?" He pulled back just enough to grab my chin and get me to look at him. "If she did that to me, do you really think you would've escaped? Now more than ever, I'm happy you escaped, even if it hurt you. You got to be free, Char. You got to live your life and be *you*. If Grandmother had gotten her hands on you, you wouldn't have stood a chance. I know you don't agree. I know you think I'm being hardheaded, and maybe I am. But Char, I've loved you my whole life. I'll keep loving you until the day I die. That hasn't changed at all, and it never will. Being apart from you has been hell, but I'd do it all again, for however long it took, if it meant you were safe from her. If it meant you got to be happy. That's all I ever wanted."

I pulled back from him, stepping away, even as I sobbed.

"That's not fair, Theo." I wiped my tears away, angry at him all over again.

"I know, Char. But tell me this: if our situations were reversed and we'd both been eighteen, and you'd been given an ultimatum and knew your parents might bind me the way they did others in your family, would you have risked it, or would you have let me go?"

My lips wobbled as I looked at him. Theo's green eyes were red. He was crying too, maybe not as hard as I was, but crying nonetheless.

This was such a fucked-up situation. This whole thing was beyond fucked up.

I didn't want to admit it, I didn't want to say it, but Theo was right.

It would've hurt like hell, but he was right. I would've let him go. I probably would've explained the situation and broken things off rather than ghost him—which I also knew was something he would've done if he could have—but yeah.

"I hate this, Theo. I hate what she did to us, what she did to you." Unable to stay apart, unable to see the pain in his face, I walked back to him and hugged him. "You should've been allowed to be free too, Theo. Not just me. We should've been happy together."

We clung to each other, mourning the life we could've had, the life that had been stolen from us. So much pain, so much sorrow.

I'd spent five years trying to hate Theo for the pain he'd caused me, never knowing he'd been hurting just as much. All because of his grandmother.

"I really, really hate your grandmother right now, Theo," I admitted against his shirt, my words slightly muffled.

"I know, Char baby. I know." His arms tightened around me as if he needed as little distance between us as possible. "And I'm sorry about that too. I know she won't be brought to justice, true justice, because of me. But Char, I promise you this, she'll never touch you again. In any way. You'll never have to worry about her."

"Okay," I said, and then I got up on my tiptoes and brushed my lips against his. He tasted of salt and tears. Probably just like I did. Still, it was a comfort and a promise. "It's okay, Theo."

"No, it's not. Not yet, anyway. But soon," he vowed.

Soon, he'd be facing off against his grandmother. If everything went according to plan, he'd assume leadership over his family. He'd have a chance to right the wrongs his grandmother did and maybe even unravel the bindings on the rest of his family.

"Oh, that reminds me!" I stepped back, immediately missing his warmth. Under Theo's confused gaze, I took the box from my pocket and handed it to him. "This is for you."

"For me?" Theo opened the small cardboard box and gasped.

With shaky hands, he pulled the MET from inside the box. I'd spent a long, long time thinking about what type of MET I could make for Theo, but in the end, I'd picked a design similar to the one he'd had. He'd kept the same one for five years, so that must've meant he liked it, right?

He whipped his head, looking at me like I hung the sun. "Char, is this ... ?"

The silver beads shone under the artificial light of the room, and when he pulled the whole thing out of the box, the little pendant I'd added at the end could be seen. Theo smiled when he saw the little scythe.

Okay, so, maybe not *exactly* like his old one, but Logan had told me about what Theo had done with the ghosts at the warehouse, how he used up all his magic to free them, and I felt the scythe fit.

Besides, at the press of a button, the scythe would

become an ice blade the size of my forearm, so that was a bonus. Theo's old MET didn't manifest any weapons. I hadn't known how to code that then.

I shrugged, feeling embarrassed. "I know you were still using the MET I gave you for your eighteenth birthday. Even though it was crazy old and outdated, you never replaced it. Logan told me the resistance broke your MET at the warehouse, so I figured ... Consider it a thank you for saving my life. I know it's not much, but it should have all those spells and more. And I chose the same design because then we went full circle, you know? That scythe charm actually turns into a weapon, by the way. That's why it's there. I just felt it would be handy. However, if you don't like it, I can make a new one soon. Either a MET or a weapon charm, I mean. For now, though, if we go to the living room, I can key it into your magical signature, and you can use it tomorrow if you—"

My words cut off as Theo wrapped his arms around me, picking me up from the floor and spinning me around like I weighed nothing. Then he put me down, gripped my face in his hands, and kissed me. "Thank you, thank you, Char," he said, in between kisses. "Thank you."

"It's nothing." I tried to brush it off, but he wouldn't let me.

"No, this is everything, Char. Thank you. Seriously. I don't deserve you. I know I don't. But I swear, I'll make this right, and then I'll spend the rest of my life trying to make it up to you. Just give me another chance, please." Then he kissed me again, and this time, I opened my mouth to him.

Our tongues tangled in desperation as we clung to each other, our teeth clattering in our rush. It was as if our bodies were trying to make up for five years without contact with that one kiss.

By the time Theo and I came up for air, we were both breathless.

"I'm not going to take advantage of you. As much as I want nothing more than to throw you on that bed and have my way with you, I have a lot to make up for. I'm going to do things right this time, Char, baby. That means talking to your boyfriends, too, before anything else happens. I don't want you to have regrets about me ever again."

## 27

## ANDRES

Char and Theo came out of the bedroom looking flustered. Their lips were red, and they were both grinning, happier than they'd been when they'd gone inside.

I knew that look, and what it meant.

"Called it!" I yelled, getting up from my place on the couch and dancing over to Gran. I only stopped when I was in front of her, holding my palm up. "You owe me twenty bucks."

Char and Theo had totally had sex. Char had sex hair, and Theo's red strands had clearly undergone the Char treatment. She loved grabbing onto our hair when she had one of us inside of her, said they made for great hand holders.

I was slightly worried about Theo's endurance, though, because they hadn't been gone long, but alas, he'd have time to work on that. Probably have to cut him some slack, too, since he hadn't gotten to make love to our girl in five years. I'd have shot my load soon, too, if I'd had to go without Char for that long. Hell, I couldn't even last a week without her. I was addicted, and I had zero regrets.

It was a good thing Char had a good, healthy sexual appetite.

None of which mattered right now, though, because I was finally winning a bet against Gran. I didn't care that I was being a sore winner. It was the first time *ever* I'd been right about something and she hadn't.

Rather than picking up her old woman's purse and paying up, though, Gran slapped my hand away.

"HA! I don't owe you shit! You're the one who owes me twenty bucks. They didn't have sex, you rascal. I knew I should've bet more money, but whatever. A win is a win. Pay up!"

I narrowed my eyes at Gran.

"They totally had sex, Gran. Just look at them! I'm not paying you; you should be paying me!" Then I turned to Char. "Char, Kitten, tell her. Tell Gran she's wrong. You guys totally went in there and had sex, right?"

Char stared at me like she wanted to murder me, but her face was as red as Theo's hair. That was all the answer I needed.

Bastille slapped the back of my head. "You're making them uncomfortable. Get a grip."

"But—"

While Gran cackled like a loon, Bast hit me again. "It's of no concern to you or *you*,"— he glared at Gran—"whether they had sex or not. Seriously, you two are worse than children." Shaking his head, Bast walked to Char, kissing her forehead. "Sorry about them. I swear, it's impossible to control them. You know how they get."

Then Bast looked at Theo, grimacing. "You'll probably have to get used to this because it's pretty much a guaranteed occurrence whenever Andres and Gran get together. They're hopeless."

"Excuse me, the word you're looking for is awesome, not hopeless!" I protested, and Gran nodded in agreement.

"It's fine, Bast. I knew he was like that when I started to date him," Char said, rolling her eyes, then she held my gaze, smirking. "And no, Andres, we didn't have sex. I suppose you owe Gran twenty bucks. That will teach you to stop trying to win bets against her. Although I can't freaking believe you two were betting on this. Seriously, did you really think I'd have sex with someone while Mrs. Alma was in the other room? That would've been super disrespectful! And just … wrong." Char shuddered, as if the mere thought of it was gross. I held my tongue so I wouldn't point out that not that long ago, she'd been squirming on Blaze's lap while we talked dirty to her, Gran very much present in the room.

I knew I had to pick my battles. Besides, I was kind of disappointed in Theo. Five years without Char, and then they were locked in a bedroom together with a million wards, and he didn't swoop her off her feet and seduced her? He should've apologized to her in orgasms.

Still, I was a man of my word, so I pulled a twenty out of my pocket and walked over to Gran, giving her the money. Logan watched the whole interaction with a smirk, but refused to comment.

"Does that mean you guys are back together?" Blaze asked quietly from his spot on the couch, staring at Char and Theo with a slight frown.

I gave him a look. We'd literally just talked about this. It was what had gotten Gran and me betting on the sex-no-sex thing. I thought Blaze said he'd accept whatever Char chose, but I guess he had a right to question or at least be worried about it.

I had to indoctrinate Blaze on the amazingness of the brother-husband phenomenon.

Char and Theo exchanged a look. "No, we're not back together. You know I wouldn't do that without talking to you guys first, Blaze. Theo and I just … "

Char trailed off as if trying to find the right words, but Theo was the one to step up. "Listen, I know I have a lot to atone for, and I plan on doing just that. I asked Char to give me another chance, and I'm willing to wait as long as it takes for her to decide. I'm not going to fuck it up this time, and I'll start by making things right tomorrow. I'm also not going to try to come between you guys or anything. I know she's yours, and you're hers. I guess I just want to be a part of what you guys have with her, you know? So long as I can be with her again."

Then Theo's cheeks and ears turned the same color as his hair. Damn, he was like a human lobster or something. Being a redhead must be hard.

"Well, if Char decides she forgives you, then we'll be happy to have you," Bast said, and Char's shoulders visibly relaxed.

Tongue in cheek, I headed to them, slinging my arm around Theo's shoulder. "I always knew you'd be my brother-husband." I started to lead him back to the couch, putting some space between him and Char so that Char could go to Blaze. She shot me a grateful smile. "Tell me, Theo, what are you, team exhibitionist or team voyeur? And what are your top three positions? If you're going to join this group, there's a lot I need to know. Oh, also, ghosts are a hard limit for me, m'kay? I don't mind being watched, but no dead people, if you please. Gotta draw the line somewhere, you know?"

## 28

## CHARISMA

Hidden by Andres's illusions and some of my own—courtesy of my brand new MET—we snuck into the Soulbinder mansion. The hardest part about it was timing things just right so that Theo didn't have to hold a door open for longer than what would be needed for him to enter or exit a room.

Unfortunately for us, we were facing more than security cameras or the eventual maid—and the Soulbinders had a lot of those. Hacking security cameras and using illusions to hide our path so mages wouldn't see us? Easy. Hiding our presence from any ghosts who might be lurking around and could report us to Esme Soulbinder? That was a fucking nightmare.

Our solution was simple and pretty effective. Theo was carrying a huge box of stuff that he would be "storing in his old bedroom"—mostly textbooks from the Academy. Because of that, the Soulbinder butler had to hold the door open for him, and that allowed all five of us to slink past. Mrs. Alma, Andres, Blaze, and even Logan had come, while Bast had stayed behind so he could monitor the spy cameras. Bast hadn't loved being left behind, but we were all worried about the consequences of revealing we had a Necromancer on our side.

We feared, and rightly so, that if she found out, she'd use it against us. If so much as a rumor got out that a Necromancer was in the city, there would be a witch hunt. That was the last thing we wanted. Bast and his people had to be protected. One day, I hoped we'd be able to reveal the truth that not all Necromancers were evil, and that they'd been living among us without harming us for years. However, it would be naive to think it could be something that could be changed in a day or even a week. We had to start slowly. First, discredit the war at the border, then insert people like Blair, who had been raised by Necros but had a different type of magic, before we could fully change the way our society saw them. I knew my guys would help me, especially now that they'd gotten to know Bast, to work with him, to see that he wasn't evil the way we'd been raised to believe. But change like that? It took years, maybe decades. And until our society was a safe place for him, all we could do was help Bast protect his secret.

We were almost to Theo's old bedroom when Mrs. Alma pulled my arm. I almost fucking jumped, startled, but managed to keep the scream from escaping me. I turned to her, wanting to know why we'd stopped.

"Ghost," she mouthed, jutting her chin to a space on my left.

I cursed mentally. I didn't bother asking her how she knew. She was a Soul Mage. Mrs. Alma may have lost her eyesight—or most of it, I was never truly sure—but she'd already proved she had ways around it.

I cast a frantic look around, trying to figure out a way to bypass the ghost or ghosts in our path. We were so damn close to the Soulbinder matriarch's office. So damn close to our goal. We couldn't be discovered now.

Before I could fully freak out, Mrs. Alma tugged my shirt again, mouthing "all clear" when I looked at her.

Thank Goddess.

I wasn't cut out for this undercover, sneaky stuff. I was a girl who did her best work behind a computer, with a keyboard and a bunch of screens. My poor little opossum heart couldn't deal with this much adrenaline. I was a Magical Engineer, dammit. When my fight-or-flight instincts were engaged, my body's go-to response was to drop to the ground and play dead. It was the opossum way. There was a reason I identified with a mailbox opossum, for fuck's sake.

I kept mentally rambling as a way to let go of some of the stress until we finally, finally made it to Theo's bedroom. He carelessly dropped the heavy box of textbooks there and then nodded.

*Showtime.*

Theo opened the door to his grandmother's office with a bang, and we quickly snuck inside. With angry steps, Theo strode forward until he was right in front of his grandmother's office desk, giving us time to scurry to a corner of the room.

Mrs. Esme's office was all white. The walls, the furniture. Hell, even her computer was white. The only specks of color in the room were the inlaid gold details in the table and chairs, which I was almost sure were made out of actual gold and not just dyed to look like it. The floors were white marble, and the motherfucking chandelier—because why not have a chandelier in one's home office—was crystal. Which, granted, wasn't white, but it reflected the color, so it totally counted, especially because the non-glass bits were, in fact, white.

It was ... a lot to take in.

Mrs. Esme sat behind her desk; her short hair was perfectly styled. Even *that* matched the color scheme of her office.

At least she was wearing color in her clothes. Well, she wore a silky dark blue blouse, and I couldn't see her pants or skirt from here, but odds were she hadn't paired it with white. I hoped not, at least. Light-colored pants got dirty with very little effort.

Upon Theo's dramatic entrance, Mrs. Esme raised an eyebrow at him, taking off her gold-rimmed glasses and carefully placing them over the files on her desk.

Her green eyes—the same shade as Theo's and Annie's—were bored when she surveyed her grandson. "Theodore, did you make an appointment I forgot about?"

Theo crossed his arms in front of him, shoulders and jaw tense. If he kept that up for long, he was going to have some serious dental problems in the future. "Grandmother. We both know I didn't have an appointment, no."

"I see," she replied, pausing and staring at the still open door. When she looked back at Theo, her tone was even frostier. I didn't even think that was possible.

Wow, she could put my parents to shame.

"And is there a reason for this ... visit? I thought you were way past the age to have temper tantrums, Theodore."

Holy shit! I just realized who Esme Soulbinder reminded me of with that attitude! Miranda Priestly! Except she didn't rule over the fashion industry, she ruled over the Soulbinders, and rather than having scared assistants; she had frightened maids. How had I never realized that before?

I didn't know if Theo was putting on a show or finally being able to express his feelings regarding his grandmother, but he stomped over to the door, closed it to ensure "privacy" and turned to face the matriarch once more.

"Grandmother, I'm going to ask this once, and please don't insult me by lying. We both know I can tell when someone is lying to me."

Wait. He could do that? I didn't know he could do that.

*Ohhh. Right. Reading auras.* No wonder Mrs. Alma always seemed to know more than anyone was telling her. I'd simply assumed it was the ghost spy network.

"Have you bound my parents' souls the way you did Aunt Kate's?"

You could hear a pin drop in the silence that followed on their side of the room.

Hidden in our pocket of wards, though, things were a different matter. It was a really good thing Logan had woven his own ward around us, the one that kept any noise from getting out because I was pretty sure I gasped.

I thought Theo would slowly build the moment or the conversation, seeing how far she'd go or take things before admitting it. I didn't think he'd just ... straight up ask her.

Ballsy. As. Fuck.

And kinda hot, too.

His grandmother's well-manicured eyebrow rose again. "What makes you think I'd do that?" she asked, her tone as flat as if they were talking about the weather or something equally dull.

"I've seen their auras, Grandmother."

Mrs. Alma cursed at Theo's answer.

So much for following the script. Theo wasn't supposed

to mention the aura reading thing because if Esme had bound his parents' souls years ago, then Theo would've technically had enough time to read them and see the changes, but he'd never brought it up. Mentioning it now meant something had changed, and unless Esme had bound Theo's parents' souls once more—recently—it was stretching the truth too much.

"I see." Mrs. Esme tilted her head to the side the smallest bit, the movement almost imperceptible. "And what if I have?"

Theo curled his hands into fists beside him but managed to keep his tone even, although not as dead as his grandmother's. "I want to know why you did it. You used Aunt Kate to set an example for us on what we should never do, and I understand the reasoning behind that," Theo lied. Well, it wasn't exactly a lie. He did understand the reason for what Esme had done to his aunt Kate. It was just that he didn't agree with any of it. "But what about my parents? What did they do to deserve such a fate?"

"Have a seat, Theodore. It seems it's about time we had a chat, don't you think?"

At his grandmother's "request," Theo sat in one of the white armchairs, keeping his posture stiff.

"Wish I could take a seat, too," Mrs. Alma grumbled beside me, staring at the all-white couch on our side.

Unfortunately, though, I was pretty sure if we sat, the cushion would become uneven or some shit and give us away.

"You guys, just because the wards can keep sound in doesn't mean you have to abuse it," Andres whisper-yelled from beside us, giving us a look. Sweat was beading his forehead, and he looked like he was starting to struggle, but he held strong. With his MET's help and the tweaking I'd done, he should be able to keep the wards and illusions up for another hour or two, but that didn't mean he wouldn't feel the effects. I'd tried to keep the magical output to a minimum, but Andres had been holding an illusion to cover five people, completely hiding our presence for almost an hour already. We hadn't wanted to risk anyone—or anything—seeing us disappearing at the front entrance.

Blaze and Logan were holding the wards, a mixture of dark matter, rune magic, and the standard warding magic any mage was capable of doing. Mrs. Alma had helped by adding a layer to the wards that would keep ghosts from trying to pass through where we were. All in all, it was a shit ton of magic and power bleeding out constantly, and it stood to reason it was taking its toll on them.

I felt almost bad that due to my low magical power, the only help I'd provided was in tweaking their METs. But as a Magical Engineer, that was literally my job.

"Sorry," I mouthed to Andres, mentally promising to make it up to him once this whole thing was done. Maybe I could give him a naked massage. Or add another blow job to the tally.

Outside our magic bubble, the silence was stretching, making me antsy. It was like watching an hour-long chess match where the players took their sweet time thinking through every move. Or maybe a Shogi match. I'd heard those things could take even longer. How anyone had the patience to sit through something like that without being bored to tears, I'd never understand. But to each their own. I was pretty sure there were people out there who thought the idea of spending all day in front of the TV or computer building the perfect hospital and micromanaging every layer of it was boring as hell. And yet, I'd gone through a Two Point Hospital binging phase where I'd played it nonstop for a week. Roller Coaster Tycoon? Boy, I didn't even know how much time I spent playing that as a kid. So yeah, I would not judge other people's hobbies ... even if I was judging the Battle-Of-Silence between Theo and his grandmother.

When Esme cracked the silence, at last, I was so wrung up with tension that I jumped, earning a smirk from the guys.

"Have I not made it clear that you are not to use your powers within the family?"

I had to blink a couple of times at the irony of Esme's question. Like. So it was okay for her to brainwash her family members and make them her puppets, but Theo couldn't read their auras to check up on them?

Although come to think of it, it was no wonder she'd prohibited him from using that side of his powers. She'd probably been trying to hide the depths of her evilness.

Theo shrugged. "It's not something I can always control. I'm getting better at it, but sometimes I don't even realize I'm seeing the auras until it's too late," he lied.

Mrs. Alma snorted. "If that were the case, he'd be as blind as I am. But that's a good enough excuse," she murmured as if speaking to herself more than anything. "Most importantly, though, that old hag is buying the lie."

"I see. You need to be careful about that, Theodore. Allowing your powers to control you is not fitting for the next Soulbinder Head."

I rolled my eyes so hard, I saw the little monkey who was in charge of my procrastination waving hello.

When Theo didn't try to defend himself or say anything to counter Mrs. Esme's claim, she sat up even straighter in her chair—I didn't even know that was humanly possible—and linked her fingers in front of her. Classic evil mastermind look. All she needed was to twiddle her thumbs together now, and she could star in the next superhero movie. "Tell me, Theodore, do you think your parents are fit to rule? Do you think they have what it takes?"

Uh. Yes? They were kind-hearted people, magically strong, and though Theo's mom was on the quiet side, she baked awesome cookies. They'd always welcomed me in their home growing up, and they'd never made me feel like less. Maybe they weren't the most outspoken and tended to avoid conflict at all costs, not that anyone could blame them. Especially Theo's dad, who had been raised by Mrs. Esme. After what had happened to Ms. Kate, too, it was unsurprising they'd drawn even deeper into their shells. Or, at least, based on everything Theo had told me during our talks recently.

Theo's answer was more diplomatic than my own, though. "It's not my place to decide who is fit to rule or not, Grandmother. You're the head of the family."

There was an infinitesimal tilt to one of the corners of Mrs. Esme's lips, and that was the only indication she approved of Theo's answer.

"Quite so. My son and his wife are lovely people, but they do not possess what it takes to rule. They're too weak-willed, too gullible. The Soul Mages need strong leadership, and I'm afraid none of my children would have been able to give our people that. They are too much like my late husband, I'm afraid. Fortunately, however, my son was able to fulfill his duty. He produced heirs, and you, Theodore, have more of me than my own children ever did. That's why you've been chosen as the heir and why I know you'll do right when it's your turn to take my place."

"Thank you, Grandmother, for the vote of confidence."

I snorted. I couldn't help it. Theo was laying it *thick*. And what was more; he was able to keep his true feelings from showing, his voice never betraying the turmoil that must be taking place inside him.

Poor Theo. When this was done, I was going to cuddle him so hard.

"Is that why you placed the soul binds?" Theo prompted. "To ensure they wouldn't make any foolish decisions?"

Mrs. Esme *actually* smiled.

It was scarier than I thought it would be.

"I knew you would understand, Theodore. The family name must be protected at all costs. It's our duty as Soulbinders to ensure our family thrives. Unfortunately, sometimes, that means we need to take matters into our own hands and choose … unorthodox methods."

I held my breath, knowing what was coming even before Theo uttered another word. Esme had just admitted to the soul binding, which was what we'd been after. It was enough to ruin her name and put a shadow on everything she'd done so far. We had her, but we were far from done.

Theo's next words were full of poison, and there was an icy rage to his tone that he'd managed to keep out thus far.

"Is that why you bound my soul, then? To ensure our family thrives?"

I saw a tint of red on his hands and was startled to realize he'd dug his nails in his palms so hard that he'd ripped the skin open. He was bleeding.

I'd stepped forward, desperate to go to him, to hug him, soothe him, kiss his pain away. But Logan physically stopped me before I could. He grabbed me, pulling me back, his arms banding around me and keeping my back pressed against his front to prevent me from ruining everything we'd built. "Shhh, baby. Let him do this. He needs it as much as you need to comfort him. Let him have his closure," Logan whispered in my ear, and I slumped against him, drawing comfort from his strength.

Just because Logan was right, it didn't mean I had to like it.

"What are you talking about, Theodore?"

Mrs. Esme may be a great robot, but she wasn't a very good actress.

"Grandmother, you know there's no point lying to me. You bound my soul. I know it, you know it. Don't try to deny it. You did it more than once, too. Why?"

A crack in the façade appeared when Mrs. Esme frowned. "How do you know? You can't read your own aura."

Still in Logan's arms, I grabbed his hand, knowing the time had come for phase two.

Mrs. Alma smiled, nodding to Andres so he'd drop the illusion on her. That part was tricky, because once Andres dropped the illusion, we'd have to drop all the wards, too. We'd no longer have the sound barrier or any of the other protections. We'd be dependent solely on Andres and his illusions. If we so much as breathed too loudly, Mrs. Esme would hear us.

I didn't even know if that would make much of a difference at this point, not when we already had the confessions on tape, but better safe than sorry.

At Mrs. Alma's nod, Andres tightened his grip on his MET and changed the illusions.

Mrs. Alma stepped forward like she was coming out of the wall. "He knows because I told him. He might not be able to see his own aura, but I can."

Any color on Esme's cheeks vanished, and she stared, wide-eyed, at Alma as one would a ghost. Except, way more terrifying since Esme could, in fact, see dead people.

Whatever had remained of the matriarch's façade shattered at Mrs. Alma's presence and her words.

"*Alma*. How?" Esme asked barely above a whisper.

Mrs. Alma smiled, but there was nothing nice about it. "Hello, old friend. It's about time you atoned for your actions, don't you think?"

*Check. Fucking. Mate.*

## 29

## CHARISMA

"Carter, I thought I told you to stay out of trouble," Christian's frustrated words over the phone were better than any hello.

I twitched in my seat. "Sir?"

When in doubt, playing dumb was the way to go.

"Esme Soulbinder just formally announced that she was stepping down as head of the family and would retire to their home in the countryside."

I tried very, very hard to play dumb. "Oh? Wow, I didn't expect that. I mean, she's old enough that she should've retired long ago, but I was starting to think she'd just stay as head of the family forever. Like some vampire warlord or something."

I didn't have to be near Christian to know he was rubbing his head at my rambling. It was there in the pregnant pause and the rustling sound of something brushing against the phone.

"Am I supposed to believe you had nothing to do with this?" he asked, sounding exhausted.

I wondered how long I could keep up the act.

"Uh. Isn't the Soulbinder Matriarch stepping down from her role ... you know ... Soulbinder business? Last I checked, I wasn't a Soulbinder. As a Soul Mage, *you* would have more to do with the whole thing than I would. I'm an Elemental Mage, and an outcast one at that." I winced. Dammit. I'd just laid it a little too thick there. Should've kept the Elemental Mage and outcast cards out of it.

"Carter, what did you do?"

What the hell? Why was it my fault?

"I went through all the resistance files just like you told me to, stayed hidden at Bast's, and stayed out of trouble? Oh, and when Blair called a few days ago, I gave her a preliminary report on my findings. Which reminds me, I should really forward you the stuff. I'm almost done with it." I should've been done a few days ago, but I'd been ... preoccupied.

Plus, going through the resistance files was *boring*.

"Carter, cut the bullshit. You're not fooling me. Fine. Here's what will happen. Is Agent Futhark with you?"

I hummed in agreement.

"Good. Have him bring you to AMIA, and we can talk in person. Bring your reports. Then you can fill me in on everything that has been going on. Be here in an hour, and I'll make sure I have some fucking donuts."

I knew a bribe when I heard one, but we both knew I couldn't resist the cafeteria's donuts. They were made out of cocaine or something because they were addictive as shit, and I hadn't had any in *weeks*.

"I'll be there," I promised, and Christian didn't even bother saying goodbye before he hung up the phone. Just like always, really.

Well. I supposed it was about time I went to pay the boss a visit.

By the time I was done recounting all the events that had taken place involving Esme Soulbinder, Christian looked on the verge of turning Super Saiyan. Minus the blond hair and yellow sparkly magic surrounding him.

If he'd seemed tired when I'd arrived, it was nothing compared to now. Christian's eyebrows were drawn together, his eyes were bugged, trying to jump out of his face, and he was gritting his teeth so hard, that multiple veins were pulsing in his neck. On his desk, there were teeny tiny pieces of paper that he'd ripped to shreds one by one as a way to rein in his stress.

"So let me get this straight," he started, carefully enunciating the words as if he was speaking a foreign language for the first time. "Esme did all that, and she's just going to walk? Theodore won't report her. There won't be an investigation; she'll never answer for her crimes?"

When he said it like that, it sounded really fucking bad. It wasn't that we didn't think she should be held accountable, though, even Theo. It was just that short of magically making it possible for others to see auras, we couldn't *prove* her crimes. All we had was the footage from yesterday, but anyone could've claimed it had been tampered with. Our plan hinged on Esme feeling the threat of exposure personally and on her feelings about the family, not on prosecution.

Besides, when it came down to it, the main victims of Esme's manipulations were her own family. So far, Theo was the only one who'd been fixed, and he wasn't willing to report his grandmother. Once he managed to unravel the bindings on his parents and his aunt, things might be different, but until then …

I sighed. "Is there another option? Short of killing her, what the hell could we do?"

Christian drummed his fingers on his desk, deep in thought. "What worries me is that we have no way of stopping her from doing it again, Carter. How can you be sure she won't bind someone else? Or even Theodore?"

He wasn't going to like my answer. "Mrs. Alma—you know her, right? She said you did." When Christian nodded that he did indeed know who Mrs. Alma was, I continued. "Okay, so, Mrs. Alma is teaching Theo how to detect soul bindings and unravel them. Esme's interactions with other people will be very limited, and Theo will closely monitor those his grandmother has contact with. Meanwhile, we're trying to come up with a ward or some way to protect people from being bound, but I don't know how much time that will take. I know it's not ideal, but it's the best we can do for now. Trust me, I really, really wanted Esme to be arrested for the shit she's done, but I can also see why Theo doesn't want his grandmother to be behind bars."

"You said Alma is teaching Theodore how to unravel soul bindings? Is he already able to do that?" he asked, bracing his arms on his desk and sitting forward.

I tilted my head, frowning at Christian's question and the glint in his eyes.

"Erh ... I don't know?" His shoulders slumped slightly. "Boss, is there anyone you think has been soul-bound?" The pieces clicked in my head. "Is that why Blair wanted Theo's number the other day?" I'd been confused as fuck about the request when she'd called me, but given her the number nonetheless.

Christian sat back on his chair, crossing his arms in front of himself and staring at me. "How much do you know about Agent Illudere's current progress in her mission?"

I racked my brain. "She just wanted to know if I had any new intel on Ricardo, which led me to believe they were hitting a wall. But it was basically me telling her what I put in the last report I emailed you, and then she asked for Theo's number." I shrugged, keeping out the fact that Blair had called when Andres and I had been experimenting with chocolate syrup. There were some things Christian did not need to know. Come to think of it, Blair didn't want to know either.

As for the intel I gave Blair, well, it was pretty lame stuff. Nothing interesting in the files from the resistance, except for the fact that all of them, literally every single one of them were dated from up to five years. There was nothing older than that, which was weird in itself, considering the resistance as a movement existed for longer.

"What I'm about to tell you does not leave this room, Carter."

Ohhh. The boss had my attention before, but now he had my curiosity too.

I nodded rather than say anything, so I wouldn't give away how much I'd perked up at the idea of some juicy intel.

"Agent Illudere and her team captured a couple of resistance members who were parading around using Ricardo's likeness."

What in the name of maggot-filled chocolates!?

"They're both currently in holding cells, but they're like dolls whose strings have been cut. I have it on good authority that they've been soul-bound, too, though Alma assures me it's not Esme's doing. It's too much of a coincidence, however, and you know how much I hate that."

My mind spun as I tried to understand all the layers of what

Christian had just revealed. Why was it that I'd gone all my life without even knowing that binding souls was a thing that Soul Mages could do—though Theo assured me only Soulbinders were supposed to be able to do that—but now, suddenly, it was the one thing we kept running across? And if Mrs. Alma was right, which she usually was, then it hadn't been Esme's doing, but then who else could it have been? Who was strong enough?

The same person who'd bound the ghosts to the warehouse Theo and Logan had stormed? That was the only thing that made sense, but just who the fuck was it, and how had they managed to stay under the radar this long? I'd been keeping an eye on the program I'd had running on all the METs related to the resistance, and I hadn't seen any more suspicious activity. As far as I knew, everyone who'd been involved and whose METs I'd been able to ping had already come forward.

I felt like Conspiracy Charlie. All I needed was a big whiteboard and a couple of hours, and then I could give him a run for his money. Except I'd need a lot more colored lines so I could have a different one for every branch of magic. Keeping things pretty and all.

I opened and closed my mouth a few times, trying to put my thoughts in some semblance of order so I could voice some of my questions, but the more I thought about it, the worse it got.

One thing was for sure, though, now that Theo was the head of the Soulbinders, regardless of whether he could unravel the bindings or not, he needed to know what was going on. He needed to know someone that strong and scary was working with Ricardo. Fuck.

"Christian, sir, are the agents working with Blair strong? I know she's badass, but if she's going against someone who can do things like that ... she might need a Soul Mage on her team."

If she didn't already have one. It would be the only way to ensure they didn't get fucked over or brainwashed like Theo had.

"Don't worry about Agent Illudere, Carter. She has some of my best agents working with her, and we both know Alma will be looking after her. Blair will be fine."

I nodded, even if unease still churned in the pit of my stomach. It wasn't like I could do something to change it, though. I only knew two Soul Mages who might be strong enough to have Blair's back, and one of them had just become Family Head, and the other was a million years old. Well, there was also Mrs. Esme, but with how evil she'd turned out to be, she was more likely to join Ricardo's bid to take over the world rather than help us stop him.

"Is there anything I can do to help? I know you didn't want me involved, but—"

"No, Carter. I appreciate the offer, but I can't risk you too. You've gone through a lot in very little time. You need some proper time off, a vacation or something. Get your life back in order. I know you haven't even found a permanent place to live. We'll be okay. Once things settle, you can decide whether you want to retire from being an agent—though we'd be sad to let you go—so you can start your official career as a Magical Engineer the way you always dreamed of, or if you want to stay with us, but only in the Engineering Department."

I narrowed my eyes at the man who was more of a father to me than my biological one. "Why does it feel like you're trying to convince me to quit AMIA?"

He surprised me by grinning. Damn, when Christian

smiled like that, he looked years younger. "As AMIA's Director, I really shouldn't be saying any of this, but you know I consider you one of my own. If I had a daughter, I'd love it if she could be even half as good a kid as you are. You're young, Charisma, and you have your whole life ahead of you. You shouldn't be tied down with the Agency. Don't give up on having a life, a family, and even children someday just so you can keep risking your hide to save the world. Change is coming to Arcane, and it'll be the good kind. You worked hard for your diploma so you could have your own life; it's time you went out there and did just that. Think about it, and know that no matter what you decide, we'll always have a place for you."

I wasn't crying. Nope. Not one little bit. Those weren't tears coming from my eyes; they were eye sweat.

My lower lip wobbled, and I felt like my heart was so full of rainbows, it might burst.

Without thinking, without giving Christian a chance to realize what I was doing, I got out of my chair and ran to his side of the table. I kissed his cheek, mindful to avoid the beard. Poor Christian, he was working so hard, he wasn't even bothering with shaving anymore. He probably didn't have time for it amid all the stress. Still, the rough look worked for him. Honestly, he should have a line of ladies at his door. If he weren't married to AMIA and his work, he'd be a womanizer.

"Just in case I never told you, you're the best pseudo dad I could've wanted. If you'd had a kid, I'm sure they would've agreed, too. Thank you for everything you've done for me, Christian. I promise I'll think about what you said. I won't make this decision lightly."

As I stepped away, I pretended not to notice that his eyes were sweating too.

"Now get out of here, and this time, please really do try to stay out of trouble," he teased.

I grinned. "I've told you before I never go looking for trouble; it just seems to find me wherever I go."

"I know. That's what I worry about, Carter. That's what I worry about."

He was such a dad.

And I wouldn't change a single thing.

# 30

# CHARISMA

"Kitten, I think it's time you met my parents," Andres said cheerfully as I made my way to the kitchen. Andres, Bast, and I were alone in the house, and it was my turn to make lunch. So peanut butter and jelly sandwiches were on the menu for the day.

I turned around so fast that I overcompensated, and my world spun a little.

Andres grabbed me before the world stopped spinning. "Wait. What? I already met your parents." Hadn't I? I was fairly certain I'd met the Illuderes in one of the times I'd gone to their house.

I'd definitely met them back when I was growing up and was still the Silverstorm heir.

Andres tsked. "No. It's time you *met* met them. As my girlfriend."

Oh, hell no. There was no way that would go over well. The fuck was I supposed to say? "Hi, Mr. and Mrs. Illudere. I'm Charisma Carter, the shunned heir who's dating your son. Oh, and by the way, I'm also dating Blaze Futhark, Logan Nightshade, Bastille Tumba—yes, that Tumba—and sort of dating Theodore Soulbinder, the new head of the Soulbinder family. It's so nice to meet you." There was no way that was going to work.

Andres laughed, pulling me into his arms and kissing my hair. "Relax, Kitten. They know about our unconventional relationship. Don't forget, my dad dated Bast's mom a long time ago. He's familiar with this type of dynamic, even if he decided it wasn't for him. They're not going to judge you for it, if that's what you're worried about. My mother might not understand, but she knows you make me happy, and that's all she wants for me. Besides," he added, lowering his voice as if telling me a secret. "She kind of likes the idea that Bast will be around me to keep an eye on me. She thinks he'll be a good influence on me." Andres rolled his eyes, and I snorted.

"Does she know that by spending more time with Bast, you're also spending more time with Gran?" I teased.

"Probably not, and let's keep it that way, shall we? Anyway. They just called, and they're inviting us to go over there for lunch. I figured you'd prefer it over having to cook."

"*Now*?" My voice was so high-pitched, it was probably on the same wavelength as those dog whistles. "You want us to go there now to have lunch with your parents? Without prior warning? With no time to get ready, freak out about it, come up with a million excuses to cancel, and overthink the outfit and interaction for a month? Are you out of your ever-loving mind!?"

I tried to remember to breathe. In and out like normal people did, but there was this pressure in my chest that made it hard to.

Andres stared at me, smirking, those adorable dimples on his stupidly handsome face. He tilted his head to the side like I was a puzzle. "Yes? They invited Bast, too. I figured we didn't have plans for today anyway, so we might as well. And, like you said, you've already met them, so what's the big deal?"

"The big deal? It's a huge moment, Andres! I need to be warned about these things a week ahead so I can mentally prepare for it!"

"Well, alright. Sorry. Do you want me to call them and cancel?" he offered, looking all caring and shit.

I hoped he stepped barefoot on a Lego.

"No, no. You already said we were going, right? Then we should go. Do I have enough time to shower?" I'd showered when I woke up, but it had been a normal, quick one and not a "meet your boyfriend's parents" type of shower. I hadn't even washed my hair. Just dry-shampooed it like a pro. I looked down and noticed I was wearing a shirt that had a kitten with devil horns and "Go to Hell" written in glittery pink. I couldn't meet his parents wearing that! I needed adultier clothes.

Andres' grimace was the only answer I needed.

"Fuck. Fine. Give me five minutes. I can be ready in five," I said and rushed to the bathroom. I needed to work a miracle, and I couldn't use illusions to do it.

*Men.*

"Charisma! It's so good to see you," Serena Illudere crossed the room to meet me with open arms. She was just as beautiful as the last time I'd seen her. Tall, dark-haired, and with golden skin like Andres.

She bypassed her son, not even acknowledging his presence, coming straight to me.

I awkwardly hugged her back, relieved when she stepped back and put some distance between us. Personal space was a basic opossum need, yo.

"Look at you! I'm so glad you could make it." She smiled at me, truly happy at my presence.

"Don't hog the girl, dear. Let me talk to her, too!" Diego Illudere exclaimed, playfully bumping his wife out of the way so he, too, could hug me.

Serena Illudere greeted Bast with the same level of excitement she'd given me.

"Charisma! So good of you to join us! Andres has been trying to keep you away, but we finally managed to get him to bring you around!"

I really, really was grateful that they were welcoming me to their family with open arms—literally—but this whole physical affection thing was freaking me out a little.

I could see where Andres had gotten that side of him, and it was heartwarming. The Illuderes couldn't be more different from my parents in that regard, and it showed.

The way they looked at each other and smiled all lovey-dovey was another major difference. Not that I thought my parents didn't like each other, there was just ... no physical affection between them at all.

However, while I was very cuddly with my men, hugging anyone else or being all touchy-feely was really, really weird. It wasn't how I was raised, and I worried if I got any stiffer, it would be considered rude.

"What am I, a ghost?" Andres protested, expertly detangling his family from me and keeping me at his side.

I gave him a grateful smile while his parents scoffed.

"We saw you just the other day, Andres." Diego rolled his eyes at his son before smiling at me. "But you? We were so happy when Andres told us you two were dating. I've always told him he needed a good woman to keep him on his toes." Mr. Illudere winked at me, and yup, I could definitely see where Andres had gotten his charm.

"Bast! I didn't see you there! Welcome back, son." Diego went to do the weird man-bro-hug thing with Bast, and I finally felt like I had enough room to breathe.

"Sorry about them," Andres said, kissing my hair. "I told you they were excited to have you being officially introduced as my girlfriend."

"It's cool. It's just ... "

Andres chuckled. "They're a lot, I know. But see? I told you you had nothing to worry about. C'mon, while they're distracted catching up with Bast, let's sneak into the dining room and take our seats; this way you can avoid another round of hugs."

He gently guided me out of the sitting room. I looked behind me, seeing that Diego was asking Bast a million questions while Serena smiled at something Bast had said.

Bast caught my eye just before we crossed the door, frowning playfully when he realized we were trying to escape.

"Looks like Andres and Char are heading in to lunch," Bast told the Illuderes, loud enough that I knew he wanted us to hear. "Why don't we join them?"

Andres cursed, closing the door behind us.

"Run," he said, pulling my hand and all but dragging me through the Illudere manor.

"Why are we running?" I asked, confused, even as I let him tug me away.

Andres didn't answer, and he didn't stop running. I tried very hard to keep up with the lunatic's pace, but it was hard. I was in heels. *Heels.* I'd dressed up like a freaking adult to meet Andres' parents, and now he was dragging me around away from them and making me risk the safety of my ankles for this.

It wasn't until we reached the dining room that he stopped, and by then, I was breathless. Meanwhile, Andres was laughing like a loon.

"What the hell, Andres?" I asked when I could speak again without wheezing.

Andres picked me up and spun me, laughing. "You're amazing. Did you know that?"

"And you've lost your damn mind. Why did we run?" I pressed the second he put me back down.

Andres' dimples were doing their best to try to distract me, but I wasn't so easily swayed ... when I didn't want to be.

"Sorry, Char. I didn't expect them to act like that. They were being weird, and I half expected Mom to bust out the baby pictures. By escaping, you avoided the inquisition, *and* we didn't go through the foyer with them. Dad would've probably told you the whole story of the Illuderes who first built this house or something. Trust me. I was doing you a favor."

"You're the one acting weird," I accused, but it was impossible to stay mad at him when he looked at me with that damn grin, his eyes full of mischief.

"Sorry, Kitten," Andres pulled me even closer and rubbed his face in my neck. He knew how sensitive my neck was, and he always took full advantage of it. "Tell you what, if my father isn't still talking about the family legacy when they catch up to us, I'll give you a tour of my old bedroom after lunch and eat you out until you forgive me. You'll be my dessert."

Oh, well. I supposed I could be swayed by those terms.

"And if he is?"

Andres' smile turned predatory. "Then I suppose you'll be the one to have the dessert."

Andres had been right. Diego Illudere had joined us in the dining room while he was talking about his great uncle and how he was an architect ahead of his time. Apparently, the Illuderes had been one of the first families to create an environment with illusions woven into it, and the illusion wonderland that was their foyer was just one of his creations.

Once we'd all been seated, though, lunch had been pretty fun. I'd sat between Bast and Andres, and the conversation had flowed pretty easily all around the table. Serena had told me stories about the havoc Andres caused as a kid, and Diego had even gone so far as to conjure some illusions to illustrate it.

It had been pretty funny.

None of the Illuderes were acting like they were worried about the Ricardo situation, but they were careful to avoid his name. Still, there were signs that everything wasn't as well as they might wish, like the number of guards at the gates and the bags under both Serena and Diego's eyes.

Andres had already warned me about that, and on the way here, he'd also told me to avoid mentioning his uncle, if possible. It was a touchy subject to them all, though Andres had made it clear that it wasn't something they were going to try to wipe under the rug or avoid forever. The Illuderes were using every resource they had in an attempt to find the rat bastard, and Blair was keeping them up-to-date on her mission. Normally, Blair wouldn't be allowed to do something like that as an agent, but circumstances were far from ideal, and the Illuderes were going above and beyond to cooperate so Ricardo could be found and arrested.

They were carefully optimistic about the outcome, though, and so was I, honestly.

AMIA was making strides to find Ricardo, and soon enough, he'd be found and held accountable for his crimes.

Once lunch was over, Serena and Diego—as they insisted I call them—had encouraged Andres to give Bast and me a tour of the house while they retired to their own room.

Andres waited until his parents had closed the door behind them before looking at me and smiling.

"Bast, out of curiosity, what did my father talk about when you guys made your way here?" Andres' gaze never left mine.

"You know damn well what he talked about, fucker. You owe me one, by the way," Bast answered grumpily.

Andres' grin only grew, though.

"So, I suppose I owe you a tour of my childhood room, huh? And dessert."

I smiled. "I suppose you do owe me that, yes," I agreed.

I was, after all, a girl of my word. I owed Andres a blowjob, and if I got to do that while riding Bast's gorgeous dick, even better.

## 31

## CHARISMA

"So, what does it feel like to be the new head of the Soulbinders?" I asked Theo, smiling at him from his office's door.

Theo hadn't moved into the Soulbinder manor as he was expected to since he was head of the family—and I doubted he ever would. He'd chosen to stay at his apartment, but he'd officially given me a key if I ever wanted to visit him ... after I swore I would not fill his house with any more miniature toys.

Joke was on him, though, because he hadn't ruled out all the other sizes of toys. Not to mention a bunch of other miniature stuff that wasn't considered a toy. Like plushes or printouts. The possibilities were endless. Not that I was planning on doing any of it, of course, but a girl had to keep a guy on his toes.

For the past couple of days, Theo had been stuck trying to catch up on his new role as the Soulbinder Head, which included having back-to-back meetings with the rest of the Council of Six. The truth was, Theo had become head at a really rough time for the families, and the guys—well, the whole council—were working around the clock to make things right.

After my talk with Christian, I'd actually remembered to ask the guys about the "good changes" Christian had alluded to and had been pleasantly surprised to find out Logan had come up with a solution that might appease the mages all around while retaining their power.

It still needed a lot of work and talking—hence all the meetings—but they were planning on creating a sub-council of sorts. One where a mage of each magical branch would be elected by the people and be in charge for a set period. Not only that, but the sub-council would get to appoint one member–which would be elected or picked among themselves–to join the Council of Six, about to become Council of Seven. The seventh council seat would also be a set term, but it should be enough to give mages a voice, regardless of their magical strength. There was still a lot that would have to be hashed out, but I was positive this would work. And Christian was right; this would be a great change in our society.

They were also carefully trying to come up with a way to end the pseudo-war at the border, but that would take some time and a lot more work. It was the first of many steps to slowly change the way Necromancers were seen in our society. The truth was that while our generation might not see the day mages wouldn't be terrified and hate Necromancers, we hoped that the day would come for future generations. And my guys were going to take the first steps to it.

It had to be enough for now.

At my voice, Theo looked up, a smile slowly lighting up his face. Theo's hair was even more messy than usual, his clothes slightly askew. When I arrived, I noticed the slumped posture and the shadows under his eyes. But as he got up from his chair and walked around his desk to me, it was like all the exhaustion vanished just by seeing me.

Really made a girl feel special.

"Char, hey! I didn't expect to see you!" He came over and hugged me in greeting, and I melted into his embrace.

It felt so damn good to be in his arms again, to have him be a part of my life.

Because of the amount of work he had to do, we'd barely seen each other since the confrontation with his grandmother, but we'd been keeping in touch. Texting and calling each other. Slowly making up for all the years we'd been apart.

The guys had even created a group chat and added him so Theo could be included. I knew it was their way of telling me they accepted Theo as part of the group since it had become pretty clear that I still had feelings for Theo.

"Surprise!" I said, pulling back just enough that I could grin at him. "C'mon, Theo, I've come to steal you away. You've been working too damn much. It's time you had some fun."

"Char, baby, I don't think you should have any more sugar," Theo chided, shaking his head, more amused at me than anything.

I stared at him over the top of my cotton candy. "Why not? I only had two funnel cakes, some ice cream, and now a cotton candy."

He snorted. "That's exactly why you shouldn't have any more sugar, you weirdo."

I blew a raspberry at him and then walked away with my

cotton candy while Theo paid for it. He caught up to me in no time, chuckling.

"You know, when you 'kidnapped' me so we could come here, I thought you were being sweet and reliving our first official date as teenagers," he teased. "I should've known your endgame was another one entirely."

Theo was spot-on in his assessment, though. I had chosen this amusement park because it had been where our first date had been. I figured, now that we were starting over and dating again, it would be a nice—if slightly bittersweet—touch.

We'd spent all day going on joyrides and having fun, stopping every now and then to stuff ourselves with yummy food.

Here, we were just a boy and a girl having a good time in the middle of the crowd. There was no magic, no council business, no pressure or responsibilities. Theo could just let go and enjoy himself.

And it was working, too. He'd been smiling from ear to ear, having fun and teasing me. Just like he'd always done.

I loved this carefree side of Theo more than anything.

"Well, I can neither confirm nor deny that I wanted to come here for the food. But the rollercoaster was a nice bonus." And so was the company.

Theo tried to grab some of my cotton candy, and I sidestepped him before running away, knowing he would chase me.

Laughing, I ran through food stalls and tried my best to avoid colliding with people, knowing Theo was hot on my tail. I ran until I reached a less busy part of the park and then slowed my pace just enough that he could catch me. Theo snatched me, picking me up from the ground and playfully biting my shoulder while I giggled.

I dropped the cotton candy when he turned me around in his arms, but I didn't give a shit. Then Theo's face was inches from mine, both of us breathing hard, smiling at each other like idiots.

"Look what you did; you made me drop my sugar!" I complained, but there was no real heat behind my words.

Theo's gaze dropped to my lips. "Hmm, there's still some here, I better clean it up for you." Then he kissed the corner of my mouth, his tongue swiping at the spot.

I clung to him, tilting my head. Theo chuckled, kissing the other side of my mouth.

I growled a bit, grabbing a handful of his hair and directing his lips where I wanted them most.

Theo's kiss tasted like sugary goodness and comfort, like having ice cream on a hot summer day.

Like love lost and found again.

Whatever reservations I'd still held, whatever pain I'd unknowingly clung to washed away as our tongues tangled with one another. As Theo explored every inch of my mouth as if he needed to be reacquainted with it.

More than anything, though, the kiss tasted like hope.

Theo and I would be alright, we'd be together.

Because that was where we both belonged.

I knew there was more we still had to work on, a new relationship to build, but I loved him, had never stopped loving him, not really. That was enough for now.

"Take me home, Theo."

## 32

## THEO

I barely remembered driving us to my place. The whole time, I'd been focused on keeping my hands off of her so I could get us here in one piece. I'd probably broken a million traffic laws, but we'd made it.

It had been one of the most torturous experiences of my life. When we'd taken the elevator, I'd kept an eye on the panel that showed the floors as if that would help it go faster. Char had laughed and teased me, but I was a man on a mission.

When we'd finally reached my floor, I'd been about ready to explode. Still, I'd finally regained control when we reached my bedroom.

I didn't want our first time back together to be frantic and desperate. I wanted to take my time with her, to show her how much I loved her.

I carefully laid Char on my bed, not even believing this was really happening. If this was a dream, I never wanted to wake up.

Char was here, in my bed, in my arms, all soft and pliant, eager for my touch, for my kisses. *For my dick.*

I never thought I'd have the chance to have her like this again. I thought I'd have to contend with just the memories of our teenage explorations.

The memories didn't hold a candle to the real thing.

Char pushed up on her elbows, lifting her head from the bed to watch while I finished undressing. We'd made quick work of our clothes when we'd entered my apartment, but I still had my boxers on.

Under Char's watchful gaze, I slid them off, masculine satisfaction filling me when Char licked her lips at seeing my cock.

"Oh, I've missed you, big guy," she murmured, eyes fixed on my dick.

How she could make me laugh when I was so hard I felt I might burst was a mystery only Char could unravel.

"My eyes are up here, Char," I teased, walking closer.

"I know, but I really missed your dick," Char replied, reaching out for me. "Come here, Theo. I need you."

Her words were my undoing.

"You have me, Char. Always." I kneeled on the bed between her open legs, hissing out a breath when she gripped my cock and squeezed like she was giving it a handshake.

"Char," I warned. If she kept petting my dick like that, I was going to embarrass myself. It had been too damn long, and I hadn't been with anyone since her. I wanted to make her come over and over again before I found my release.

Rather than stopping, Char smiled and slid her hand over me, gently pumping and using her thumb to gather the pre-cum from my tip.

I had to close my eyes to stop from thrusting forward.

"Listen, Theo, we'll have the rest of our lives to relearn

each other's bodies, but right now? Right now, I really need your dick inside of me. I've had enough of foreplay."

To illustrate her point, she pumped me again.

*Fuck.*

With a growl, I pounced on her. Grabbing her head for a bruising kiss, I settled between her legs and rubbed my fingers on her clit. Char arched in my arms, pushing her breasts up.

I broke the kiss so I could take one of them in my mouth, circling her nipple the way I knew she liked.

Char grabbed my hair with both hands, finally letting go of her tight grip on my cock. "Theo. *Please.*"

I spread her lower lips and inserted a finger.

She was so wet, so ready for me.

I picked Char up in my arms, rolled, and laid on the bed with her on top, straddling me.

"Then ride me, Char, baby, show me how much you missed my dick. Take what you want." It was more a request than an order, but it worked.

Char wasted no time lining herself up and guiding me home, slowly sinking onto me until I was fully sheathed.

"You feel so fucking good, Char baby."

So wet, so tight for me.

Char's eyes were closed, her mouth half open in pleasure. I gripped her hips, helping her move on top of me. Char kept a slow, almost torturous pace, raising up on her knees until I was almost completely out of her before sinking back down. I watched the way her tits bounced with every move, dying for another taste of them.

Char placed her hand on my chest for support, bending forward, gasping when she found the perfect angle for her. Every time she moved, her clit rubbed against me, getting her closer and closer to the edge.

My balls tightened with the need to come, her wet heat feeling so good squeezing my dick, I knew I wouldn't be able to hold off much longer.

I raised my head, taking one of her tits in my mouth, gently pulling on the nipple. Char gasped in pleasure, arching into me, pushing her breasts closer.

I loved how responsive she was.

Wanting her to feel even better, I slid my hand between us and slicked my fingers over her clit.

It wasn't the best angle, but I was rewarded by Char's breathy moans.

She rode me faster, harder, until her inner walls fluttered around my dick.

Char came with a scream, her rhythm faltering, and I grabbed onto her hips, slamming in and out of her, letting her ride her orgasm and milk me until I couldn't hold back anymore.

I came hard, pumping into her until we were both spent.

Then Char was lying on top of me, her head on my chest as she sighed dreamily.

I kissed the top of her head, trailing my fingers in her hair.

I had the woman I loved back in my arms, and this time, I wasn't going to fuck it up, no matter what.

## 33

## CHARISMA

*Ian and Elizabeth Silverstorm are proud to announce the engagement of their daughter, Charisma Silverstorm, to Lucien Brant.*

I couldn't read past that sentence. The full-page spread was all over the news and internet, and I was pretty sure it would go on about the Silverstorms and the glory of the family and whatever other bullshit my parents had told them to print.

I just ... I couldn't believe the *nerve*.

Had I hallucinated my last visit there? I had very clearly and specifically said I would *not* be going along with their plan. I wouldn't marry Brant or anyone else they picked for me, and I was not Charisma Silverstorm. I hadn't been for five years.

I wasn't just mad. I was freaking *livid*.

Who did they think they were? Did they honestly think I'd go along with it because they announced it everywhere? Fuck that.

I was going to march over there right now, and I'd make it very, very clear that they were delusional. Even if all I did was give them another piece of my mind, I couldn't just let them get away with this shit. They had to *know* this type of behavior wouldn't fly with me. Not anymore.

I stomped to the door with a clear goal in mind, but when I opened it to leave, there were three pairs of concerned eyes staring at me.

"She knows," Logan said, the second he saw me.

"Shit. I'd been hoping we could break the news to her slowly. You know, maybe after a bunch of orgasms." Andres winced at whatever stormy expression he saw on my face.

"Somehow, Andres, I don't think that there would be enough orgasms in the world that would keep Char from going on a murderous rampage." Blaze's comment had me narrowing my eyes at him.

I wasn't so far gone that I hadn't noticed that out of all my boyfriends, the trio standing in front of me were the least likely to be hanging out together, which meant whatever meetings they'd gone off to for the day had required the presence of all of them. The Council of Six had probably met again.

I'd ask them about whether or not there had been any progress later. Right now, all I cared about was that if the Council of Six had held a meeting, my parents had attended, and they should be on their way home right about now.

The timing would work rather well.

"If the three of you are talking about the announcement of my alleged engagement to Lucien Brant? Then yes, I saw it, and I'm pissed. I'm going there right now to demand they fix this shit." Seriously, like, it made me wonder if they'd even bothered *asking* my alleged fiance if he even agreed to this charade.

It was a pity I didn't have Brant's number because if I did,

I would call him and ask, then we could both storm there and force my parents to call the reporters and rectify their delusional statement. I didn't know Agent Brant very well, but I doubted he'd be okay with getting married to someone he was not in a relationship with.

The people I *was* in a relationship with, however, were not expressing the appropriate level of anger at my parents' latest scheme, and that only added fuel to my fire.

"Why are the three of you blocking the door instead of bracing to go to war with me?" I asked when I noticed they were literally doing just that. All three of them, shoulder to shoulder. They hadn't been like that when I'd opened the door, but the second they'd seen my face, they'd moved. I hadn't even realized they were barricading me inside until it was too late.

"Kitten, listen, you know I love you, right?" Andres carefully took a step forward as if he was approaching a wild animal or something.

He was right to fear me.

"We all do, but we really, really don't think you going out there and storming your parents' home because of that piece is a good idea. Just ... let it go. Soon enough, when it becomes clear you're not actually engaged or married to Brant, things will calm down, and the gossip will die. In fact, it'll probably become one more thing your parents will be ridiculed about. Isn't that better?"

Andres looked almost hopeful, and he kept making these weird hand gestures like I was an angry mare he was trying to calm down.

It only made matters worse, not better.

I put my hands on my hips, eyebrows raised. "You think I should just do nothing? Andres, that's exactly the type of behavior my parents expect. I can't just ... I need to do this, Andres. You guys don't have to understand, but I'd appreciate it if I could have your support."

I knew that by the time I actually made it there, I'd have a grip on my anger, and in spite of my initial reaction, I didn't *actually* want to set fire to their house. However, I needed to show them, to tell them that I wasn't going to let them bully me into compliance.

"Very well." Logan surprised me by being the first to acquiesce. "If you feel that's what you need, then we won't stand in your way. But can we go with you? You don't have to face them alone, Charisma."

Dammit, was it any wonder I'd fallen for him?

"Please, Little Spitfire. Let us go with you, or at least one of us. It'd help show them we have your back and that their interference won't be tolerated."

"As a bonus, they'll see you have all the heirs to the other families wrapped around your little finger. You might get to see them keeling over," Andres chipped in, cheerful at the idea of mischief.

I considered the idea, and I couldn't lie; it had a lot of appeal, but ... I bit my lip, and Logan sighed.

"You want to go alone, don't you? So you can show your strength." He wasn't really asking, but I nodded anyway.

"I guess I'll just wait in the car again," Blaze grumbled, but he took my hand when I went past him, and I knew he didn't mind it all that much.

"Thanks, guys. Now let's go so I can wreck my parents' delusional plans once and for all."

I didn't bother ringing the doorbell to my parents' mansion. I technically didn't *have* to, and I really didn't want to involve James or some poor maid in this mess. Besides, I had a key. They'd never bothered asking for it back when I'd been kicked out, and I hadn't bothered returning it.

I unlocked the door, not bothering to lock it behind me. I'd be quick enough that it shouldn't make a difference. I'd get in, yell at my parents, tell them they were delusional, force them to correct their statement in the news, and then I'd get out. It would be cathartic.

Easy, efficient, and with minimal amount of stress. If they didn't agree to it, well, I supposed I'd have to take matters into my own hands and discredit their claim my own way. They'd hate that, too, but I'd rather not have to go through the hassle.

I hated public speaking.

The one good thing about having lived here for eighteen years was that I knew my parents' routine, and I doubted it had changed. They'd been doing the same thing since I was little, and they'd probably continue to do so until the day they died.

So, the second I walked into their house, I headed up the stairs. After any lengthy meeting, both of my parents would be in the sunroom unwinding. It was one of the few rooms in the whole house that had a bar. My father would head straight to it, pour himself a dose of whiskey, and sit down to enjoy it. My mother, on the other hand, would ring for tea and surreptitiously doctor it. Why she thought she had to keep up appearances when she'd been doing the same thing for years, I'd never know, but if she wanted to pretend everyone wasn't fully aware she took her tea with one part tea-three parts whiskey, then that was her prerogative.

Only when I reached the door to the sunroom did I realize I hadn't run into anyone. Had they dismissed the maids for the day? It wasn't even five in the afternoon.

Hmmm, maybe my parents were in a bad mood, and the staff were making themselves scarce. That was actually a lot more likely. Anyone who'd worked for my parents for more than a few weeks quickly learned to stay out of my mother's way when she was angry at something. Mostly because she tended to make the temperature in the room literally drop, and nobody wanted to face frostbite. I could hardly blame them.

With my hand on the doorknob, I took a deep breath, reminding myself why I was here.

*No more being a doormat, Charisma. Not to your parents or anyone. Ever again.*

I opened the door and gasped at what I saw inside.

There was glass everywhere. My mother's fancy tea set was shattered, split into pieces, and her prized golden tea cart was haphazardly knocked on the floor. And, worst of all, my mother's unmoving form slumped near the mess. She was sideways, her arms at odd angles. But the most concerning fact was the big, angry, red gash on her forehead and the trickle of blood coating her face.

I stepped into the room, and that was when I saw my father. Ian Silverstorm was facedown on the floor, his body half-concealed by an armchair. There was glass near him, too, from his broken cup. It was as if he'd just finished pouring himself a drink and been on his way to his seat when someone had knocked him from behind.

Grabbing my MET from the back pocket of my jeans, I rushed inside. I knew I had to call for the Healers, but I had to first make sure my parents were okay. Or alive at least.

Goddess, please let them be alive.

They might be assholes, and the most cold-hearted family one could possibly have, but they were still my parents. I didn't want them to die. I just wanted them to leave me alone to do my own thing.

I went to my mother first, since at a glance, she seemed to be the one with the worst wound. Careful not to jostle her too much, I took her wrist, feeling for a pulse.

Relief filled me to my very core. Her pulse was a bit weak, but it was there. She was alive. And from up close, the wound on her forehead didn't look as terrible as it'd seemed from afar.

I didn't know what the fuck had happened here, but right now, I didn't care. Once I made sure they were okay and called the Healers in, I would worry about that.

I got up to go to check on my dad, but once I turned, I noticed there was someone at the door.

Fucking Cara leaned against the frame, her once perfectly styled platinum blonde hair in complete disarray, her silver eyes *furious*. She wore well-fitted jeans and a black, long-sleeved crop top, looking like she'd just been strolling around instead of running and hiding from AMIA for the past few weeks. I kept a wary eye on the golden bracelet on her left arm. Her MET.

"Cara, what have you done?" I asked, tightening the grip on my MET and slowly blocking my psycho cousin's view of my mother.

There may be no love lost between my family and me, but they were weak, vulnerable, and I didn't trust Cara wouldn't take advantage of it.

I should've called my guys the second I saw my parents on the floor, but I'd been worried about the blood and hadn't fucking thought straight. Now I worried if I tried to reach for my phone in my pocket, Cara would strike.

I had a better chance if I focused on disarming and apprehending her first.

*So much for staying out of trouble.*

"What have I done?" Cara scoffed like I'd asked her the most ridiculous question. "What have *they* done? Did you really think, after everything I went through, after everything I did to secure my place as the next Silverstorm heir, that I'd let them just cast me aside so they could replace me? And with what, a mutt like you, who isn't even strong enough to be a Battle Mage? I don't fucking think so." She flicked her hair over her shoulder, full of self-righteous fury. "They're going to pay for what they've done, cousin dearest. They'll learn they can't fuck with me. And so will you."

"So, what, you knocked them out and left them, and that's how they're going to pay?" That didn't make sense. Cara was a psycho with delusions of grandeur, but even she should be smarter than this. Just knocking them out wouldn't get the revenge she clearly thought she was owed. Killing them would've worked—though I was fucking glad she hadn't done it—but the room had been empty when I'd arrived, and neither of my parents were dead. At least, I assumed my father wasn't either.

Cara laughed like only an evil psychopath could. "Just how stupid do you think I am?"

I bit my tongue to keep from replying with *very*. Antagonizing her during her evil speech would only make it worse, and I wanted to find out what her game plan had been and whether or not she was working alone. Christian had said Cara and Ricardo had parted ways, but that could've just been a setup.

Cara narrowed her eyes, and I cursed my lack of a poker

face. "You *bitch*. Don't worry about it, dear cousin. By the time I'm done making them suffer, they'll be begging for death. Killing them will be a mercy, really. Not that you'll be alive to see it. You're nothing but a waste of space, and you're not even worth the effort of killing you."

Was that supposed to be insulting? Some kind of sick burn? Because if so, she seriously had to up her game.

Still, I really didn't want to have to fight her. I just wanted to take my parents to the Healers and then enjoy cuddles with my guys, dammit.

"Cara, you know that killing them, killing us, won't change anything. Everyone knows you were involved with the resistance. You won't be able to take over the Silverstorm seat at the council. Nobody will allow it." Why, yes, I was trying to reason with crazy even though I was almost sure it was pointless. Still, it allowed me to mentally go through the best way to take Cara down while protecting my parents. Just in case.

Cara smiled, and I'd never realized how creepy it was until now. Maybe she'd done a better job of concealing her true self than I'd ever given her credit for, or maybe she had just really lost it for good because she looked *unhinged*. "Poor, naive Charisma always believing the best of everyone. I don't give a shit about a seat in the council. I'm not like you; I have ambitions, and ways to make them happen," she bragged. "Well, cousin, as much as I've enjoyed this little chat with you, I'm afraid I have better things to do with my time. Be a good little mutt and stay put so I can kill you quickly, yeah? I promise, it'll barely hurt."

Then Cara reached for her MET, and I acted.

Knowing I wouldn't have time to key an entire sequence, I pressed the "panic" button on the side of my MET, and multiple flaming orbs flung at her.

Cara rolled her eyes, almost bored, and batted the orbs away as if they were pesky flies, not even bothering to use her MET.

"Is this the best you can do, mutt? You really are pathetic."

People really should know better than to underestimate me. Sure, my spell may have been easily dismissed, but it had served its purpose. All it was supposed to do was distract my target and buy me time, which it did wonderfully.

My fingers flew over the screen of my MET as I cast spell after spell. My first order of business was to protect the vulnerable, so I cast a couple of dome-like wards to protect my fallen parents. Then I kept a steady stream of fire, ice, and black matter projectiles flying toward Cara from multiple directions.

My cousin cursed and grabbed her MET, creating a thick ice barrier around her that kept the attack at bay.

Then she threw a fireball the size of my *face* straight at me. I ducked, wincing when I heard a crash behind me.

It was like Cara had decided she'd fight fire with fire—literally—all the while one-upping me to show who had more magic.

The thing was, I *knew* she was magically stronger. She didn't have to prove it to me.

But there was one thing I was, other than a closet badass; I was *sneaky*.

Finally finding the opening I'd been looking for, I placed an illusion of myself running away while simultaneously activating the illusion that would make me vanish.

"Pathetic to the end, dear cousin." Cara mocked as she used her magic to break her ice barrier, transforming it into actual spears and sending them my way.

Or, towards my illusion, at least.

While hundreds of ice spears closed in on my fake self, I snuck around Cara. My cousin realized her mistake right before I knocked her out with a well-placed karate chop on the carotid artery.

K.Fucking.O., bitch.

## 34

## BLAZE

For the second time in less than a month, I was sitting in my car, parked just outside the Silverstorm gates, waiting for my girl while she faced her parents by herself.

This time, though, I wasn't alone. Logan sat in the passenger's seat beside me, the picture of casual elegance while he worked from his phone, and Andres was in the backseat being his usual annoying self.

Not for the first time, I wished we'd left him at home. Andres was remarkably bad at being patient, and he'd already complained more than a five-year-old on a long road trip with his parents.

I was two seconds away from using Rune Magic to shut him up for good.

Logan's phone vibrated, and he sighed. "Tomorrow's meeting just got pushed back to two in the afternoon. AMIA's Director will be joining us for it."

I groaned. That was going to be a long one.

Logan, Theo, and I had been spending a ton of time together, not only because we were all dating the same girl, but because we were attending multiple council meetings.

Even though I was technically not required to, my father had decided that since the Soulbinder leadership had changed, it was about time I continued to take on more responsibility and attended even more meetings.

I was pretty sure he just didn't have the patience for the increased demand of his time—before this, the Council of Six used to meet once a week at most—and that was why he'd thrown me to the wolves. However, this worked better with Logan's plan and the changes he was trying to get approved by the council. My father was old school and would not favor the idea of creating a sub-council, much less adding a seventh seat to the main governing body. Too bad he wasn't attending any of the meetings and didn't bother asking me how they were going.

Meanwhile, Andres tended to stay home with Char and Bast since he wasn't required to attend the meetings, though he'd gone to quite a few. He could have some good ideas when he stopped joking around and actually participated. I felt bad for Bastille, though. We all tried to keep him up-to-date on what was going on, and were slowly putting a plan in motion that would help him and all Necromancers, but it would take time.

"Do you guys think we can call the Silverstorms out on the bullshit engagement tomorrow?" Andres asked from the backseat. I looked at him through the rearview mirror, and he was smiling. That did not bode well for Charisma's parents, but I honestly didn't give a shit.

Ian and Elizabeth Silverstorm were scum. Not only had they treated their daughter like dirt her entire life and fucked-up with Cara—though I wasn't sure I could blame that on them completely—they constantly opposed the changes we were trying to bring to the council. They didn't want to lose power or their status and seemed unable to understand they already had very little of both.

"If you think Charisma would benefit from it, then go ahead. However, I'm sure by the time we have the meeting tomorrow, the announcement will have been rectified, and the Silverstorms will be ridiculed even more. I wouldn't be surprised if the challenges started to pour in for them soon. In fact, the only thing I'm surprised about is that they haven't already started."

Logan was right. Not only that, but I was sure the reason they'd announced Char's engagement to Brant and her return to the Silverstorm family was to try to buy more time.

The only reason the Illuderes—and Andres—weren't being challenged left and right was because Andres had just won a public duel against Ricardo, wiping the floor with his uncle. So far, nobody had been foolish enough to think they could win against him, and I hoped things stayed that way.

My phone vibrated with a call, and I smiled when I saw Char's name on the caller ID.

"Put her on speaker phone!" Andres demanded.

I rolled my eyes at him but did just that.

"Hey, Little Spitfire, you ready to go?" I asked.

"We've been missing you, Kitten," Andres cooed from the back.

"Hey. Uh. Would you guys mind coming in here? I've already called the Healers, and I've alerted AMIA, but I could use a little help." Char sounded shaken.

We were all immediately on alert.

"What happened, Charisma? If you're able to, fill us in. We're on our way." Logan grabbed the phone while motioning for me to turn on the car.

I drove through the open gates of the Silverstorm estate,

grateful whoever was on guard had recognized my car from when I'd dropped Char off.

As Char's retelling of what happened made me sick to my stomach, I drove as fast as possible until, with tires screeching, I stopped right by the doors.

We all jumped out of the car and went inside, running as quickly as we could so we could check up on our girl.

Fuck. We shouldn't have let her come in alone. We should've known better.

Fucking Cara. I swore to the Goddess if she'd hurt even one strand of Char's hair, I'd *end* her.

All three of us had our METs ready when we burst into the sunroom, even though Char had kept talking to us the whole time, trying to assure us she was okay. We'd only believe her and be able to relax when we had her in our arms.

Logan went through the door first, with me hot on his heels and Andres taking the rear. So when Logan suddenly stopped, I barely managed to stop bumping into him. Andres wasn't so lucky. He crashed into me like a freight train, pushing me forward.

"Ohh shiiit," Andres cursed.

Oh shit, indeed.

The momentum from the bump sent me forward, and I took Logan down with me.

By the time we managed to detangle and get up from the floor, Char was staring at us and laughing.

"What kind of rescue party from hell is this?" she asked, amused.

"*Heey* Kitten, care to join our cuddle pile? We're short on soft skin and pretty curves." Andres *finger waved* at her from his place on the floor.

As if we hadn't just embarrassed ourselves in front of our

girl. As if she hadn't just gone through some major trauma while we'd twiddled our thumbs. As if her cousin wasn't currently a heap on the floor, not too far from where Logan was, bound and gagged with rope Char had found only the Goddess knew where.

Char snorted at Andres' antics. "I think I'll pass this time, but thanks." Then she turned to me. "I don't suppose you could use that little trick you used on me to tie Cara up and make sure she stays that way? I don't trust the rope, but it was the best I could do on short notice."

I grimaced. I really, really didn't want to use the rune I'd created to spice things up with my Little Spitfire on freaking Cara.

It felt wrong. Like it would taint it somehow.

"I can do you one better," Logan offered, getting up from the floor and brushing imaginary dust from his clothes. Then he picked up his MET, pressed a couple of places, and suddenly, a dark matter cage materialized around Cara.

Andres whistled.

When I caught Logan's eye, I nodded in thanks. He answered by raising an eyebrow.

Smug bastard.

I got up from the floor and offered Andres a hand just as we heard sirens approaching. Good, AMIA was here. That meant soon enough, we'd be able to take our girl home.

## 35

## CHARISMA

Cara hadn't just knocked my parents down; she'd also poisoned them, using the same nasty stuff Ricardo had used on Diego.

Apparently, Cara really had planned on torturing my parents until the poison took effect and killed them. It was a sick and completely twisted evil plan I hadn't expected from her, though it was no wonder she hadn't been worried about going on and on about her plans when I'd gotten her talking. She'd known their time was limited.

It was damn lucky timing I'd gone there to give them a piece of my mind. Who would've known that my parents' delusional attempt at saving face in our society would've ended up saving their lives?

The irony wasn't lost on me.

The Healers had arrived at the same time AMIA did and, under Christian's watchful gaze, they'd been able to save my parents, drawing the poison out and healing the gash on my mother's forehead.

Later, Christian had called and informed me Cara had poisoned their whiskey. Not only that, but they'd found evidence that she'd been hiding at the Silverstorm mansion. It seemed Cara had been staying in the basement, using the room I'd once been trapped in whenever my parents had tried to force my magic out.

I shuddered just thinking about it.

*All that matters is that Cara is now behind bars, Charisma,* I reminded myself.

That, and my parents were on the mend. They'd tried to contact me, but I'd refused their calls. I wasn't ready to talk to them just yet, and I didn't know if I ever would.

However, I'd finally realized that was okay, too.

Thankfully, even though I didn't get to confront them about the engagement, when I woke up today, I saw that my parents had retracted the announcement. News about what had happened yesterday was starting to spread, too—at least, the AMIA-approved version of it—and it was quickly drowning out any gossip involving my love life.

I'd finally be able to turn a new page in my life, this time with my found family.

Just thinking about my guys made me smile. Andres had gone to pick Gran up for game night, and they should be arriving soon. He was supposed to invite Blair, too, so most of my new family could be together, but Mrs. Alma had said Blair had her hands full with her men and wouldn't be joining us. I may have squealed when Gran had said that, and I couldn't wait to talk to Blair and ask her all about it. I had no idea what Blair's type was—probably people just as awesome as her.

Meanwhile, Theo, Logan, and Blaze were on their way here. They'd been at another council meeting, although this time, the main topic discussed had been the Silverstorms. According to the text Logan had sent me, the council had decided to hold any and all challenges my parents were receiving until they got out of the hospital.

When news broke of Cara's attempted murder on the Silverstorms Head, challenges started to rain down like crazy to the point that the council had to intervene. My parents would have a month to recover and get their act together, and then there would be a dueling championship of sorts. Basically, anyone who wanted to challenge to take their place would have to participate. Rather than every Elemental mage fighting my parents, they'd fight each other until there was only one winner. Then, the winner could choose between becoming the heir and learning from my parents or challenging them and becoming the Head of the Elemental Mages.

I should probably feel bad for them, but honestly, it was poetic justice.

"Char, can I move the boxes on the table?" Bast called out from behind me.

"Su—" I started to answer until I remembered what was in the boxes. "No, wait!" I yelled, jumping up from the couch, dropping my phone and the Switch controllers in my hurry to get to him.

Fuck fuck fuck. With everything that had happened, I'd forgotten to give Bast his present! I'd been waiting for the right moment since I wanted to make it special for him, but things kept happening, and I'd just ...

Shiiit.

Bast looked adorably alarmed when I rushed to him, picking up the box before he could. He tilted his head to the side, puzzled.

When I hid the box behind my back, he raised an eyebrow. "Are you keeping secrets, my love?" Bast asked in a growly voice, walking forward and caging me in between him and the table.

Was it possible to come just from a look? Because I was pretty freaking sure, I'd just done it.

There went yet another pair of underwear.

I couldn't answer, could barely even think. All I could do was stare at Bast's lips, desperate for a taste. Bast bent his head as if he was going to put me out of my misery and kiss me, but at the last second, he changed course, gently biting my earlobe. "My love, if you keep looking at me like that, I'll take you right here, right now."

Uh. Was this supposed to be a threat? Because I was fully on board with that plan. In fact, my vagina was so into it that she was doing a little dance.

"I volunteer as tribute," I said, dropping the box on the table and wrapping my arms around him.

"Hmm," Bast hummed, kissing the spot below my ear. "You sure you want Gran to get here and see the show?"

I pushed Bast away from me so fast, he had to take a few steps back so he wouldn't lose his balance. Laughing, he showed me what he had in his hands, and I didn't know whether to bite my sneaky boyfriend or drag him into the bedroom and lock the door, visitors be damned.

Probably both, to be honest.

"Now, let's see what you were trying to hide, shall we?" Bast teased, eyes laughing at me.

Even though I was planning my revenge, I couldn't deny I loved this side of Bast. He wasn't as playful as Andres, but he was definitely a close second. It was just that, more often than not, Bast was busy trying to reel in Andres and Gran, so he had his hands full. Still, playful Bast had been the one I'd seen most often over the years, back when we'd just been online gaming buddies and then friends. It had been the first side of him I'd fallen for.

I said nothing as Bast opened the box, and then it was my turn to watch in amusement as he stared at the contents, confused.

He looked at me, picking up the dark purple controller in his hand. "Why were you being so secretive about this? Did you plan on revealing it tonight for game night, and you didn't want any of us to steal your new toy?"

I snorted. "Bast, that's not a controller."

He looked at me, then at the hardware that was—in fact—shaped exactly like a controller, with all the buttons and even the analog sticks. Bast was too nice to say he thought I'd lost my mind, but it was clear on his face.

I couldn't stop my grin. "It's a MET, Bast. Your MET. I made it for you," I said, taking pity on him.

His eyes widened, and he stared at me like he was trying to understand what I'd just said. "Sorry, I must've misheard. I thought you said—"

"That that's your MET. You didn't mishear me. That's what I said. Happy early birthday, Bast."

I was unprepared for how watery his eyes got. For a second, I worried I'd done something bad, but then, slowly, a boyish smile took over Bast's whole face, lighting it up. "Char, this is. I have no words. I ... thank you."

Then he was picking me up and kissing me, saying over and over how thankful he was, and it was my turn to get teary-eyed.

I cupped his cheek. "I love you, Bast. I'm sorry it took me this long to make your own MET. If you want, we probably have enough time for me to key in your magical signature and talk you through how it works," I offered.

Bast shook his head, still smiling at me with so much

love it made my heart feel like it was about to burst. "Nah, I love the gift, Char, and I love you, but we can do that tomorrow. For now, I just want to hold you and show you how thankful I am."

"But Gran—"

Bast grinned. "I'll call Andres and tell him to take the long way here."

This man. He really knew the way to my heart. All my guys did, really.

I'd always hoped that once I graduated as a Magical Engineer, that I'd finally be able to find my place in the world. Little did I know that graduating had just been the first step into living the life of my dreams. With my guys, I'd found a family for myself and more love than I'd ever thought possible. I'd found the place I belonged, and it had been worth all the pain I'd suffered to get here.

I had my Ohana. My family. My men. And there wasn't a single thing I'd change about it.

My men accepted me with all the little quirks that made me who I was. They didn't care about the strength of my magic. All they cared about was *me*. And I loved all of them as much as they loved me.

Whatever the future held, we'd be able to face it because we were together.

# EPILOGUE

### Charisma

*Months later...*

"Here, Kitten, we need you to put this on." Andres offered me a piece of cloth, and I stared at it.

"Uh, Andres, can kinky sex wait until we're home? You know we can't get frisky in the car. Remember what happened last time." Andres and I had gotten a little ... carried away in the backseat while Theo had been driving once, and he'd almost crashed the car. Since then, the guys had instilled a new "no car sex" rule which I thought was pretty wise.

And even though Logan was the one driving today, not Theo, I still wasn't sure we should risk it.

"Worth it," Andres sing-songed, chuckling. "But no, Kitten. This time, it's not for kinky reasons. Although, if you want, we can totally use the blindfold later, too, for sexy times." He waggled his eyebrows at me while the guys groaned.

"We have a surprise for you, Little Spitfire," Blaze said from beside me. We were in the backseat of one of Logan's cars—the only one with enough space for all six of us—and I was in a delicious Blaze-Andres sandwich. Logan was driving, Bast was in the passenger seat, and because Theo had lost the rock-paper-scissors round, he was stuck on the extra seat in the trunk.

"A surprise?" I asked, trying to sound nonchalant and failing miserably.

Bast turned his head to look at me, smirking. "Only if you're a good girl and put on that blindfold, my love."

Well, when he put it that way.

I took the fabric from Andres and covered my eyes with it. Andres, being Andres, started to wave his fingers in front of my face, asking me how many fingers he was holding up in an attempt to determine if I was cheating.

I totally was, but I wasn't about to tell him that.

"Naughty little thing, aren't you?" Blaze asked in my ear, and I shivered.

Blaze cupped my cheek and fixed the blindfold, so I was no longer able to peek. The spoilsport.

"There. *Now* she can't see," he said.

I made it to the mental count of five until I couldn't hold back the questions anymore. "Sooooo, anyone want to tell me where we're going?"

"Patience, Char baby. We're almost there," Theo said from behind me, gently running his fingers in my hair the way I liked.

I was many things, but patient was not one of them. They should know that by now. It wasn't like I'd ever tried to keep it a secret or anything.

I started to test the blindfold by tilting my head this way and that, trying to see if different lighting would help. The guys laughed, and Andres—at least, I was pretty sure it was Andres since it came from my right—kissed me.

"Okay, Kitten. Are you ready?"

Fucking *finally*.

"Born ready!" I fully expected the blindfold to be removed, but instead, the engine cut off, and the guys opened the doors to get out. Blaze carefully guided me out and, knowing who he was dating, picked me up and carried me to our destination.

It didn't take long.

He gently placed me down and stepped back. I raised my hands to get rid of the blindfold, but someone gripped my wrists.

Someone's hard body pressed against my back, the grip on my hands still strong.

"Always so eager, Charisma. Andres had the right idea. I can't wait for us to get home so I can test the limits of your patience. I bet the others are just as eager." Logan's dark promise in my ear made me gasp.

We'd walked around the line, but so far, we'd never all been together. Either because they were busy with work or, sometimes, just bad timing. Because of the lack of room at Bast's apartment—which was still where I was living—it was hard for all of us to actually spend the night together. Usually, the guys took turns staying over, or I went to one of their places. I was starting to have clothes and stuff spread over five apartments, and it was beginning to be confusing for me. I'd tried to search for a bigger apartment, one we could all move into, but it was hard. Mostly because none of the places I'd been to felt *right*.

"Okay, Logan, you can take her blindfold off now," Andres called, sounding a bit far.

Logan didn't waste time removing it, growling "Later" in my ear.

He would totally keep that promise, too, just like he'd done the first time. Just thinking about it made me wet. Well, wetter.

I blinked a few times to get used to the light and gasped at what was in front of me.

A house. No, house was too bland a word. It was a two-story *dream home. My* dream home.

Big, spacious without being overbearing, it had floor-to-ceiling windows on the ground floor that would let enough light in even during the winter to make sure anyone was cozy. It had a big front yard with enough space for a dog—or five—and with enough space between it and the neighbors for privacy.

I was dying to look inside, but I was pretty sure I knew what I'd find. All the things I'd dreamed about and hoped for as a little girl. Things I'd only ever told one person. Whenever we played make-believe, I liked to describe what I imagined my dream home would be. From the way the outside would look, with the big yard and space, right down to the number of rooms—though as a kid I had insisted the perfect house needed not one, but three game rooms. Even as a kid, I had my priorities straight.

My eyes grew watery as I tried to fight the overwhelming emotions churning inside me, but I knew it was a losing battle.

The guys were spread around me in a loose semi-circle, all smiling expectantly at me, waiting for my reaction. But my eyes went to Theo.

There was no question in my mind he'd been responsible for it. He'd been the only one who knew.

"How?" My question was barely above a whisper. I was too choked up to say anything else.

Smiling, Theo shrugged. "I found it one day, a few years ago. I've been keeping an eye on it since then, but it never went for sale. When I mentioned it to Logan, he made it happen. We put in an offer right away. They took it, and we've been setting it up ever since."

I was totally ugly crying. My heart felt so full I worried I might burst. Not only was Theo the catalyst for making one of my earliest dreams come true, but he was sharing the credit of the moment with others. The boy I'd known and loved since I was a little girl had grown, and he kept surprising me.

"Kitten, you're crying but you haven't even seen the inside of the house yet," Andres complained, bouncing on the balls of his feet, unable to stay still any longer. "I mean, I'm thrilled you're enjoying the surprise, but you haven't even seen the *best part.*"

"Then why don't you show me?" I suggested, smiling so big that my cheeks hurt. In a very unladylike gesture, I used my shirt to wipe away some of my tears until Blaze offered me a packet of tissues.

My tearful snort was totally sexy.

Bast smiled softly at me and then pulled a key from his back pocket, opening the door for us with a flourish.

Andres grabbed my hand and led me inside, hopping from room to room, barely giving me enough time to process everything I was seeing.

There was a living room, a *game* room—I was willing to bet money Bast had been the one to insist on that—and a dining room. The kitchen was so beautiful that it made even me, Culinary Enemy Number One, want to cook something.

Then Andres dragged me to the basement, and my mind was blown.

They'd set up the ultimate tech room for me. A setup I could only ever dream of, with multiple computer screens, a comfortable as fuck chair, and an entire storage area. More than that, Logan had clearly pulled some strings because there was a brand-new Magiscan.

Andres tried to continue with the tour, but I dug in my heels.

"Holy shit. No way." I tugged my hand away from his and raced into the room, crouching near the Magiscan and lovingly caressing it. "You are so, so pretty and all mine, my Precious. I can't wait to play with you," I cooed.

This was just. I couldn't come up with the words to describe it. The house, the space, the geeky haven, the *equipment*. Even if I didn't take the rest of the house into consideration—which must've cost a small *fortune*—this room alone would've cost more than all the insurance money I'd gotten from my old apartment. Not only that, but every single piece of it had been clearly thought-out and planned by the guys with me in mind.

Their way of showing support and encouraging me. I'd officially quit working for AMIA just last month, having decided to follow Christian's fatherly advice, and I'd stopped taking commissions as "Onyx". Instead, I'd slowly but surely been building my own name—my own brand, so to speak—as a Magical Engineer. The guys had wanted to boast the fact I'd designed their METs to help boost my reputation, but I'd asked them to keep it quiet. I wanted to earn my clients' respect and not be seen as a tool to get an "in" with my men.

"Do you want us to leave so you can have a moment

alone with it, Char, baby?" Theo teased from the door, and I turned to find all five of them smiling in amusement at me.

"I'll come back for you, my pretty," I promised the Magiscan, getting up from the floor and going to my guys.

"I just realized I haven't said this yet, so I'll do it now. Thank you. Seriously. I just. Thank you. You guys blow me away."

Then I went to give each of them a kiss.

I didn't make it past Andres. The second I stepped away from him so I could kiss Logan, Andres picked me up, throwing me over his shoulder.

"You're taking too long. Let's go upstairs so I can show you the best part," he said, carrying me up the stairs like a sack of potatoes. "I've been *dying* for us to break in the new bed."

Well, when he put it like that.

The guys rushed behind us, not wanting to be left behind.

"You assholes better keep your dicks away from me." I heard Blaze saying, and I laughed.

Every time I thought I couldn't be happier, my men surprised me. Was it any wonder I'd fallen for them all?

# AFTERWORD

Char's story may be over, but the Arcane world isn't.

Blair's story has just begun.

For more of Blair, Gran, and AMIA, start the Arcane Agent series with Deadly Illusions.

Oh, I almost forgot! If you're currently cursing me because the orgy scene wasn't in this book, don't worry! I'll be releasing it as a bonus epilogue soon. Just keep an eye on the newsletter. ;)

# ACKNOWLEDGMENTS

Thank you so much for reading the Arcane Mage series! Whether you only just started or you've been following it since Chaotic came out two years ago, I just wanted to say thank you, from the bottom of my heart.

It feels so weird to be saying goodbye to these characters after all this time. I'm not going to lie; Charismatic was hard to write because I simply wasn't ready for it to end. But I'm really glad I did. I feel like Char and her guys deserve their happily ever after, don't you? And I'm happy I could give that to them. I promise, though, that even though her story is over, I have a few other series planned out in the same universe. That also means everyone's favorite mailbox opossum might be making an appearance, so you guys will be able to check up on her. Those who have already started the Arcane Agent series have already seen a lot of familiar faces—including Gran—and know there are more shenanigans to come.

So thank you, my dear readers, for giving my books a chance. You guys made it possible to live my dream, and I'm beyond grateful. Back when I started Char's story, I just wanted to write a story with a main character people could identify with, one that would make people laugh, but I never expected so many of you to fully embrace the mailbox opossum life; and I couldn't be happier.

There are a few other people who have helped me and

supported me while I went on this crazy ride, and I want to thank them, too.

Colette and Rachel, thank you for having my back and helping me whenever I was struggling with something. You guys are amazing and I love you for all the support, even if sometimes you had to bully me into writing.

Marie, Candice, Stacey, thanks for sprinting with me and making sure I could hit all my deadlines, even while you continuously reminded me I was being crazy.

Kelly Bennet, Janet Williamson, Rachel James, and Cindy Aleo, thank you for taking the time to beta read for me even with the crazy schedule.

Steph Rawlins @RawlsReadsAuthorServices for being an awesome editor. And Lorie Collin for being such a terrific proofreader. You guys rock.

And last, but not least, a huuuge thank you to Gatti, my awesome partner, who not only has always supported me when I decided to start writing, never doubting and always offering to lend me a year—not to mention helping with all the engineering stuff—but who also kept me fed while I wrote these books. And who also kept a steady supply of chocolate around as brain food. I love you a lot.

# ABOUT THE AUTHOR

A scientist at heart, T.S. Snow lives in a land far far away, secluded from most authors and readers (rumor has it that if you open your wardrobe you can find her hiding in there trying to take a nap). T.S. has a thirst for learning new languages, even if she is mostly worried about finding out new curse words in them. She has an amazing support system that include a loving partner, her family, friends, and her loyal–if completely lazy–dog. When she's not writing, T.S. can often be found causing complete chaos with her friends on social media, inhaling unhealthy amounts of coffee, or napping. Mostly napping.

T. S. Snow Reader Group on Facebook
https://authortssnow.com/

# ALSO BY T.S. SNOW

**The Arcane Mage Series**

Chaotic

Hectic

Erratic

Frenetic

Ecstatic

Charismatic

**Arcane Agent Series**

Deadly Illusions

Fractured Illusions

**Darker Shade Series**

Rise of Shadows

**Knotty by Nature**

*RH Omegaverse with Colette Rhodes*

Allure Part 1

Allure Part 2

**Shared World Standalone**

Sleepy as a Koala (Society of Shifters)

Stolen Hearts (Mischief Matchmakers Series)

Printed in France by Amazon
Brétigny-sur-Orge, FR